BREAKING THE ICE

PART ONE

AVERY
1995

Chapter One
DECEMBER 1995

"Avery, so help me God, I'm *this close* to punching you in the boobies. Stop arguing. We're going out tonight. I'll pick you up in an hour."

I hung up the phone with my best friend Casey and then promptly flopped backwards onto my bed. I wasn't in any mood to go out that night, but then again, I wasn't much in the mood to go out *any* night.

Especially not to *Johnny's*.

The bar itself was cool enough. It's just that Johnny's was right down the street from the local hockey rink and was a known hangout for the players. It just so happened that our local hockey rink was the Brendan Byrne Arena and the players were the New Jersey Devils.

My father was their General Manager, so I knew a bunch of those guys personally and was friends with a lot of them. Even the guys I didn't know too well seemed okay, but a select few were downright assholes. I guess the constant exposure to professional athletes desensitized me to the godlike status some people had bestowed upon them, because ultimately, they weren't different from any other guys as far as I was concerned.

Every September, there was a Welcome Back dinner, a chance for all the players, coaches, and their families to get to know each other before the season officially started. It was normally held at some stuffy reception hall, a place where everyone could pretend to be normal, upstanding citizens. I'd missed the dinner this year because I had just reported to my campus, but I'd been to the meet-and-greet practically every year prior.

After the formal dinner, all the guys would usually go out to Johnny's for a night on the town. Last year was the first time I'd ever joined them; Casey had some fake I.D.s made for us and we'd been sneaking into places ever since. Prior to that, I was always "The GM's daughter," one of the many team mascots who hadn't yet come of age. Once I turned eighteen, however, it was like I was being let into a secret club.

The gentle giants I associated with at those civil family dinners turned into absolute lunatics on the ice and even bigger monsters in the bar. A casual night out almost always devolved into a raucous evening of free-flowing booze, exaggerated tales of glory, and all too eager hookups. It was fun for a while, but only one short year later, I was already growing tired of that scene.

Don't get me wrong—the guys were essentially very respectful toward me. But seeing the way they were with any of the *other* girls was pretty disturbing. The women would typically lurk around the arena and *always* at the bar, hanging all over the players, some of whom were married. I'm not going to name names, here, but a few of those married guys were more than receptive to the women's attentions. It was a bit of a rude awakening; I babysat some of their kids, for godsakes.

The rookies were positively the worst, though. They were all cocky and conceited, every last one of them. Treating the bar like it was their own personal buffet, thinking they were God's gift, having sex with anything that moved.

I grew up around the game, basically breathing hockey from the day that I was born. I liked the sport well enough, but Casey was practically rabid with her fanaticism. I knew she'd been spending a lot of time at Johnny's lately, because her letters to me at school always talked about her adventures at the place. She'd recruited our mutual friend Dana for her missions while I was away, but

I'd been there with her a bunch of times myself, if for no other reason than it was a fun place to hang out.

And now she wanted to head there to play jersey-chaser.

It was my first night home from college, on leave for Christmas break. I still had unpacking to do, and after a four-hour drive, I wasn't much in the mood to play wingwoman for my friend. I'd called Casey soon after I got in, under the mistaken delusion that she would be content to just come over and watch a movie or something. I was excited to see her, and I couldn't care less what we did so long as we were together. But it was Friday night, and she was not only astounded that I wanted to stay in, but insistent that we hit the bar. She wouldn't take no for an answer.

The thing was, I'd just *come* from Party Central; I was in my freshman year at Penn State. It's not as though I indulged my inner wild child every minute or anything, but there was no escaping that atmosphere even when a girl like me went out of her way to avoid it.

Let me be clear, here: It's not that I was anti-social. I had lots of friends and managed to get out amongst the living on a fairly regular basis. I just didn't *major* in partying the way some other kids did.

That mindset went out the window whenever Casey came to visit. She never went away to school, a fact which she bemoaned at every opportunity. Because of that, she'd visited me on campus quite a bit, and when she did, I knew she expected me to put my boogie shoes on. And when she wasn't out road-tripping to Pennsylvania, she was waiting for me to come home to continue the party here.

Basically, there was no way to get out of going to Johnny's tonight.

I hauled myself off my bed and started to get ready. I grabbed a quick shower, then debated what to wear. It was the first day of winter, but the weather was fairly mild, not cold enough to require a pair of jeans. Johnny's was always so hot and stuffy anyway. I threw on a black miniskirt and a stretchy, vee-neck top that displayed my Y-necklace to perfection. Pairing such a borderline skimpy outfit with my knee-high black boots was a bit out of my comfort zone, but they looked really cute, so I went for it. Besides, if I knew anything about the kind of girls that went to Johnny's, I figured I'd fit right in.

I switched out my huge satchel purse for my black wristlet, just packing the necessities:

Fake I.D.? Check.

Lipstick? Check.

Cash?

Hmmm. Probably not enough.

Casey was due any minute, and I didn't want to hear her gripe about having to stop at the MAC machine. I went into my parents' room and swiped twenty bucks out of the cash box my father kept in his nightstand drawer, replacing it with a signed I.O.U. Dad was always pretty cool about letting me borrow money, provided I could account for it and pay him back in a timely fashion. I wasn't exactly raking in the millions at my coffee shop job near campus, but I normally made enough to fund a decent social life.

By the time I finished getting ready and Casey picked me up, we didn't roll into Johnny's until after eleven. The smell of the night air was crisp and smoky, with only the slightest chill. Kind of weird for December in New Jersey, but I wasn't going to complain. I pulled my leather jacket a little tighter around myself as we made our way across the parking lot.

One step inside the front door, my ears practically exploded from the noise. Johnny's was a huge bar, but on the nights when the Devils had a win, it was packed wall to wall. We sliced through the dark, hazy room, trying not to lose one another, unable to hear ourselves think over the blaring music. Johnny's was a peanut-shell-on-the-floor type of club, and I almost twisted an ankle on my way across the crowded room to the bar. I was usually much better thought-out than to wear spiky heels to this place.

We got a couple beers and managed to nab a table on the edge of the ruckus, in the raised platform area near the dance floor. The brass rails that surrounded it turned that section of the club into a giant playpen. Fitting, because the people contained within it normally acted like toddlers. A few of the players were right nearby, whooping it up and toasting their win. I recognized some of them, but even if I didn't, it would've been easy to pick the NHL guys out from the crowd. All you had to do was look for a random pocket of squealing girls and *poof!* There they were.

Casey had been eyeing up Simon Sorensen ever since the beginning of the season. He'd knocked around the minors for a couple of years waiting to be called up, and we'd finally acquired him in the spring. She figured she had a decent chance with him, since he wasn't yet as famous as some of the more seasoned guys who had shot to the top of the groupie wishlist.

"You are such a puck bunny," I said once we were situated.

"I am not!" Case shouted back at me in open-mouthed shock. "Just because I love hockey, and just because the majority of hockey players happen to be extremely hot… that doesn't make me a puck bunny."

"You're right. You're not sleeping with any of them," I said. "I guess you're only an *aspiring* puck bunny."

She rolled her eyes. "We're hockey fans. Plain and simple."

"Correction," I shot back. "*I* am a fan. *You* are a stalker."

"I am not a— Oh shit. He just looked at me."

I busted a gut laughing at my friend. We'd arranged our positions so that my back was toward Simon's table, allowing Casey to spy at him over my shoulder. Apparently, her covert ops were paying off.

"Oh my God. Avery. He's waving me over. Oh my God. What should I do?"

"You should go over and talk to him, weirdo. What do you *think* you should do?"

"Marry him and have his babies?"

"Let's go, crazy girl."

I couldn't understand why she was being so hesitant. Talking to Simon was the whole reason we came out tonight, wasn't it? Yet, I had to physically grab her purse to get her to follow me. I plunked it down at his table, saying, "Hi Simon."

"Hey Avery. Hi Case. You ladies are looking rather lovely tonight." Simon leaned back in his chair and checked us out from head to toe. God. I really hated the frozen foods section of the meat market. Hockey players could be so... *blunt*. I wasn't necessarily an extroverted kind of gal, exacerbated by the fact that I'd spent the majority of the past three months in my little college bubble. I was learning to deal with the party crowd there, but I was out of practice with how to run with the even faster crowd here. Thank God I only had to deal with this scene while I was home.

We took over the unoccupied stools at his table just as a waitress came by to take our drink orders. I was only half-finished with my beer, but figured it might be a long wait before I had the chance to order another one, so I took advantage while I could. "I'll have another Coors Light, thanks." I turned toward my friend and asked, "Case?"

She just nodded her head and offered a barely-audible, "Yes."

God. What was *with* her tonight?

Simon said, "Okay, so that's two Coors Lights, I'll take a Bud, and… hang on."

He leaned back on his stool, twisting around to consult the crowd standing behind him. The group was one of the aforementioned pockets of girls, surrounding some dark-haired guy I could only see from the back. I watched the guy give a thumbs up, and Simon turned back toward the waitress, holding up two fingers. "Let's make that two Buds. Thanks."

Simon put his forearms against the table and leaned in to face Casey. "You left early last week."

Her eyes lit up at his words, and I knew she was probably freaking out at Simon's acknowledgement. She'd told me all about their encounter last Saturday night. After weeks of hanging around hoping he'd notice her, he finally did. They apparently spent a good portion of the night chit-chatting, and Simon had asked for her number before she left. He hadn't called her yet, though.

I waited for Casey to say something, but when she didn't, I filled the space. "Sooo… great win tonight, Simon. I only caught the end of the game, but you guys looked good out there."

"Thanks."

It was kind of an awkward conversation to have. Simon wasn't seeing much time on the ice, so I didn't know if I should be congratulating him on a win he didn't have anything to do with. Couple that with the fact that my father was the particular general manager who had hired him to seemingly do nothing more than sit the bench, and I felt that maybe Simon would have had reason to view me as the enemy.

Not that you'd know it by the way he was staring at my legs.

He saw my raised eyebrows and knew that he'd been caught. "Nice boots."

"Thanks. They're Casey's," I burbled out in a moment of inspiration, trying to give her an opening.

"Oh yeah?" he asked, while my friend sat on the stool next to me like a lump, completely clueless as to how to act like a normal human being. Jeez. She must've really had it bad for this guy. Casey wasn't normally the reserved type. That was my job.

I gave her a snap-out-of-it kick under the table, but the only thing she added to the conversation was, "Ouch!"

Like I said: clueless.

At least I was able to divert Simon's attention back in her direction. "You okay?" he asked.

Case finally found her voice. "Yes. I just hit my shin on something under the table." She shot me a dirty look and then leaned down to give a rub to one of her skinny, little legs.

Casey was a tiny sprite of a girl. Tiny frame, tiny hands, tiny feet. Huge brown eyes, short brown hair. She was like a smaller-scaled version of a regular person, like Jada Pinkett or Cheri Oteri or Prince. Not just short or skinny, but *downsized*. Whenever I referred to her as a "seven-eighths person," she was not amused.

She was, however, finally talking at least. She held Simon's focus as they laughed and relived some funnier moments from the weekend before. As I was not there during their apparently fabulous evening, I found myself awkwardly smiling along, my attentions wandering.

When I heard the unmistakable sound of exaggerated laughter, I checked out my immediate area. Simon's friend was flailing his arms around, obviously in the midst of some entertaining narrative. There were a couple other guys listening, along with five or six girls. One of the girls sipped her drink daintily through a straw and batted her eyelashes at him as he spoke. I'm not kidding. Legit, straight-up, *batted her eyelashes*. Gag me.

I saw the moony looks on the girls' faces and wondered what they found so fascinating. "Who's that?" I asked Simon.

Simon tore his eyes away from Casey's cleavage long enough to respond, "New guy. Came up in September. Wanna meet him?" Before I could decide, he yelled out, "Hey Maniac! Come meet my friend."

I caught a brief glimpse of his profile when he shot a look over his shoulder at Simon, and I figured I was in trouble.

But when he excused himself from his group of admirers and turned fully in our direction, I knew that I was toast.

I swear, my stomach dropped clear out of my body and landed right there on the floor. He was gorgeous, and he was standing only two feet in front of me. Dark hair that hung over his forehead, luscious pale eyes that were staring at me appreciatively, a mouth parted in what looked like surprise.

I almost died.

Simon's voice halted my impending heart attack. "Maniac, Avery. Avery, Maniac."

"Nice to meet you, Avery," he said in the most magnificent voice. Rainbows appeared over his head. Angels sang.

Damn. I suddenly regretted my lack of attention to the games this season. I couldn't believe this beautiful man had been here just waiting for me all these months, and I didn't even know about it. Well, not *waiting for me*, but you know what I mean.

"You too… Maniac?"

He gave a confident smirk and shot back, "Maniac's my name on the ice. Zac is what you can call me in bed."

The rainbows disappeared. The angels wept.

I was sure my eyes rolled right out of my head. He was standing there wearing a cocky grin, assuredly expecting me to rip my clothes off right there in the bar. Oh Jesus. One of these. Why should I have even been surprised. "Okay, then, *Maniac*. Good luck with that."

I got up from my seat and walked off, with all intentions of heading back to my safe little table in the corner of the playpen; maybe I'd even call a cab and split for home altogether. I already got Casey talking to Simon. She could do quite well on her own from here on out.

"Hey, whoa! Avery, hold up!" Zac was on my heels, and I couldn't decide if I was angry or overjoyed about it. I never expected that he'd bother to follow me, so I guess what I was feeling most was *surprised*. He put a hand at my elbow, which caused me to turn toward him abruptly and cross my arms over my chest. I was sure the move came off as haughty, but I was only trying to recover from the electric shock his touch had sent down my skin. Dammit.

"Where you running off to?"

I gave a quick rub to my arms and answered, "Look, Zac. I know all too well what this scene is about, and it's not who I am, okay? I've been around guys like you my whole life."

"Guys like me?"

"Yeah. You know… Guys who aren't… serious." *Not serious* was the most passive way to categorize a lot of those NHL guys. I figured it was a less antagonistic label than *colossal man-whores*.

16

His lip twitched at that, before he tucked his chin into his chest, lowered his eyebrows, and said in a deep baritone, "I can be very serious."

I found myself sputtering out a laugh in spite of myself. He may have been an arrogant ass, but there was no denying that he was funny. And extremely easy to look at.

Before I could fumble over the right thing to say, he launched into an apology. "Hey look. I didn't mean to freak you out back there. I was just goofing around."

I ran a hand over my hair and met his face. Wow. In this light, I could see that his eyes were a beautiful, brilliant green. Like freshly-cut grass on a summer's day. Bright and earthy, with a splash of gold near their centers.

He looked sincere enough, and I supposed I *did* overreact a little bit. "It's okay. I'm sorry for getting so snotty so quickly. I've been around these guys too long, I guess. I've seen too much."

He raised his eyebrows. "Is that so?"

I ignored his leading question. For one thing, it wasn't as though I was going to offer details, for godsakes; I was quite sure he was well aware of exactly what I meant anyway. For another, it was becoming increasingly difficult to maintain a conversation with the guy. I was at eye-level with the white, long-sleeved T-shirt straining to contain his sculpted chest and stretched taut around his bulging biceps. His face was chiseled out of solid marble but there was an intriguing scar across his chin which added a welcome ruggedness to his beautiful features. He was so gorgeous, it was almost painful.

And I'd been staring at him for far too long.

I grabbed a lock of my hair and averted my eyes, trying to make it look as though I was simply inspecting my split ends while I changed the subject. "So… you're new?" I asked, like an idiot. Of course he was new. Even if Simon hadn't just told me about him, I already knew most of the guys on the team, and I most definitely didn't know *him*.

"That I am."

"They playing you?"

He crossed his arms over his chest and leaned back on his heels, staring me down from his commanding height. "I get my fair share of ice time."

"Guess I haven't caught too many games this season." That was the truth. While I grew up loving the game, I'd just been so caught up in my new college life that hockey wound up on the backburner.

His lips quirked as he replied, "You should. I'm quite the sight to behold."

"Wow. You're way too modest. Show a little hubris, for godsakes."

His gorgeous eyes crinkled at the corners as his face split into a wide grin. I wondered if the teeth were actually his or if he just had a really good dentist. "Hey, look. I was truly only screwing around before. Let's go back over to the table. No need for you to cut your night short just because of this."

He was right. It took me an hour to get ready and we'd only been there for thirty minutes. It would have been a waste of an evening, not to mention a really cute outfit. What did I really think I was going to do anyway? Stomp out of the bar like a big baby just because of one little offhanded remark? I'd heard much worse out of those guys over the years. Why did Zac's comments ruffle me more than theirs ever had?

I wondered if everyone had seen my hasty attempt at an exit and wasn't much looking forward to slinking back to the table with my tail between my legs. But there was Zac, my supposed antagonist, offering the olive branch. His apology gave me an easy enough excuse to go back to my evening without losing face. I stood there debating my next move way longer than was necessary, until I caught Zac's adorable grin and hesitant eyes. "We cool?"

My shy smile must have been enough of a capitulation, because he put a hand at my elbow and escorted me across the room, saying, "Good. I'd hate to think we won't be friends just because I said something offensive." I was busy trying to downplay my racing heart at his touch during our walk, and also attempting to dismiss the dirty looks I was receiving from his female entourage as we approached, so it caught me off guard when he added, "But if you plan on hanging out with me, you may need to get used to it."

Man, the guy really knew how to blow an apology.

He deposited me back at Simon's table, and then promptly left me flat while he made his way back into the crowd.

"You two make nice?" Simon asked.

"For now," I replied flatly.

"What's the matter? He get pissed when he couldn't talk you into bed?"

"No," I laughed out, trying to seem unaffected. "It wasn't like that. He didn't even try."

Simon shot an incredulous look at me and huffed out, "That's a first."

Newsflash: ZAC WAS A DOG. Not that I hadn't already figured that out on my own, but Simon's comment basically affirmed my assessment.

Great.

I guessed Casey must have found her voice while I was gone, because she piped in with, "He is simply adorable, Avery. You should work on that."

I didn't appreciate that she was not only calling me out in front of Simon, but that she was treating my dating life like it was a job. *Work on that?* Falling for someone should be easy. There shouldn't be battle lines drawn within the first minute of meeting someone. And judging by the girls fawning all over Zac at the present moment, I realized I was in no position to try and fight through that army in order to make it to the front lines.

Besides, I was only going to be home for four short weeks.

There really was no point in trying.

Chapter Two
JANUARY 1996

I was caught up in the holidays the first few days I was back home, so Case and I didn't get the chance to go out again until almost two whole weeks had gone by. She and Simon had been talking nonstop over that time, and they'd even had their first official date a few days before. So, on Simon's request, we chose Johnny's as our destination for the night.

Because of that, I'd have to admit that I was more than a little excited about our impending evening plans. It had been ten entire days since the last time we'd been to the bar, ten entire days since I was hit with the bag of bricks otherwise known as Zac McAllister.

We were at Johnny's for all of two minutes before I spotted him, and another thirty before I realized I'd been staring like some sort of lunatic stalker. Of course he was the focus of the crowd surrounding him and of course that crowd consisted mainly of women. He devoted a hell of a lot of energy toward flirting with them, and I found myself wondering which one he'd pick to take home at the end of the night.

Truth be told, I found myself wondering what it would be like if he picked *me*.

Not that I had anything to worry about regarding *that* unlikely scenario. He hadn't even said hello yet, and I started to get the impression that he didn't even know I was alive, much less in the same room. When you spend most your life trying to be invisible, the fallout is that sometimes you succeed. Basically, I wasn't the type of girl to just go barging into the middle of his group of admirers and demand his attention. I didn't have any right to it anyway.

But that doesn't mean I didn't like to look.

So, I sat and I watched and I waited. I sipped my drink. I chatted with my friends. I made small talk with anyone who came by the table to say hi. I listened to the band.

And I watched. And I waited…

And I realized I was being pathetic.

I'd been there for two whole hours, and the majority of that time had been spent waiting to find a way to talk to Zachary McAllister.

I took a look across the table to see that Casey and Simon were enthusiastically sucking face, and I felt like a third wheel.

I needed air.

Excusing myself from the table, I made my way to the side door, pulling on my hat and gloves in the process. There was a fenced-in patio outside with a bar that was only opened during the warmer months. Last summer, Casey and I indulged in a few too many Fireball shots and we had to call a cab to take us home. Live and learn.

The booming music from inside was merely a garbled hum out here, emanating from the building along with the excited frenzy of the people that occupied it. I brushed off the light dusting of snow to take a seat on one of the stools, turned my head up to the sky, and let out with an expended sigh. I watched my breath curl into a cloud of smoke over my head, and when it dissipated, I caught sight of the starry night above.

At first I was glad to be alone, but then the warring thoughts took over my brain. I loved being home, seeing my family, hanging out with my friends. Heck, I even liked coming to Johnny's with the team. I'd always leave my house feeling optimistic about the evening ahead, even though by the end of it, I always left deflated. As much as I liked hanging out with the guys, there were times I wished it wasn't always as their *mascot*. I was bored living life on the outskirts. After years of being friends with Casey, you'd think some of her outgoing nature would have rubbed off on me, but I was still the same old Avery Brooks I'd always been. Was I destined to spend my life on the sidelines?

A burst of music blasted out in a brief crescendo, and my attentions turned toward the door.

Zac.

"Hey! You cutting out so soon?"

I gave a rub to my arms and answered, "Nope. Just taking a break. You?"

"Nah. I just noticed you were gone and—" He shot a hesitant look over his shoulder into the club, trading alternating looks between the crowd inside... and me. He seemed to be considering his options. A slight thrill ran through me as he let the glass door close behind him and came over toward the bar. Apparently, between whatever was so fascinating inside and the company that awaited him outside, he'd chosen me. I knew I shouldn't have cared, but the fact that I was all alone out there with him kinda made my heart stop beating.

I swiped a gloved hand over the stool next to mine, and Zac sidled onto it, facing sideways. He draped one elbow over the back of the seat and the other on the bar, his knees pointed in my direction. "It's kind of dangerous to be out here all by your lonesome."

"Why?" I asked, jerking my head toward the door. "All the predators are in there."

That made him chuckle.

He leaned in a bit closer and offered in a conspiratorial whisper, "Don't fool yourself, baby. I'm the biggest threat there is."

Tell me something I don't know.

I was already aware of the way he joked around and figured he was only kidding. And thank God for that, because I was feeling too vulnerable to be able to deal with him if he was flirting with me seriously.

"And yet you're out here with me instead of trolling the club for your next victim. Taking it easy on the helpless prey this evening?" I asked, unable to hide my smirk.

"For now." His eyelids lowered, shooting me a dirty look, daring me to doubt him. Then his lip quirked into a crooked smile as he said, "I just thought I'd come out here to let you know what everyone's been saying behind your back."

Oh, this should be rich. "What's that?'

"Nice ass."

Zac couldn't contain his smile as I snorted out a laugh. "Ouch. You sure can toss out a line. Did you study some sort of handbook or something?"

He ignored my jab and reached his hand over to pinch a corner of my scarf, rubbing it between his fingers as he changed the subject. "What is this? It's nice."

"Yeah, no. It's wool," I said flatly.

"Huh. Coulda fooled me. It feels like girlfriend material." He raised his eyebrows and shot a wide grin at me, nodding his head, obviously impressed with himself.

That he managed to blindside me yet again with such an obvious pickup line had me cracking up. "Stop! Okay. You roped me right into that one."

"Yeah. Can't believe you fell for it. You must get stuff like that all the time."

"Sometimes," I admitted.

"Lemme hear one."

"What, a line?" I asked, incredulously. "What's the matter, Zac? You run through your whole catalog already tonight? Need some new ammo?"

He lowered an eyebrow at me. "I don't use lines."

"What are you talking about? You just tossed out like thirty of them!"

"I don't use them *seriously*."

"Oh really? Then how do you manage to leave with a different girl every night?"

The question slipped out before I realized just exactly what I was revealing. Great. Now he knew how aware I was about his stupid sex life.

Thankfully, he didn't offer commentary on my slip and just answered the question. "Like I said, I don't use lines. I use *honesty*."

Ha! As if!

My expression must have relayed my skepticism, because Zac said, "Don't believe me? Fine. Let's play a game. You give me the worst pickup line you ever heard, and I'll give you one of my sure-things. We'll take turns."

Gleaning some insight into Zac's world-class hookup skills was too tempting an offer to pass up. But even still, I couldn't believe he was prepared to invite me into his brain. "You serious?"

He smacked his bare hands together and gave them a rub, cupping them against his mouth and blowing before answering. "Sure am. You ready? You can go first."

As a living, breathing, single woman who found herself out amongst some red-blooded males on occasion, there was no avoiding the cheesy pickup lines. It's not like guys were constantly throwing themselves at me, but I'd heard enough bad come-ons to play along.

I shifted in my chair, nodded in his direction, and asked, "Let me ask you something first. Did it hurt?"

Zac stopped rubbing his hands together and stared at me with scrunched brows. "Did what hurt?"

"When you fell from Heaven."

He groaned, half in pain, half in laughter. "Oh man. That's bad. You got me. I didn't realize we were starting."

"Payback's a bitch. Now it's your turn."

He didn't even wait a beat before lowering his lids to half mast and eyeing me up and down. The look on his face was thrilling enough, and I could see how any girl would be helpless at the mere sight of those green eyes traveling along her person. Hell. *I* melted into a puddle easily enough.

He leaned a bit closer and raised a hand to my cheek, tucking a stray curl back under my hat, his fingers swiping behind my ear and raking down the line of my hair to the ends. He gave a playful tug to the strand in his grasp before twirling it around his finger, refocusing his attention back to my face. His touch sent shivers through me as his eyes bored into mine, and I was panicked at the thought that he was going to kiss me. My fight or flight response had taken an extended vacation, and I was left staring into those smoldering green eyes as a small smile broke from his beautiful lips, sending my heart racing into overdrive.

And then, God help me, he added his honeyed voice to the equation. "What's your sign? Because I think we should fuck."

"*What?*" I immediately found myself busting up; that was *so* not what I was expecting him to say. "Oh my God, that's *horrible*," I laughed out, not sure if I was grateful or heartbroken with the recent turn of events.

He laughed back. "Your turn."

I was still trying to recover from the lightning bolts running under my skin, but the fact that he had me laughing managed to loosen me up a bit. I guessed he wasn't going to take this game as seriously as I thought. No matter. This version was way more fun, and a hell of a lot safer.

Hunching my shoulders like a caveman, I offered in my sleaziest Jersey-guy voice, "That's a nice outfit. It would look betta on my bedroom flaw."

"Cute shoes. Let's fuck," he shot back.

"You have beautiful hair. I can't wait to see what it'll look like sprawled across my pillow."

"Hi, I'm Zac. Wanna fuck?"

"I'm sensing a pattern here."

We both cracked up as he shrugged. "I told you. I'm honest. Women respond to that."

"Yeah, sure, women who are looking to…" Even though he'd just dropped a handful of F-bombs in my presence, I couldn't find a way to say it back to him. "…looking for the same thing as you, you mean."

He stopped laughing at that, giving out a heavy breath as he turned in his seat. "Yeah, I guess." He put his forearms against the bar and focused on his clasped hands, surprising me when he sighed, "Actually, I don't *know* what I'm looking for, Ave."

My heart sped up involuntarily when I heard him say my name. And heck, not even my name, but his very own personal nickname. *Ave!* Oh God. It sounded so much better coming from his lips than it should have.

I was so elated at his words that it took me the extra second to recognize the weight behind them. I broke out of my own euphoria when I realized what he'd said and registered his defeated pose. His shoulders were slumped and he was swirling the snow on top of the bar into a little pile with his fingertips. I never imagined he was capable of being so... *contemplative.*

"Are you alright?" I asked.

"Yeah," he said to his hands. "It's just that sometimes... I don't know. It gets *tiring*, you know?"

"What does?"

He didn't bother to answer, and simply snapped out of his sullen mood as he turned toward me. "Hey. You must be freezing your tail off out here. Let's go back inside."

I didn't care how cold it was out there. I would have welcomed the frostbite if it bought me a little more alone-time with him. Not that I could say that, however.

I was still concerned about his brooding comment, but he didn't seem as though he was looking for some big heart-to-heart, so I let it go. "Yeah, okay. I didn't even tell Casey and Simon where I was going. They might be worried."

The old Zac was back as he chuckled, "Yeah. Especially if they knew you were out here with *me*."

I was in the process of hopping off my stool, but his comment stopped me cold. "Why do you do that?" I asked. "Why do you put yourself down like that?"

He'd stood up, but he wasn't going anywhere. He looked at me blankly and said, "I don't."

"You do," I answered back. I'd only known him for little over a week, but that wasn't the first cutting jag I'd ever heard from him. "I'm starting to think your humor is three parts shock value and one part self-deprecation."

"So?"

"So, I guess it makes me wonder if you're happy."

"Of course I'm happy. I'm a Devil on the ice and a god between the sheets. What's there to be *un*happy about?"

I could tell I wasn't going to get anywhere, and I let out a sigh. "My formula was missing a key component. I forgot to dip the whole specimen in conceit."

He smiled, seemingly impressed with my evaluation. "C'mon. Let's go."

We made our way back to the table to see that our friends were still connected at the lips. Zac gave me a nudge and said, "I don't think they've come up for air since we left. Yo, Sorenson!"

Simon managed to tear himself away from Casey's face and address us. "Oh look, babe. There are other people here."

Casey giggled and rested her head on Simon's shoulder. I'd say that their schmoopiness was sickening, but they were actually pretty adorable together. I took my hat off and smoothed my hair back down, gathering it into a ponytail with the tie at my wrist. It wasn't my best look, but it was easier than dealing with static-head all winter.

"Where did you run off to?" Casey asked.

"Ah. So you *did* come up for oxygen long enough to realize I was gone."

Simon gave Case a quick smooch on the top of her head. "Who needs oxygen when a beautiful girl steals your breath anyway?" He punctuated his rhetorical question with a huge grin aimed at Casey's smiling face.

I went to shoot an eyeroll at Zac, but he hardly looked as though he was sharing the joke. For one split second, I caught the intense stare he was focusing on my mouth. Almost immediately, his eyes met mine as his lips quirked into a slight grin, snapping his expression back into casual mode.

Good for him and all, but *I* was feeling anything but 'casual' at the moment.

It was hard to feel laid-back when my new friend had just pulverized my insides.

"Bottoms up, Buttercup."

Zac clinked his glass against mine and we both threw back our shots. It was his bright idea for us to "kick off the season in style," which would explain the fact that we were presently chugging back a couple of twenty-dollar whiskeys as if they were Wild Turkey.

We'd met up at the Welcome Back dinner earlier in the evening, and now we were cutting loose at Johnny's with the rest of the team. Casey was our designated driver, so after the reception, she shuttled me, Simon, and Zac over to the bar.

We'd become an unofficial foursome over the months, and a lot of the time, Zac and I wound up together, seeing as our best friends were normally joined at the lips. Casey and Simon had been dating pretty steadily over the past year, and I was really happy to see things happening between them. It looked as though he was going to turn out to be one of the good ones—a rare commodity in the NHL world. Oh, sure, I'd met a few. But a committed hockey player was about as rare as a Bigfoot sighting. For the most part, they simply didn't exist.

Zac sure as hell wasn't looking to settle down anytime soon.

He and I had been in each other's company a lot over the past year, and sometimes, the two of us would pair off by ourselves to take a breather, like we were doing now. Our encounters were normally in a group setting, though, so more often than not, I was relegated to nothing more than a member of his adoring entourage. I didn't gush all over him like the other girls—at least outwardly—so I was sure Zac figured he didn't have much use for me beyond our newly-solidified friendship. He generally only utilized his social skills in order to further his sexcapades, and I had no intentions of ever being part of one of them.

He liked new meat whenever possible, but sometimes, he'd take his pick from one of the regular groupies. Truly, I didn't judge. If they wanted to be passed around from guy to guy every other night, that was their business.

It just wasn't a scene I was into.

It was pretty painful having to watch him leave with a different girl every night, but it was even worse when *Julie* was one of his options. She was a girl from Zac's real life who would show up every now and again to hang out. She was nice enough, but it didn't stop me from disliking her. After all, she was the only one of those women that ever seemed to have any sort of relationship with him, and yet, she always gave off the vibe that she couldn't have cared less. I supposed that's why he let her hang around so often.

She lived in the city, and according to Simon, she and Zac were just friends. Yeah, right. The girl was gorgeous. Maybe it was a friends-with-benefits situation? But then, I couldn't understand why he bothered. He had plenty of *benefits* whenever he wanted them. I figured he must have really liked her to invite her out so frequently, even if they weren't actually "a couple."

So, it's not as though I ever considered dating the guy. Even if I allowed myself to consider it, I'd have to get in line behind a whole string of girls, and who the hell wants to be someone's last choice?

But the thing was, even though he was an unrepentant dog, he was *fun*. He was an entertaining guy to be around. I enjoyed our nights out together—or at least I did right up until the minute he'd leave with some other girl. It's not that I could even be jealous about it or anything, because I'd made it a point to keep him at arms' length since the first moment we met. And why wouldn't I? The dude had 'devastation' written all over him. I mean, seriously. I'd seen the boy in action and I knew what he was all about. Even if the stars aligned and by some miracle, we actually *did* hook up or something, I was well aware that he wouldn't stick around for more than a single night. And one single encounter would be completely self-destructive, because being left in the dust like that would just completely break my heart.

But even knowing that, I still found myself daydreaming about it. A girl could dream, couldn't she?

"Damn!" he growled, slamming his glass upside down on the bar. "Want another?"

I was still recovering from the burn of the first one, but managed to laugh out, "No, thank you."

He flashed me a dazzling grin and ordered us a couple beers before asking, "So how's school? Learning anything out there in the sticks?"

"Believe it or not," I countered, "even those of us who didn't go to some snobby university in a major city can still manage to pick up the random bit of knowledge every now and again. Hell, *some* of us even graduate."

He smirked at my jab. We both knew that leaving Boston College to play for the NHL was the best move he'd ever made. He had one hell of a season last year and was shaping up to be one of the breakout superstars of the team.

I'd started paying more attention to the games again since the past winter, and I suppose the reason why was fairly obvious. I knew it was probably pretty stupid and pointless, but seeing

Zac—even on my TV—was my new favorite form of entertainment. He'd racked up over two hundred penalty minutes during his rookie year and wasn't showing signs of letting up anytime soon. No wonder his nickname was "Maniac."

It's not that he was a dick on the ice, he was just an extraordinarily aggressive player, and managed to get called out for it at every turn. Hooking, slashing, boarding... But the most entertaining theatrics were witnessed when he was diving. The guy was a decent actor, and could sometimes manage to draw the penalty from the opposing team. But when he didn't? He'd protest the embellishment call until he was red in the face, then slam the boards with his stick on the way to his time out. And that was just the anger he displayed before ever receiving the fines.

Even when I wasn't glued to my TV, I still thought about him (despite my better judgment), and always looked forward to seeing him in the flesh. It wasn't every day that I found myself in the presence of someone *that* good-looking, and it was always thrilling during the occasions when I did. There was just nothing like that flippy feeling you got being around a gorgeous guy. Even when they were jerks, the butterflies in your stomach would betray you.

So, I didn't beat myself up about watching all those games. I loved hockey, it was my father's job, and catching a glimpse of Zac was simply a bonus. Just because we'd never be together didn't mean I couldn't *look* at the guy, right?

Looking at him never disappointed, but tonight, he was even more delectable than usual. He was wearing a dark gray suit which made him look less like the wild athlete he was and more like a suave, respectable gentleman.

A totally hot one at that.

"Well, that's good. I'm glad you're doing well out there." He tapped his bottle against mine and added, "I'm actually surprised you came tonight."

His lips quirked, trying to repress a smile. As if he was trying to get me to admit that I'd come back to see *him*. Fat chance.

"Yeah, well, my father asked me to be there. He wasn't too thrilled that I skipped it last year."

"He likes to show you off."

I picked at the bar napkin under my drink, trying to will myself not to blush from Zac's adorable grin. "He's proud of me, if that's what you mean."

"I can see why." He raked his eyes over my floral dress and added, "You've sure got some... *assets* to be proud of."

For as much time as we spent in each other's proximity, it was inevitable that I'd find myself on the receiving end of Zac's flirting. I always tried to take it with a grain of salt, though, knowing his playful comments were just a part of who he was.

As fun as it was to play along, I think I liked seeing the serious part of him more. He didn't let it slip out too often, but I loved those moments. For all his life-of-the-party personality, it was nice to get the rare glimpse of him just being himself every once in a while. I got the impression that I was one of only a very few people that he ever allowed into his real life.

"I'm going to hit the bathroom..." I diverted, sliding off of my stool and making my escape.

It was on my way back that I literally bumped into an old friend. Coming down the hallway just as I was leaving it was Nick Stradlater, a guy I used to date in high school.

Nick was a year older than I was, and was known to everyone in town as The Devirginator. I'm not going to go into detail here, but let's just say I'm able to report the validity of his moniker from firsthand experience.

We'd only dated for a few months, long enough to get the job done before he shipped off for college. Considering the main reason I even dated him was to get my deflowering over with, I wasn't terribly heartbroken when we broke up.

"Avery Brooks!" he laughed out, throwing his arms around me like we were old pals.

"Hey Nick," I said with the last breath of air in my lungs.

He finally released his boa-constrictor hold on me to step back and say, "I haven't seen you in years."

"Three years, Nick. It's only been three. How are you?"

I eyed him cautiously, trying to gauge how the years had treated him. He was still tall, obviously. Messy dark hair. Wearing a pink Izod, frayed along the bottom, which earned him fashion points in my book for pulling off a preppy-yet-rockstar look. He looked good, but I was hardly overjoyed to see him. I mean, it was embarrassing to have to confront someone who once saw me naked. And based on the way his eyes were presently scrutinizing every inch of my body, I started to believe he was envisioning me in such a state right now. Jeez, the guy was still a cad.

"I'm great! Just transferred over to William Patterson, so I'm home now. You?"

"Penn. Just started my junior year."

I was peeking over his shoulder, clearly looking to get back to the bar, but Nick's towering form was blocking my escape. He was practically wedged at the mouth of the narrow hallway we were standing in.

"Junior year, huh?" He shot a toothy sneer at me as he added, "Correct me if I'm wrong, but wasn't it your junior year when you and I...?"

"*Dated*?" I finished for him.

"I was going to say 'fucked.'"

Of course he was.

"Well, correct *me* if *I'm* wrong, but we did a lot more than just... that. We were together for four months!"

"Guess I just choose to remember the good part."

If I thought for even one second that he was only kidding, I would have spent a few more minutes catching up with the guy. But because I knew he was entirely serious, I decided to put an end to the conversation.

Before I could, however, he chucked me under my chin and said, "Smile, sweetheart. It can't be that bad."

Ugh.

Normally, nothing pissed me off more than when some dude tried to tell me what facial expression I should be wearing. But I got the impression that maybe Nick just needed a little help in the tossing-out-a-line department. I chuckled to myself when I thought about how Zac could offer a class or something.

"Well, it was good to run into you, Nick. I guess I'll be seeing you around."

I started to step around him, but he made a big show of blocking my exit. "Hey, whoa! What's your hurry?"

"Umm... I was just going back over to my friends."

"I thought *I* was your friend," he slithered, stepping forward, requiring me to take a step back. "At least we used to be. Don't you want to be friends again?"

Not wanting to encourage nor antagonize him, I amended in as civil a tone as I could muster, "Actually, I'm just heading back to my *boyfriend*." I mentally tried to transmit that said imaginary boyfriend was very huge. And jealous. And short-tempered.

His grin turned into a leer as he reached out and ran a hand down my bare arm. The touch caused me to shiver, and not in a very good way. "Aww. You're not using the old 'fake boyfriend' line on me, are you?"

"I'm not using anything on you."

I could smell the beer on his breath as he dipped his face closer to mine, causing me to jerk my face away as I dodged. But I was quickly running out of room in that little hallway and wasn't able to put as much distance between us as I would have liked. You know, like a continent or two.

Trying to laugh it off, I said, "Whoa, Nick. This isn't happening. It was good to see you, but I have to go."

"No, you don't."

He grasped me by my hips and backed me against the wall to the bathrooms as I tried to register just what in the hell was happening. Things were hey-howdy-hi-how-are-ya only a minute ago, and now suddenly, this little reunion was escalating all too quickly into creeper territory. He'd obviously changed in the years since I'd seen him, and not for the better. The guy was always a blowhard but I'd never found him *intimidating*. Until now. I wasn't quite in panic-mode just yet enough to make a run for it, but I definitely did not like where things were heading.

I attempted once again to talk my way out of his grasp. "Okay, honestly? I don't know if you're just screwing around, but you're starting to scare me here. I'm leaving now."

I knew I said that last bit with a little extra snippy in my voice, but I didn't like the feeling of being trapped in some dark, abandoned hallway with a guy who obviously didn't know how to take 'no' for an answer.

When I stepped to the left, he stepped in front of me, and when I tried to slip past him on the right, he grabbed me around the waist, snickering, "If you wanted to dance, all you had to do was ask."

Okay. I was officially skeeved out by this guy. I was just about to forcefully remove myself from his grasp when Zac appeared around the corner.

When he saw the tangle I was in, his eyes turned into daggers. I tried to defuse the situation when I sputtered out, "Look, Nick. I told you. I'm here with my boyfriend. He's right behind you."

"Nice try," he scoffed, before smashing his lips to mine.

I squirmed against the onslaught, shoving my hands against his chest to no avail. I went to knee him in the crotch, but I missed and only grazed his thigh.

Zac grabbed Nick by the shoulder and spun him around. Nick was trying to recover from my near-fatal ninja moves when Zac asked, "What the fuck is going on here?"

Nick must have recognized Zac right off. "Mind your own, Maniac."

A muscle was pulsing furiously in Zac's jaw as he seethed, "You're about to find out why people call me that." The next thing I knew, a barreling fist was landing squarely on Nick's jaw.

Things got a little blurry after that.

The hallway filled with Zac and Nick's traded fists. It was a tight fit, and I found myself backing into the corner—willingly this time—to avoid them. Zac shoved him into the main part of the bar, and once everyone realized what was happening, the place turned into a scene from *Smokey and the Bandit*. The booming voices of the cheering spectators drowned the music as a few of the rowdier guys started fights of their own. Chairs were toppled; tables were relocated.

I don't know how long the fight lasted, but once the bouncers got involved, it was over pretty quickly. They pulled people apart and threw out the most troublesome of the troublemakers, Nick included.

A few people were patting Zac on the back as I made my way through the crowd toward him. As soon as he saw me, he threw his arms around my waist and pulled me to him in a smothering hug. He was sweaty, and he smelled like a brewery from the beer that had spilled on him, but that didn't stop me from hugging him back. As if it could.

"Are you okay?" he asked. He pulled back and checked me over, looking for any damage to my person.

I was shaking, but I was unhurt. Physically, at least. "Yeah. I think so," I answered, as I returned the scrutiny. His hair was a tangled mass of black, sticking out in every direction, and his tailored shirt was torn at the shoulder. I took note of his injuries—aside from a bloody lip, he was only sporting a few scrapes and some raw skin on his cheeks and knuckles. "Are *you* okay?"

"Never better," he grinned.

"What about *that*?" I asked, pointing to his mouth. "Will you get in trouble at work tomorrow? How are you going to explain the split lip?"

"I'm a hockey player, Avery. No explanation needed beyond that. Are you sure you're alright?"

"Yes, I swear. Freaked out, but I'm okay."

No one had ever 'defended my honor' before. I probably should have been disgusted or horrified, but honestly? All I could seem to feel at that moment was *grateful*.

And not just because Zac had stepped up to play Batman.

He'd pulled me in for another hug, binding his arms around me tightly, trying to still my shivering. Problem was, being that close to him was most of the reason why I was still shaking in the first place. His heart was beating like crazy, leftover adrenaline from the fight. *Mine* was only racing from being wrapped up in his arms.

I picked at a stray thread from the torn shirt at his shoulder, playing the brawl over in my mind. I closed my eyes against the vision and I was instantaneously reminded of a much more entertaining moment from the fight.

"You're about to find out why people call me that?" I chuckled against his chest, busting his chops.

I couldn't contain my giggles as he shot back, "They're not all winners, baby."

Chapter Four
MAY 1997

Zac's family owned a bar a few towns over, and he'd gotten the guys to go there a handful of times over the years. Johnny's was their home base, but they liked having another option every once in a while.

I hadn't gotten the chance to check it out until tonight, however.

We walked into *The Westlake Pub* and I was immediately smacked with the smell of warm food and beer-soaked wood. The building was a large, open space with high ceilings accented by weathered, wooden beams. Even the walls were adorned in wood, framing the few rectangles of decrepit sheetrock plastered with beer ads and band posters.

There was a large square bar on one side of the room, and a long bar along the opposite wall. It faced a wall of windows which looked out onto the lake out back, but as it was already dark out, I couldn't see more than some random lights along the perimeter. It must've been beautiful during the daytime. I made a point to get back during daylight hours someday in order to appreciate the view.

A bunch of guys from the team were already there, but the place would have been crowded regardless. People of all ages occupied the stools along the bars and gathered at the hightop tables in between. The tables sat in the middle of what looked to be a repurposed dance floor. Two minutes in the door, and I could already tell that a place like this had no need for such a thing. It was *not* the type of bar where people came to dance.

Casey nabbed a booth just as a group was leaving from it, sliding onto the vinyl seat before the last person had even left. Commandeering a good seat at a bar sometimes required guerilla tactics, and Casey's little body was the perfect size to sneak in under the radar.

Simon grabbed us a round and we settled into the booth. I was facing the long bar, and I could see Zac behind it, enthusiastically holding court and serving drinks. He seemed comfortable enough behind the taps, but I guessed since he'd grown up in this environment, some of it had rubbed off.

There was a large chalkboard behind his head, listing a dozen drink concoctions. They were named after different sports terms and made up of a bunch of different liquors, some of which I'd never even heard of. There were Slam Dunks, Double Dribbles, Alley-Oops, First Downs, something called a Safety (that was mostly juice), Slap Shots, Penalty Shots, and my favorite: The Game Misconduct. It had about a million ingredients and was served in a glass fish bowl. It was also served with a warning that a customer was only allowed to order one, because it supposedly put the imbiber "out for the night."

The tables at the booths were all carved up and doodled on with people's names, bits of wisdom, and a few bad jokes. I guessed such behavior was not only tolerated, but encouraged, because there was a Sharpie hanging from a small hook at every station with a long chain attaching it to the paneling. Simon was busily scratching his and Casey's initials into our table with it when I excused myself to the bathroom.

On my way back, I took a moment to check out some of the framed pictures. The Westlake was a sports pub through and through, and the photos on the wall reflected that. There were numerous clippings from the local newspapers, shots of high school football games and YMCA basketball teams.

I was eyeing up an eight-by-ten of Zac, on the ice, his stick in mid-swing, when I heard a voice behind me. "That's one of my favorites."

I turned to find an older man standing there. Salt and pepper hair, warm smile. Handsome.

"It's a great shot," I answered back.

The smile grew a bit wider as he said, "I suppose I'm a little biased. That's my son. He plays for the Devils now."

"Oh, this is your place! You're Mr. McAllister."

"Yes. You know Zac?"

"Yeah. I sort of came with him."

"Really?" he asked. "Well, I shouldn't be surprised. He always knew how to find the prettiest girls."

Oh crap. The guy thought I was dating his son. "No. I mean, I sort of came here with him… and a bunch of other people. We hang out sometimes. As friends. With other friends." I knew I was babbling, but I was only trying to make it clear that I was *not* Zac's girlfriend, in spite of my occasional wishes to the contrary. "I'm sorry. My name's Avery. Brooks, actually."

His kind grin put me at ease as he held out his hand for me to shake. "Oh, so you're Benny's daughter."

"Yes, sir."

"Well, that pretty much makes you my son's boss, now, doesn't it?" His comment made me giggle as he added, "And it's Rudy. Please don't call me Mr. McAllister. After all, we're practically family."

I gave a shy smile as he put an arm around my shoulders, directing my focus to the wall once more. He pointed to all the pictures in turn, explaining what each person had done to make it onto his Wall of Fame. There were local guys who had excelled in their chosen sport and some girls who had been part of various Olympic teams. There were pictures of everything from professional sports figures right on down to the little leaguers who'd made it to the state finals.

He lingered over the photos of his sons—I was reminded that there were *four,* God help him—telling of their myriad accomplishments in great detail; the beaming pride in his voice was unmistakable. It would have been embarrassing if I hadn't found it completely endearing.

I'd been so enraptured listening to all of Mr. McAllister's stories that I didn't even realize Zac had joined us.

"Moving in on my girl?" he asked, handing me a fresh beer as he took a sip of his own. "Don't listen to a thing this guy tells you. It's all lies, I promise you."

"Hmm," I answered back, shooting a conspiratorial grin at Zac's father. "So, you *weren't* MVP of your high school hockey team? You *don't* hold the all-time school record for most goals scored?"

Zac gave a sheepish smile as he corrected, "I meant don't believe anything *bad.*"

His father shot me a sidelong smirk (which reminded me an awful lot of his son) as he said, "Aww, Zac. You've always been an angel. Everyone knows that."

The comment had me sputtering out a laugh. Too bad I was mid-sip at the time. I cupped my hand to my chin and swiped the beer from my lips as Zac and his father chuckled at my predicament.

"Drinking problem," they both coughed out in unison, which just had me cracking up all over again.

Chapter Five
JANUARY 1998

I pulled into the lot at Johnny's just as David Bowie's "Changes" came on the radio. It was blasphemous to go inside without listening to it in its entirety, so I rolled down the windows and hopped up onto the hood of my Jetta. Lounging back against the windshield, I watched the stars as a few snowflakes flurried onto my face. I closed my eyes and sang along, trying to fully enjoy the warmth of my car at my back and the chill of the night along my front, but my brain wouldn't shut off.

I was leaving to head back to school the next day, and my mind was consumed with seeing Mike once I got back there. We'd been friends since my freshman year, but just started dating a few months ago. He only lived a couple towns away from me here at home, but he'd spent the Christmas break skiing out in Colorado with his family, so I hadn't seen him since we drove home from Pennsylvania together.

I knew I'd see him tomorrow, though.

And I wasn't much looking forward to breaking up with him.

He was a great guy, and he was super cute, and really funny but… I don't know. I wasn't sure why someone who checked all the boxes didn't send my heart racing whenever I thought about him. Shouldn't I have felt more… well, *more* for him?

It figured that at that exact moment, a certain familiar voice broke my reverie. "Wow. A hot chick listening to Bowie? I think I'm in love."

I didn't open my eyes and simply broke into a smile as I said, "That's funny coming from someone with a cold, dead heart."

"Ouch. Now that hurts, Ave." I giggled as he added, "What are you doing out here?"

"Thinking." I finally cracked my lids to see Zac standing over me. "You're blocking my sun," I teased.

"It's January. And nighttime. And you're wearing way too many clothes." I laughed as he gave a tug to my ski hat, pulling it over my eyes. "You bring up an interesting point, though. How come I never get to see you in a bikini?"

It was true that we didn't ever hang out during the off-season. I didn't even know why that was. Our association had always revolved around hockey, I guess. Summer was always the time for players to go back to their *real* lives.

"It's January. And nighttime," I teased back.

He shot me a dirty look as he took my hand. "C'mon, Nanook. Let's get you inside."

I let him haul me off the car, then I locked everything up before following him into the bar. He was still holding my hand as we searched the room for Casey and Simon. Thank God I was wearing my mittens, because I was so nervous about this interesting turn of events that my palms were getting sweaty.

When we finally found our friends, I gave Casey a wave with my free hand.

"Well, look what the dog dragged in," she busted.

I laughed at her play on words. "Hey guys," I greeted as I slid into the booth.

When Zac skootched me over to sit down, I realized that we'd be playing foursome again. It looked as though tonight was going to be one of those atypical evenings where he spent more of his time with his friends instead of going on the prowl for his next conquest.

Even though his conquests weren't too difficult to come by.

"I already ordered you guys a round," Case said as she flagged down the waitress. "What took you so long?"

Before I could respond, Zac jumped in. "I found her out front trying to freeze to death."

Casey tried to hide her smile when she said, "Nah. Avery has built up an immunity to the cold."

I knew what she was leading up to. I glared at her as I removed my coat and hat, trying to contain a grin as I warned, "Case, don't say it…"

"Hey, Avery. Why don't you tell Simon and Zac about that night you spent in the penalty box!"

"What?" the guys laughed out, waiting on my explanation.

I shot Casey a dirty look. "It wasn't the *whole* night," I defended, twisting my hair into a ponytail.

Zac leaned back in his seat and crossed his hands over his stomach. "Oh, now I just *have* to hear this one."

I groaned through a laugh, figuring there was no way to get out of telling the story. I waited for our server to finish unloading our beers onto the table before starting in. "Okay. When I was little, I used to spend a lot of time at the arena."

"You spend a lot of time there now," Zac said.

"No. I pop in on occasion. When I was around ten or eleven, I was there *all* the time."

"Okay…"

"Well. I used to putter around the building after practices, score some free snacks from the concessions, play with the air-dryers in the bathrooms, stuff like that. Basically, Dad always knew where to find me when it was time to go. This one night, I snuck off and went to hang out in the rink—I loved being in that big, empty space by myself—and I guess I was waiting there for so long that I fell asleep. By the time my father was ready to leave, I was nowhere to be found. He went crazy searching for me in all my usual spots. No one had seen me. They called arena security, and eventually, the Rutherford police."

"Shut up!" Simon laughed.

"One of the janitors finally found me hours later in the penalty box, sleeping like I didn't have a care in the world. Problem is, I'd been in there so long, they thought I fell asleep because of hypothermia. I kept saying I was fine, but they brought me to the hospital anyway to make sure."

Zac was grinning like an idiot as he asked, "And...?"

"And, clean bill of health. They sent me out of there with this weird silver blanket, and I went home, good as new."

"Awww, Diddums," Zac faux-sympathized.

"Hey, I got a new bike out of the deal. I'm not complaining. I just always feel bad for doing that to my father! He was worried sick."

"Jesus," Simon chortled. "I think that qualifies you for some sort of record. Even McAllister hasn't spent that many minutes in the bin!"

Casey shook her head. "Avery, I swear to God, you're such a wacko sometimes."

I laughed, but didn't get the chance to deliver an appropriate rebuttal, because Zac put a hand over mine and shot back, "Why do you think I like her so much?"

The bones of my hand turned to mush at his touch, but the rest of me positively melted when I saw the look on his face. He was aiming a crooked smile in my direction, his gorgeous green eyes raking over me in appreciation.

I'd seen that same look a few times over the past two years, and it always knocked me out just as much as it had that first time, the night when he was trying to show me how he 'didn't need lines.'

With that smoldering mug staring me down, I became well aware that he certainly did not.

I didn't know what I'd done to warrant "the look" tonight. We'd spent a lot of time in each other's company, and he often flirted with me, but that was only because he flirted with everybody. The sex appeal was just a huge chunk of his personality... not like I was going to complain. You remember that little dinosaur in *Jurassic Park* who spit the acid in Newman's face? Yeah. That was what it was like being around Zac. You'd just be hanging out, minding your own business, when *SPLAT!*

Dead.

"You only like her because you thought she wanted to jump your bones," Simon said.

I almost choked on my beer. *What the fuck, Simon?* How would he even know something like that? It's not as though I ever told him how I felt. I barely even mentioned anything to Casey, for godsakes, and she was my best friend! Were my feelings just that obvious? *Oh God. Kill me.*

Thankfully, Casey jumped in to cover. "What the hell are you talking about? She hated him that first night and has barely tolerated him since!"

Simon cracked up at that. It wasn't every day that Zac got shot down, so I was sure his friend found it amusing when he did.

"You've *tolerated* me?" Zac asked.

I aimed a what-the-hell look at Casey. "Why would you go and say something like that?"

Sure, I'd kept my distance. But I didn't mean for him to think it was because I didn't like him. I was truly happy with the friendship we'd formed, and impressed with the guy I'd discovered under all that swagger.

I turned to Zac, hoping he wasn't actually insulted. "Tolerate is the wrong word. So is hate, for that matter. I think you and I have always just had... differing goals for how we think our evenings should go."

His mouth gaped. "You think I'm a slut."

Simon laughed out, "Who are you kidding, sitting there all hurt? You love when people think you're a slut."

"No..." I answered. "I don't think that. I—"

"I thought *you* were an *angel*."

That is not as complimentary as it may have seemed. "The Angels" were a self-named assemblage of hockey groupies that had been coming to this bar for years.

"You thought I was one of the *Angels*?"

Zac stared blankly at me for a second too long, then let out with an uneasy laugh. "Well, you were wearing that tight shirt and those sexy boots. Why *wouldn't* I have thought you were a groupie?" He chuckled again as he added, "But then you got so offended when I put the moves on, I figured out pretty quickly that I read you wrong, and changed up my M.O. There I was, showing you my softer, chewy-nougat insides, and it turned out you were off-limits anyway."

"What?"

"Sorenson didn't tell me you were Brooks' daughter for three whole weeks." He looked over at Simon and added, "Asshole."

Simon was wearing a shit-eating grin as he cracked, "I thought it would be funnier if I didn't."

"Dickhead."

Chapter Six
DECEMBER 31, 1998

With only months remaining before I graduated college, I was looking forward to getting a real job that paid some real money. But for now, at the age of twenty-one, with my room and board paid for, I basically only needed enough to cover incidentals and beer money. But seeing as I was off the clock at *Beans* over holiday break, I wouldn't see my next paycheck until closer to February, and my stash was already wearing thin.

That didn't stop me from buying a new dress anyway.

I couldn't help myself. The thing was practically screaming at me from the display at *Nordstrom's*, where I'd done some Christmas shopping for my mom. Unfortunately, I was there to exchange the present I'd gotten her as she already had a blue pashmina. I scored a new pink one for her… and a slinky gold gown for myself. I figured the dress would be perfect for Casey and Simon's wedding next fall.

Except this morning, they'd thrown a wrench in their original plans when they hopped a plane for Vegas instead.

Casey called me from a payphone at the airport to spill the news. I was shocked, and more than a little heartbroken, but ultimately, I couldn't be anything other than happy for her. They'd just gotten engaged at Thanksgiving, and I knew she immediately found the whole wedding thing overwhelming. As much as I was looking forward to helping her plan, I was well aware that they needed to do what was right for *them*. I was sad that I wouldn't be there for it, but the more she explained their decision, the more I became impressed with her logic.

"We just started asking ourselves why we were driving ourselves crazy with the thing, you know?" she asked at one point.

"No, I get it. I know you weren't enjoying any of the decision-making."

"Exactly. That's your department."

I snickered, but acknowledged that she was right.

I'd become quite the party planner over the years. Birthdays, sorority balls… you name it. I was a very organized person by nature, and such skills came in handy whenever there were plans to be made. Aside from the fact that I totally reveled in the details, I loved having the control to make the decisions. Even during my sorority's committee meetings, I found most of the members would simply delegate all authority to me, and I was more than happy to take the reins. It might sound stupid, but after years of blending into the background, it felt empowering to finally stand out for my accomplishments. Even if said accomplishments were nothing more than pulling together an awesome party.

"Oh, whatever," I appeased. "Yes, I would have loved to help you plan the best wedding ever, but I completely understand why you're choosing to skip it."

"We know we love each other. Why should we wait?"

"You shouldn't." I figured her parents might have felt a bit differently, but then again, they were pretty laid back people. Maybe they'd even be relieved. "Oh my God. The next time I see you, you'll be married!"

"Eeek! I know! Oh God. Wish us luck!"

"Good luck! Tell Simon, too."

"I will. Love you!"

"Love you, too."

I hung up the phone and slunk down onto the bed. When Casey first told me she and Simon had gotten engaged, I was surprised. But thinking about the fact that she was actually going to be *married* within a matter of twenty-four hours was positively surreal.

My brain tried to register the new information as I eyed my new dress. It was hanging from my closet door, still with the tags on it, still returnable. Long, slinky, shimmery... sexy, but chaste enough for a formal occasion. I'd tried it on in the store and fell in love with the skinny straps, the fitted bodice, the dropped-cowl neckline that made me look boobier than I actually was.

I realized that even though I was Maryann... I could still rock one hell of a Ginger dress.

My plan was to show it to Casey for final approval. One of the only decisions she'd made was to have me as her sole bridesmaid, and because of that, she was planning to let me pick my own gown. But I wanted to make sure she liked it before getting my hopes up about keeping it. Shame of it was that I knew she'd say it was perfect, but now it looked as though I'd be returning it after all.

I walked over to the gown, and before I could think about the ramifications of my actions, I ripped off the tags and threw them in the garbage. It was New Year's Eve, and what better way to kick off the new year than in a fabulous new dress?

* * *

Johnny's was hopping already and it was barely nine o'clock. I assume it was the new dress that gave me some much-needed

55

confidence, because I went there alone. I knew the whole crowd would be there, as they weren't scheduled for another game until January 3, giving them three whole days to blow off some steam.

It looked as though the party was well underway.

I ditched my coat and grabbed an unoccupied stool at the bar next to Guillaume, not far from where the rest of my hockey friends were congregating.

"Hey, Guy! Happy New Year!" I said, as I leaned in for a quick peck on the cheek.

He looked at me appreciatively, letting out with a whistle. "*That* is some dress."

I blushed from my head down to my toes. "Thank you. It's New Year's. I figured I'd live a little, you know?"

"Well, I'm glad *you're* living. I think my heart just stopped."

I gave him another kiss for that.

I ordered a glass of champagne from the bartender, and while I was waiting for it to be delivered, a searing heat made its way down my spine. I turned to find Zac standing there, but I didn't need visual confirmation that it was him. From the electric charge I was feeling along my skin, I already knew it was his hand at my back.

"Happy New Year," he said, all smooth and Zachary. It wasn't standard protocol for him to beeline in my direction the first minute I showed up, and I was suddenly *very* glad I'd worn my new gold dress out that night. I decided right then and there that I would wear the thing every waking moment for the rest of my life.

"Happy New Year, Zac."

His beautiful green eyes held a trace of apprehension as he leaned in to kiss my cheek, and I became aware of the fact that I was throwing him off guard. Me. Avery Brooks. *I* was throwing *him* for a loop. That had never happened before.

Thank you, God, for alluring dresses and captivated men who smell like peppermint.

Guillaume grabbed his drink and offered Zac his seat. "Don't do anything I wouldn't do," he said with an evil grin.

"That doesn't leave much," Zac spat back. He slid onto the stool and waited for the bartender. "Flying solo tonight?" he asked, scanning his eyes around our immediate area.

"Yep. Did you hear about Simon and Casey?"

"Sure did. Got the call from the airport."

"Me too."

He swiped a hand through his hair and said, "Jesus! I can't believe they're actually going through with it."

I looked at him curiously. "Why would you say that? They were planning to do it anyway, now they're just doing it sooner."

"I don't know," he said, shaking his head at the floor. He raised his eyes to mine and explained, "Simon and me are the same age. It's just hard to imagine getting married at twenty-three."

I huffed, "Well, of course *you* can't imagine it."

"Hey, whoa. It's not that I *can't*. It's that I *choose not to*. Most guys my age feel the same way."

"Most girls, too."

"Bullshit."

"Huh?"

"Come on," he said, lowering an eyebrow. "Most girls I know have only one goal and one goal only." He nodded his head in the direction of a group of bunnies fawning all over Guillaume. "Marry some rich guy and spend all his money."

"How optimistic of you."

"It's the truth."

"No it's not! It's not the truth with Casey, and it's not the truth for me. I happen to have much bigger goals, and none of them require 'some rich guy' to make them happen."

"Oh yeah? Like what?"

"I don't know yet," I laughed, absently running a finger around the edge of my champagne flute. "But who knows? It's a new year, right? Anything can happen."

He clinked his bottle against my glass. "Here's hoping."

* * *

"Crap. I missed."

I stood upright after taking my fruitless shot and noticed a bit of wobble in my legs. I placed a hand on the table and used my cue to steady myself.

Yeah. I am definitely buzzing.

Zac and I had been playing pool for over two hours. He suggested we team up, and when we did, we became a force to be reckoned with. Challenger after challenger got smacked down as we dominated the billiard room.

Our latest contenders were Travis and Selene. Travis was one of Zac's teammates, and Selene was one of the Angels. I knew her well.

"My turn!" she let out, before moving into position and bending over the table. I watched as Travis gave Zac a nudge and nodded at her ass.

I shook my head at the two of them, then called them out. "They're checking out your butt, Selene."

She gave a flirty look over her shoulder. "Well, I should hope so. I didn't wear this tight little dress for nothing."

We all shared a good laugh at that as she took her shot.

"Yippee! Made it!" she exclaimed as she spun around and I gave her a high-five. I was giggling at her word choice. Who the hell says *yippee*? She must have been more excited than actual words could convey.

"Hey! *I'm* your teammate, remember?" Zac asked.

How could I forget? I'd had his undivided attention the entire night. I was normally a decent pool player, but I made a point to play better than I ever had in my life, because every time we won meant we got to play another game in order to defend our championship. And every game we played meant another chunk of time together. As partners. Teammates. A *couple*, by the loosest definition of terms.

Even though our relationship was planted firmly in The Friendzone—and I was content with that, truly—it didn't stop me from crushing on the guy. Especially when he looked so hot all dressed up.

I took a look over at Zac and Travis, two incredibly beautiful men leaning against the wall together. Zac's dark good looks were offset by Travis's light brown hair and eyes. Zac was wearing a black, button-down shirt, and Travis had on a chambray snap-up with white piping (and a white cowboy hat to match). Night and day. City meets country. Damn. It was quite an enticing vision.

I smiled involuntarily at the sight and explained, "Just showing a little sisterhood solidarity." Although, since I was feeling the buzz from all those glasses of champagne—and two Lemon Drop shots—I was sure my words came out more than a little garbled.

"Oh, darlin'. I think you need another drink," Travis suggested in his honeyed drawl. He was a regular good ol' boy, that one. I didn't know too many cowboys, much less ones who played hockey, but he was a really great guy, not to mention a damn fine athlete.

He waved the waitress over and asked her to hang on while Selene sank the 8-ball. She dropped her cue onto the table and threw her arms in the air. "Whoooooo!"

Travis came over and wrapped his arms around her, lifting her off the floor as he put in his order to the waitress. "Well, I know I'll be having another beer. And this little winner here will have…"

"A white zinfandel!"

"You heard the woman. You can deliver them to our table, thank ya kindly. Oh, and make sure you put it on McAllister's tab," he added with a wink in Zac's direction before carrying Selene out to the bar.

The waitress followed them out as Zac came over by me. He tossed his cue onto the table and said, "Well, partner, we gave it our all. Looks like we finally have to hand over the trophy. Good game." He held his hand out to me and I shook it.

"At least we drank for free all night!"

"That's true," he agreed, before rolling his beer bottle over his forehead, trying to cool off. I was feeling a bit hot and bothered myself. He was such a sexy bastard. He didn't even need to try. It was just who he was.

Maybe it was the booze lightening my inhibitions, but I suddenly came to an indisputable revelation: Standing right there in front of me was this gorgeous guy who made my heart do somersaults in my chest, and yet I'd been keeping him at arms' length for years. *Why did I do that?* I'd only ever let him be a friend to me, as opposed to the manwhore he was with the rest of the world. But why was I so afraid to let him be both? How come I never even *tried?*

And that was it for me. That was all it took. That stupid bottle was like a switch being flipped in my brain, a split second that changed everything. You could spend your life thinking a certain way, just following the status quo. And then BOOM. Just like that, the most inconsequential thing would have you rethinking everything.

He lowered the bottle and leaned against the pool table. I went to do the same, but I misjudged its height and fumbled a bit before getting situated. Zac watched me in amusement and asked, "Just how much have you had tonight, anyway?"

I didn't know where the hell I found the nerve, but I ran a hand across his and teased, "Why? Worried I won't be able to get it up?"

The comment actually floored him. Hell. It floored *me.*

He looked at me in open-mouthed shock and laughed out nervously, "You shouldn't joke around like that, Ave. A guy could take things the wrong way."

He'd been flirting with me all night; hell, he'd been doing it for three years. Teasing me into oblivion was pretty much his default mode, but this was the first night I ever let myself flirt *back.* I don't think he knew how to take it.

He tried to go back to joking, tried to bring things back down to friend level. "We should get you some water."

I was definitely not drunk. Tipsy, but not full-on, head-in-the-toilet, falling-over drunk. At least not on alcohol. I'd become high on the idea of getting him alone, and I was suddenly hellbent on doing everything in my power to make it happen. "We should get out of here."

That threw him. He scanned my face, trying to see if I was putting him on, but I didn't waver, didn't even crack a smile. I knew he could tell I was one hundred percent serious. *I* could tell he was fighting it. He wanted to believe me... and was scared shitless about it.

I loved every second of confusion on his face.

Finally, tentatively, he raised a palm to my jaw. His fingers brushed under the hair at my nape; his thumb feathered against my lips. I almost fainted, I swear to God. But I knew he was testing me, seeing just how far I was willing to take this little joke.

When he could see that I wasn't going to break, his grip tightened as his teeth clenched, and like some sort of holiday miracle, he hissed, "Screw it. Let's go."

Yippee!

Prince's "1999" was playing for the third time that night as Zac walked me out the door. It had to only be a few minutes until midnight, but I couldn't care less. I came out for the evening to hang with my friends, but I'd suddenly found a much better way to ring in the New Year.

We got to my car and I fumbled with the keys. I was kind of in shock that this was actually happening, and my shaking hands were so obvious that it was embarrassing. Zac's hand closed over mine, and when I looked up, he was wearing that adorable lopsided grin. His eyes met mine as he slid a palm behind my neck and into the back of my hair. We stood there like that for a moment, my stomach threatening to explode, Zac giving me one final chance to change my mind. As if I would.

He waited for just one extra beat before backing me against my car and lowering his lips to mine.

Holyshitholyshitholyshit!

My heart started beating like crazy, but my arms managed to wrap around his shoulders. Thank God, because my body was about to crumple into a useless heap right there in the parking lot.

He broke away for a moment, looking at me in what I can only describe as *amused shock*.

"*Jesus, Ave*," he whispered, stunned but pleased, before pressing his mouth to mine once more.

Oh God. Kissing him was the sweetest thing in the world. He tasted like candy and sunshine and Johnny Walker Blue. He smelled like winter chill and peppermint. He felt like… Heaven.

He pulled me tightly against his length as his lips moved tenderly across my own. I knotted my hands in the back of his hair and opened my mouth, pressing myself against him as his hands slid down to my ass, pushing me against the car again, his mouth devouring mine, his hips grinding against me.

My breath was coming out in an unsteady gasp; my heart was pounding against my ribcage. The feel of his firm lips against mine and his insistent hips and his possessive hands… Whoa. I mean, just, full-on, mind-numbing *whoa*.

He took half a step back, wearing that stunned look on his face again which was quickly becoming my new favorite expression. "I tried," he said, lowering his head and giving it a good shake. His eyes raised to meet mine as he added, "I really did try to stay away from you."

A warmth spread throughout my entire body at his words, warding off the winter cold. He'd been… *trying* to stay away from me? He wanted this as much as I did?

I found that completely too good to be true. My brain simply wouldn't allow me to believe there was any way he was as into this as me.

But still, his admission gave me the confidence to accept that this was actually going to happen.

This was sooo going to happen.

I stepped away momentarily in order to unlock the car, sliding behind the wheel and starting the engine just to get some heat flowing through the frosty space. "I hope you don't expect me to drive anywhere."

Zac was leaning in the opened driver's side door. His lips pursed together and I could see a muscle twitching in his jaw. "So, you *are* drunk."

Is it bad that I found his devastation positively exhilarating?

"No, Zac, I swear. I'm only buzzed. Too drunk to drive, *not* too drunk to know what I'm doing. Okay?"

He searched my face for a minute longer than necessary, assessing the situation. His lips curled into a dangerous grin as he realized I was telling the truth. "Get in the back."

I took him up on his invitation, ditched my coat, and maneuvered myself into the backseat as tactfully as possible. Not exactly the easiest thing to do while crawling on my hands and knees and wearing a dress. It was long, thankfully, but there was a slit that ran from hem to thigh, and as I sat back on the seat, the damn thing betrayed me. I hadn't planned to *present* myself to him quite so boldly. Not just yet, anyway.

Zac's eyes locked onto my bare leg, and I swear, he practically licked his chops as he climbed onto the floor of the car.

He slammed the door behind him, ran a palm up my exposed skin, then bent down to kiss my thigh. "*Fuck*," he scratched out. "Your legs have been driving me insane *forever*." He gave a light bite to the spot he just kissed, adding, "And Jesus. They taste as good as I hoped."

Okay. Zachary McAllister had been wondering what my *legs tasted like*? I'd say I would've been willing to die happy at that second, but the truth is, I wasn't quite ready to check out just yet. I wanted more of him first.

I put my hands on either side of his head and pulled his lips to mine once more. My Jetta didn't necessarily allow much space to move, but he managed to find a way. His body slid up the length of mine before settling himself right between my legs, and oh my God, what did I ever do in my life to deserve *this*?

His tongue swept into my mouth as his hand glided along my side. I felt a groan escape from his chest and rumble against mine, the weight of him on top of me stealing my breath. He pulled a strap of my dress off my shoulder and kissed me there, my skin on fire from his touch. His hand was in a fist at my arm as he moved his lips over to my collarbone, peppering soft kisses along the swell of flesh above my strapless bra.

I was in a complete daze from the surreal events taking place right there in the backseat of my car. But when his hand slid between my legs, I became more than aware of what was happening.

Trust me. I noticed.

He pulled my panties to the side and slipped a finger across my sensitive skin. I gave out a shaky sigh and he raised his head to smile wickedly at me... and then slid his finger inside.

Oh my God. Just... Oh my *God*.

I closed my eyes and let my head fall back, giving myself over to the sensations he was stirring within me. My nails dug into his muscular shoulders as my body pressed involuntarily against his hand. His movements were slow, tender, and I guess I never expected him to be such a patient lover. The reality was much better than my expectations. Much. Much. Better.

I didn't think anything could feel more incredible than what he was doing to me right then.

I was wrong.

He slipped a second finger inside as his thumb joined the party, and by the time his lips met mine, I was ready to completely fall apart. He groaned against my mouth in an aching voice, "*Jesus,* I want you *so bad*, Ave."

Oh God. You have me. I'm yours.

I could feel how badly he wanted me by the insistent knot pressing into my thigh, and I moaned back, not even trying to hide the effect he was having on me. I kissed him then, rough and wanting, feeling his fingers moving inside me and the growl stirring in his chest.

The electric charges started to run along my skin; I don't know why I should have been surprised, but it snuck up on me. Zac's mouth let out a groan against mine... and that sound is what put me completely over the edge. I held on for dear life as the pressure built into a cataclysmic storm of epic proportions before completely exploding; every synapse of my brain igniting as every nerve ending in my body caught fire.

I absolutely fell apart. Died a thousand tiny deaths. Shattered into a million little pieces.

Zac chuckled as I caught my breath, fairly pleased with his accomplishment. I swiped a hand through my sweaty hair and then abruptly pushed him down to lie across the backseat, immediately covering his body with my own. The movement startled him, but I only registered his surprised expression for a second before slamming my lips against his. His hands went around to my back and undid my zipper, pulling my dress and bra down to my waist and grasping at my breasts.

This wasn't over yet.

I was exhausted and out of breath, but his touch gave me a second wind, and I found my hands moving on their own, sliding down his chest as I undid each and every button, unwrapping him like a present. I swiped his shirt open to reveal his sculpted chest, all bulging muscle and unblemished skin, just the slightest tuft of hair between his pecs. I kissed his smooth skin as his hands knotted into my hair, then ran a tongue across his ripped abs.

He chuckled at that, pulling me up by my hair to kiss me again.

It's not as though I was some innocent virgin, but I sure as hell had never been the demented sex-kitten that was currently possessing my body at the present moment. I'd never felt so uninhibited before. I'd never felt this *anything* before.

I unzipped his jeans quickly, then slipped my hand inside to wrap around him. He let out a heavy breath at my touch, and all I could think at that second was how exciting it was to get a little payback. I wanted to see him completely lose his mind.

I was off to a good start, apparently.

My tongue was moving inside his mouth; my hand was moving inside his jeans. He groaned against my lips, and I moaned back, his hips rolling against my touch, my bare breasts against his chest.

He lifted up my dress, enough to slide a palm underneath and across my ass, kneading the flesh there, his thumb under my panties. I didn't know if I should stop what I was doing to take them off or if I should let him do it for me.

"*I need to fuck you,*" he gritted out, and I almost passed out from the sound of his voice, all hungry and wanting and craving. Before I could answer with a resounding *Okay!* he clenched his teeth together and said, "Not here, though. We're not doing this tonight. Not like this."

I knew we weren't in some fancy place in some comfortable bed, but I also knew that it didn't really matter to me. I was reluctantly impressed that it seemed to matter to him.

All thought ceased after that. My hand was working him over; his hands were everywhere else, sliding along every inch of my body within reach like a sex-crazed ninja octopus.

When one of those hands slid down to wrap around mine, I almost died at the sight. I watched our joined hands working together to get the job done—no pun intended—and wondered what would happen if I simply nudged myself out of the way…

Holy shit, he's flying solo right in front of me.

I grabbed him behind his neck and kissed his throat, licking and tasting and biting, shooting the occasional surreptitious look at what was doing south of the Equator. There was so much power in his movement, from his clenched jaw to his flexing bicep to his fisted hand, and I found it hard to tear my gaze away. It was the hottest thing I'd ever witnessed, and there was decidedly some new precipitation moving into my own southern hemisphere.

I watched him in a daze, his strokes building speed, his breaths turning choppy. I grabbed a tissue from the box on the floor and he held my hand over his length as he flinched and unloaded into it.

"*Fuck,*" he snarled, panting and laughing as his movements slowed and his body sank back on the seat. He grabbed a few more tissues to clean himself off before buttoning up, then grabbed me toward him to brand my lips with a searing kiss.

I settled myself on top of him, the both of us trying to catch our breath, my fingers lightly dancing over his naked torso. I laid my head on his chest, hearing his racing heart under my ear.

He let out with a cleansing breath and growled, "That was insane."

Yes. Yes, it was. It was the most incredible non-sex I'd ever had in my life.

I was still out of my mind, but the real world slowly started to creep back in. Led Zep was singing "Tangerine" on the radio, and I figured it must have been well past midnight if the stations were back to playing slow songs. I curled up against Zac's side as his hand brushed a sweet caress along my bare skin. The back of my Volkswagen wasn't exactly the most comfortable place to snuggle, but somehow, we made it work.

Out of nowhere, he said, "I'm kind of crazy about you a little bit."

Holy crap, it sounded like he really meant it.

"What?" I asked incredulously.

I felt his chest rumble as he let out with a laugh. "It's true."

I nervously tried to make light of his proclamation. "You're just proud of yourself for getting me naked."

"No. Stop joking around. I'm serious, Ave. I liked you right off, and actually had to work really hard to stay away."

I couldn't believe the words coming out of his mouth. "Then why did you?"

"Well, for starters, I didn't think you wanted anything to do with me. You made it pretty clear from the get-go that you didn't do the groupie thing."

That was true. I didn't do the groupie thing, but it didn't mean I wasn't into the *relationship* thing. I was just unglued enough to actually tell him as much when he spoke up before I could. "But then, you know, we became friends. I figured we were both staying hands-off because of that. Why did *you* stay away?"

"Pretty much the same reasons as you. I guess I was playing it safe."

"Until tonight." He shot me a wink at that, and I burrowed into the nook of his arm, my fingers flitting across his chest as he let out with an exhale. "I gotta tell you, when I found out who you were… I was crushed. Truly. You were the General Manager's daughter, for godsakes. I had to keep my distance. I busted my ass all those years on the ice…"

He trailed off, but I didn't need to hear the rest of his sentence; I already understood. Of course I did. Hockey was his whole life. There was no way he could risk blowing his whole career just for a random hookup. But then what was so different about our situation now? Was it just easier for him to cave once I finally threw myself at him? The thought had me chuckling to myself.

"I'm still the GM's daughter," I teased. "This could very well be career suicide for you if he ever finds out."

He brushed a thumb across my cheek, sending shivers across my skin. He raised my chin so I could look him right in those beautiful green eyes as he said, "Something tells me you'll be worth it."

You'll be. Not *you were.* Oh my God. Did that mean…

He lowered his lips to mine and kissed me. "I can't do it anymore. I can't stay away."

"You're serious!" I let out in disbelief.

"I am." He was smiling ear to ear, as if his admission had removed a heavy weight from his shoulders, set his spirit free.

"You're happy."

"Yes. I am. Are you?" he asked, most likely aware that I hadn't yet agreed to the "you'll be" portion of his statement, this future he had planned for us. It was always incredible to see a bit of his serious side, catch a glimpse behind the cocky, ego-driven façade that he presented to the rest of the world. But seeing him so *vulnerable?* My God. It almost had my heart busting out of my ribcage.

And he wanted to know if I was happy.

How could he even ask? I was happier at that moment than I'd ever been in my entire life. Not just because I was curled up in his arms right then, but because *I was the one who made this happen.* Sure, maybe I had a little help from a bit of alcohol, but the fact is, I had come out alone tonight when it would have been easier to stay home. I'd worn a gold dress as a superhero cape, giving me the strength necessary to assert myself. After years of pushing him away, I finally let myself go for it... and the payoff had turned out to be totally worth the risk.

Until this moment, the only intention I was shooting for was to get my hands on him. I didn't back down and I didn't relent until it happened, and I never thought to expect anything more. But the fallout was that I'd achieved a goal I never in a million years ever allowed myself to hope for.

I'd made Zachary McAllister mine.

"I don't know if 'happy' even covers it," I answered, smiling into his eyes.

He was smiling back when he kissed me.

Chapter Seven
JANUARY 1999

I woke up with a slight hangover the next morning, but even still, I was singing to myself and bouncing around the house.

I went downstairs to slam back a huge glass of water and to call a cab. I'd abandoned my poor car in the lot the night before and supposed I'd better get it back before it was stripped completely bare. But when I passed by the front door... my car was already sitting right there out in the driveway. I was only wearing a pair of shorts and a T-shirt, but I ran out into the freezing morning to grab my keys. They were sitting on the driver's seat along with a note from Zac, explaining that he'd taken care of it. He wished me a good day, and suggested that I meet him at Johnny's again after practice that night.

Actually, he didn't suggest it. He *demanded* it.

Sure, buddy. Twist my arm.

I spent my day counting down the hours until I could see Zac and waiting to hear from Casey. I was confident about the former and not so much about the latter. The wedding was happening today, for godsakes. I figured my friend would be a little too busy to check in.

I tried to wait until a reasonable time to head to Johnny's, but I must have been too excited, because I ended up getting there before the team. So, I sidled up to the bar and ordered a beer, figuring they were due any minute.

But no one showed.

It was kind of awkward sitting there all by myself, but I did it, thinking maybe practice had just run long. Once I finished my drink, however, I figured something must have come up, and decided to go back home to check my machine... but there was no message. I had Zac's number and I could have called him but it was already late and I figured it'd just have to wait until tomorrow.

Dammit.

* * *

The next morning, Casey woke me out of a sound sleep to tell me all about the wedding.

"We got the Elvis package. It was hysterical!" she reported. "Simon and I were laughing so hard, I can't believe we made it through our vows."

"That's so funny! It sounds awesome, Case. Congratulations!"

"Thanks."

"What did you wear?"

"Well, you might laugh, but I went pretty traditional with my dress. Simon bought me this gorgeous white sheath of a thing. I looked just like Carolyn Bessette-Kennedy. Only, you know, short and brunette."

"Aww. I'm sure you looked gorgeous."

"What did *you* wear?"

"Huh?"

"New Year's Eve! What did you end up doing?"

I was excited to tell her about Zac, but didn't want to look like I was trying to trump her big news. Besides. I didn't even know where to start. I got tipsy and threw myself at him until we hooked up *in my car*, for godsakes? At twenty-three and twenty-one, I would have figured we'd earned the right to hook up on a mattress, for crying out loud. We'd have to come up with a better plan for next time.

"Oh, I ended up at Johnny's. It was a good night. Played some pool, drank, the usual."

"Well, good. I was worried you'd stay home without me there."

"Believe it or not, I do have a social life outside of you, brat."

That made her laugh. "I know, I know. Hey, we're coming home tonight, so I'll come over and show you the pictures, okay?"

"Sounds like a plan."

We were winding our conversation down, but then suddenly, she said, "You know... I didn't want to ask about Zac, but I'm surprised you haven't said anything."

Jeez. Word sure travelled fast. "I wasn't trying to keep it from you. I just figured I'd fill you in on the details when you got home."

"Well, he already called Simon and told him everything."

That was unexpected. But I was curious to hear what he'd said. "He did?"

"Yeah. He sounded really pissed about it."

"Wait," I said, confused. "What are you talking about?"

"Dallas, Avery! What do you *think* I'm talking about?"

Dallas? "Case, I may be a bit slow on the uptake here, but I have no idea what Dallas has to do with anything."

"You don't know? Oh Jesus." Case expelled a deep breath before continuing. "Avery, Zac got traded to Dallas last night. He's probably already on a plane there now."

My stomach sank straight out of my body. "Zac's been traded? He's gone?"

I'd seen his evasive maneuvers with every other girl he'd hooked up with, so it's not as though I should have been surprised. But we were friends, for godsakes. Did one single hookup put me in the Must-Dispense-With-Immediately Club? Actually up and leaving town without telling me? Even if the trade was a surprise, he could have at least *called*. But he didn't say anything about it.

He never even said goodbye.

I couldn't stay on the phone an extra minute. I needed to find out if what she'd just told me was the truth. "Hey Case? I've got to go." I felt sick, but I didn't want her to worry, so I added, "I can't wait to see you."

"Me either. I'll come over as soon as we get back."

Good. I was going to need my best friend with me during something like this.

"Looking forward to it. See you then."

There was a hesitant pause on her end while I waited for her to say goodbye. "Hey Avery?"

"Yeah?"

"I'm really sorry. I thought you knew."

We hung up the phone and I sat there staring at the floor while I caught my breath. The news was churning my stomach, and I couldn't make sense of it. As badly as I wanted some verification, I was too afraid to make it real.

I needed to talk to my father.

I went downstairs and found him sitting at the dining room table, going over his roster—or, as he normally referred to it: his bible. I repeated the words that had been swirling around in my brain for the past ten minutes. "Hey, umm… McAllister's traded?"

Dad didn't look up from his book. "Yep. Dallas."

I already knew it was the truth, but hearing Dad say as much actually confirmed it. I tried to remain calm as I asked, "Who'd we get for him?"

"Boucher. From Montreal."

"Boucher is good."

"Yep."

I stood there flipping my slipper on and off my heel. "Did he… Did Zac *want* to leave?"

"He wants to win a championship, just like any other player." Dad looked up from his bible and finally gave me his full attention. From the look in his eyes, I wasn't sure I wanted it. "Avery, what is this? You seem awfully interested in my job today."

I gnawed on my bottom lip as I checked my cuticles.

Dad wasn't buying my attempt to look unaffected. "I thought you knew better than to get involved with any of those guys. McAllister is one hell of a player, but I can't imagine…" Thankfully, he didn't finish that line of thought, and simply let out a sigh. "Look, honey. He was good for me, but he *wouldn't* be good for you. Understand?"

Oh, I understood it perfectly.

I couldn't believe I'd actually fallen for his line of bullshit. I knew he was a dog the first night I met him, and he'd only proven it to me a million times in the years since. Hell, he went out of his way to *show* me how he did it, how easy it was for him to talk a woman into bed.

Though, I supposed if I was going to be honest, I guess *I* was the one convincing *him* the other night.

And oh God! The way I looked at him! All adoring and pathetic, virtually confessing my love for him in the backseat of my freaking car for godsakes! Three whole years I spent building up an immunity to his advances, and after a few drinks and some wooing words, I was practically begging him to sleep with me.

I couldn't believe he was only lying when he said all those amazing things. I couldn't believe I bought into it so easily. If this was how he treated his friends, I couldn't imagine how he treated his enemies.

"No, yeah. I know. I just didn't see him out last night and was wondering about it."

Dad's attentions refocused on his bible. "Well, no need to wonder about it anymore. He's gone."

Yes, that was true. I knew it all too well.

He was gone.

PART TWO

ZAC
2003

Chapter Eight

"Goddammit, Brodeur! Block the shot!"

I threw a towel into the sink and brought my fist down on the bar. Jerry Winters moved his drink out of my line of fire and let out a low whistle. "Take it easy, Maniac. It's only the first period."

I topped off his beer and brought my attention back to the TV. Only the first period. Yeah, I got it, but every second of this game could make the difference between a win or a loss, and they had one hell of a chance to actually make the finals this year. I supposed I was a bit more invested in this battle than your average sports fan, seeing as how I used to play for them. And even if I got shit-canned well before my prime, I didn't hold that against the team. Some of the guys out there on the ice were actually my friends.

Out of pure routine, I took a quick scan down the bar to make sure everyone's glasses were filled, even though Denny was on shift and the stools were hardly filled. I wasn't a bartender anymore, but old habits die hard. I spent way too many hours slinging drinks just to turn it off when I was on the other side of the taps. It was hard to stay out from behind the bar.

I was the owner and self-proprietor of *The Westlake Pub* in the tiny suburb of Norman, New Jersey. Second generation in ye olde family business, which I inherited a few years ago. My old man first bought the place back in seventy-eight, and it hasn't changed much in the twenty-five years since then. It was a large but ancient structure situated on the west shore of Lenape Lake, a small community within the larger town of Norman.

The neighborhood had undergone some major renovations over the years, the tiny vacation bungalows razed in favor of the ostentatious McMansions which every newly-suburbanized up-and-comer seemed to require. All that construction may have elevated the beauty of the landscape, but was nothing compared to the heightened egos of its dwellers. Through all the changes, The Westlake remained untouched. It was still the same, broken-down dive that had been the bane of this community's existence since Day One.

I grew up thinking it was the coolest place in the world.

My brothers and I spent every summer of our teen years working the kitchen or as bar-backs and every winter skating on the ice of that very lake on which this building sits. I knew every inch of this place almost better than I knew myself. Every leaky pipe, every dusty corner. The Westlake was a true "old man bar," a beer-and-shot joint, and I wouldn't have had it any other way. Let the snobs tip back a martini at the country club one town over; The Westlake was where the *real* humans went. Some of those 'real humans' were absolute drinking machines, and I'd be lying if I said I wasn't appreciative of that. My regulars were the ones who've kept this place afloat all these years.

Well, that and my father.

Every day after school, I'd come in to find him either holed up in his little office upstairs or serving drinks down here. He couldn't seem to stay out from behind the bar, either. It was addictive. Not the liquor, but the environment itself. Because even though he was surrounded by alcohol practically twenty-four hours a day, my father rarely touched the stuff. I got it. You couldn't watch all those boozehounds getting their drink on night after night without becoming the slightest bit disgusted. The same guys, day in and day out, stopping in for a drink or twelve at the end of their shifts, trying to put some space between their miserable jobs and their miserable home lives. It wasn't uncommon to find an angry housewife come storming through the door at any given moment in this joint. There were a few guys that just didn't know when to call it a night, but most of my regulars were actually pretty cool.

My four best were presently sitting at the bar.

There was Jerry Winters (better known as Jerry Liverwurst, named after his favorite sandwich), a transplanted, retired security guard from the Scrapple factory down in Philly who practically lived here. He commanded the same stool from three o'clock every afternoon to six o'clock every night. Then it was home to the wife for a leisurely dinner before he headed right back here for the evening shift, nine to closing.

Every. Day.

Most often occupying the stool to his left was Roy Bread. I don't know his real last name, but he drove the bread truck, so that's what everyone called him. He had dyed black hair and a Snidely Whiplash mustache, the kind that hasn't been in style since back when guys threw medicine balls around the gym and referred to everything as "the cat's meow."

Nobody really knew Richie Rum-N-Coke's story. He worked full-time down at the industrial park off Main, some sort of machinist or something. He put in a lot of hours *here*, though, I'll tell you what. He would come to the bar straight after work, and stay until we locked up for the night. Sometimes, he'd even stop in during his lunch hour.

The last member of the quartet was The Incredible Hank. Don't ask why everyone called him that, because I don't know. Maybe he was a *really amazing* HVAC repairman? A good guy, but down on his luck, so he couldn't really pour the same amount of booze down his gullet at the equal rate as his friends. He spent his time drinking water or club soda, anything that didn't cost too much but would allow him to hang out for a little while, and he *always* left a tip. The guys would normally spot him a couple beers on their tab, and more often than not, I'd make sure Denny "lost count" on the totals.

There were some secondary regulars—Chuckie Fabulous, Joey Tile (not to be confused with Joey Bricks), Frankie Zero, Garbage Day, Jimmy Crooner (who never spoke a word, much less sang a note), and a bunch of others—but they were only part-timers. Pikers, if you took stock in Jerry's assessment.

Whether any of them came in for one drink or twenty, I didn't judge. It wasn't up to me to decide how much was too much, except when it was time to call one of them a cab. I was just happy they kept coming back.

Even with all its drama, I was mostly grateful that I had this place to fall back on. My whole life had been built around hockey, and that motivation left little room to impart any sort of failsafe in case it didn't work out.

But it's not as though failing was even an option in my mind. Hockey was the only thing I ever wanted, so it was the only thing I ever concentrated on. Why in the world would I have pursued a degree in finance when I could make a living on the ice?

I dropped out of Boston College two years shy of getting my diploma and took the Devils up on their offer to come play with them. I went in the first round, eighteenth pick in the '95 draft, which was pretty fucking phenomenal in terms of validation. I couldn't believe it. The frigging Devils! The team that made me fall in love with the sport to begin with. My home team.

All of a sudden, I was one of them. I was one of the pros. Bobby Orr, Wayne Gretzky, and now Zachary McAllister. My name was going on a goddamned NHL sweater.

The elation only lasted about ten minutes, however, because then it was time to focus on making it to the show. A lot of guys, even if they're good, don't see much action their first year on a pro team. I didn't leave myself too much room to celebrate when there was still work to do.

And work I did. I busted my ass every practice, gave it my all, left everything I had on the ice. No one would ever be able to say I coasted through those early days. I rode the pines more than I would have liked during pre-season, pissed off and insulted that I was so close to tasting the dream, yet not quite there yet. I put my time in, paid my dues, and then kicked ass during every moment they let me off the bench. All that work finally paid off, because miracle of all miracles, I was put on the first line during our very first matchup, where I stayed throughout the bulk of my career.

My rookie year in the pros was a dream come true. I was part of a winning team that had just come off a championship the season before.

And now, eight years later, my team was a contender for the Stanley Cup once again.

Preoccupied with the game on my TV, I was only mildly cognizant of the sound of the bell ringing over the door. The thing jangled a million times a day and rarely captured my attention anymore. Just another thirsty customer, and Denny was quite capable of handling it. I topped off Jerry's beer again and went to wipe down the hightops. The bar rag slipped free of my belt loop on the walk, so it was in the midst of crouching down to retrieve it that I heard a woman's voice ask, "Zachary McAllister?"

I raised my head at the sound, just enough to see a pair of black fuck-me heels, and followed a tantalizing line of flesh as my eyes took in a gorgeous pair of legs. By the time I finally met her face, I'd already taken this girl to bed twenty ways to Sunday in my mind.

Only, she wasn't just any girl.

Sitting on a stool in my bar, eyeing me with raised brows and a scowl that let me know I'd been busted, was Avery Brooks.

The Girl Who Got Away.

Chapter Nine

"Zac?"

At the sound of her voice, I shook myself out of the stupor and finally found my bearings. "Avery."

The corners of her lips turned up slightly, seemingly pleased that I actually remembered her. How could I forget? Sweet, but shy. Smart, but fun. Down-to-earth… but extremely fucking beautiful. The kind of girl that could give a guy a physical reaction just from looking at her, if you know what I mean.

Unfortunately, she was also the kind of girl who could give a guy the boot the second he got kicked off her favorite team. I'd do well to keep that in mind.

I cleared my throat, mimicked her raised brows, and asked, "Slumming this afternoon?"

Any hint of her tiny grin disappeared at that. She adjusted the belt at her waist and sat up a bit straighter, her eyes narrowing as she responded, "I'd like to talk to you, actually. Do you have a minute?"

"Running this place doesn't normally allow for much free time."

She scanned her eyes down the bar, taking note of all four of my customers. "Clearly, you're swamped. I should have called first."

Her lips were clamped together, assuredly fighting the urge to smile. Shit. Now I had to find a way to save face.

"I guess I can break away for a few." I called down to Denny, "Den, You got this? I need to talk shop for a bit."

Denny looked at me as though I'd lost my mind. "Uh, yeah. I think I can handle it."

Of course he could. What the hell was I doing? Trying to seem so goddamn *significant* just because Avery Brooks had walked back into my line of vision. As though Denny couldn't manage the bar without my *supreme guidance*. Jesus. I was being such an ass.

I mentally chided myself and jerked my chin toward the far end of the room. "Let's take over one of the booths. We'll have more..." *privacy*. I couldn't say that, though. If I gave her any indication that I was looking to get her alone, she'd probably run screaming for the hills. Kind of like how she did all those years ago. "...We'll be able to talk better over there. Can I get you a drink?"

Her pouty lips were formed into a perfect O as she considered my easy question. Shit. Why was it so hard for us to have a simple conversation with each other? The both of us were wound way too tight. We didn't used to be this way with each other. We used to be pretty decent friends. I mean, yeah, sure, toward the end there, I thought she could be more, but—

"I'll have a club soda with lemon, thanks."

She grabbed her leather briefcase from the stool next to her and headed over to the more private booths along the wall while I hopped behind the bar to grab her drink. As I was filling the glass, I tried to pull myself together. I wasn't having much luck.

Avery Brooks.

Avery Fucking Brooks was here. In my bar. To see me.

After four whole years.

While I still carried a pretty big chip on my shoulder regarding the way things were left off between us, I couldn't deny that it was still exciting to see her again. Maybe she was here to hash all that stuff out finally. Better late than never, right?

I grabbed her club soda with one hand, a bottle of water for myself in the other, and set out for the booths. I stopped short, though, when I saw those bare legs peeking out from one of them.

Jerry elbowed me in my side, giving me his raised-brow approval as he nodded his head in Avery's direction and whispered, "Nice stems on that one. You're lucky I'm not twenty years younger, boy-o. You'd have yourself some competition."

I scowled and dismissed his insinuation. "I'm not... She's not..." but I couldn't find the right words to shoot him down properly. Deciding it wasn't worth getting into the whole story, I just shook my head at him in exasperation as I headed over toward Avery.

Placing the drinks on the table, I slid into the bench seat across from her. It's not something I took notice of every day, but suddenly, I became aware that the wooden tabletop was dinged and scratched; the green pleather cushions had seen better days. The seats were cracked and torn in a few places, the half dozen rips repaired haphazardly with green duct tape over the years. That's the thing about dive bars. We took our title seriously. And The Westlake was a textbook dive.

Avery was rifling around in her briefcase, seemingly unaware of her crappy surroundings. I took a quick second to look her over, to note the changes that the years had taken on her. The girl in front of me was a hell of a lot different than the one I remembered from back in the day. She was still stunning—no denying that—but she seemed... stiffer than I remembered. Aside from the high-heeled shoes and the tailored miniskirt that showed off her incredible gams, she was wearing a white, button-down blouse under a black, fitted blazer.

It's almost summer, sweetheart. Lighten up.

She'd only been here for five minutes, and I could already tell that this Avery Brooks was a far cry different from the timid and unsure girl of my memories. This Avery looked as though she'd just stepped off the pages of *Fortune* magazine.

Okay, fine. I could play all-business, too.

"So. To what do I owe the honor of your presence today?"

Avery found whatever she was looking for in her briefcase and tossed a black folder onto the table between us. "Nice to see you, too, Zac."

Shit. I was so intent on playing it cool that I completely skipped over common courtesy. I started picking at the label on my water bottle. "You're right." I offered an apologetic smile before amending, "Hello. How are you? How have you been?"

Her eyes finally met mine, and holy shit if that didn't send a jolt right fucking through me. I'd been so mesmerized by those killer legs that I'd forgotten all about her gorgeous eyes. Light brown irises with flecks of gold, outlined in a deep chocolate. I suppose if I was a total pussy, I'd refer to them as *topaz eyes*.

At least I would have if I were describing them years ago. Today, they were more tiger-like than warm and inviting.

She tucked a strand of auburn hair behind her ear, causing the ends to kick out from her neck. She'd cut it short, just above her shoulders. Business-like. Ball-bustery. "I'm good. I'm an event planner now. Working my tail off at it, but otherwise... I've been good. You?"

I stopped picking at the label and started rolling the scattered scraps of paper into balls with the tips of my fingers. "I've been good, too. This place keeps me on my toes. It's uh, it's normally a little busier than this, especially once the happy hour crew gets here."

"I remember."

Shit. Of course she did. "Yeah, well, it used to be a *lot* busier. These days..." I trailed off, not knowing how to explain the lack of customers. We still had decent weekends, but even then, the money we brought in was nothing compared to what it used to be. But why the hell was I letting her know *that*?

"I was sorry to hear about your father."

My throat clenched at the mention of my old man. He'd been gone for four years already, but there wasn't a day that went by when I didn't feel the sting of his loss. It's not easy to find out your childhood superhero is actually a human.

Fuck cancer.

"Yeah, it uh… it was rough. Figured I'd try to keep his legacy alive by keeping this place afloat, you know?" I made myself meet her eyes to add, "Failing fucking miserably, however."

I gave a harsh snicker at that, less embarrassed than I thought I'd be about admitting my shortcomings. To her, anyway.

Avery looked as though she didn't know what to say. A flicker of sympathy broke across the steel reserve in her eyes, and it was enough to make me want to end this little reunion. What the hell was it about her that had me spilling my guts all of a sudden? We *used* to know each other. We *used* to be friends. She knew my dad, but...

She knew my dad. I guess that's all it was. I'd been through this routine with every single patron of this bar. Listened to their stories and endless reminiscing about my old man, the individual accounts each and every person had to relay those first few times they came back through the door. Eventually, the stories turned into mere mentions, a sentence here and there, a quick snippet about my father's life recalled in tiny anecdotes, a few well-meaning, nostalgic words. Four years after his death, and people didn't feel the need to talk about him anymore. They'd gotten over it.

But Avery and I hadn't been through this song and dance yet. And hearing her talk about the guy just brought all those old frustrations back to the surface. It's no fun watching someone you love fade away, not being able to do a damned thing about it.

I was steeling myself for the conversation that was sure to follow: her telling me what a good man he was, how he was at peace now, blah, blah, blah. But instead, she just gave a nod in acknowledgement and changed the subject. "Well, maybe we can help each other on that front."

I snapped out of it enough to ask, "What? With the bar?"

"Mm hmm. It's why I'm here."

I suddenly realized that what I'd believed to be a little social call was nothing more than a professional visit, and fuck me if that wasn't an unexpected revelation. Because here I thought she'd come back for *me*.

Zac, you're an idiot.

Chapter Ten

I looked Avery over, wondering what "business" this pristine vixen in a designer suit could possibly have with a shithole like this.

She folded her hands over the black folder on the table and got right down to it. "I'm sure you're aware that the Devils are in the playoffs."

Who isn't? "Uh, yeah, I think I may have heard something along those lines."

"And, I'm sure you're also aware that if your boys bring The Cup back to Jersey, there's going to be just a bit of cause for celebration."

I was both touched and peeved that she'd referred to my old teammates as *your boys*. "Just a bit."

"Well, I'm here to arrange that the celebration be held here."

That threw me. "Here? At my bar? Why?"

"By request."

I supposed any number of people could have requested my bar for their venue. I got my teammates hooked on this place as one of our regular hangouts back in the day. Johnny's was the closest bar to the arena, but The Westlake wasn't too far of a trip whenever we wanted to change things up every now and then. I was still friendly with a few guys in that circle, and heck, my bar was the preeminent hockey-themed pub in the area. Just because it was the *only* hockey-themed pub didn't take away from that dubious honor.

To say that it was the obvious choice for their party may have been taking things too far, however. It sure as hell wasn't obvious to *me*.

My initial elation over the idea of a victory party being held here was overshadowed by my encroaching apprehension. I'd started playing with the team the season right *after* their 1995 win, and was handed my walking papers the year *before* their 2000 win. Talk about a missed window.

Adding insult to injury, I'd been sent to the Dallas Stars back in that winter of '99. Texas, for chrissakes. It was like being shipped off to another planet. But hey. I guess things could've been worse. Fact is, a few months after I'd joined their team, *they* ended up winning The Cup.

Too bad I was in a hospital and watching it on TV.

Not only were my Championship hopes shattered, but so was my knee, ensuring that my career was crushed right along with it. My injury guaranteed that I'd never be playing for any other pro team ever again. After a lifetime of working toward my dreams, they were suddenly cut short. Three and a half years. That's all I got. I came home to convalesce and brood about it, but that was just about the time my father received his diagnosis.

Within a matter of months, the two things I'd loved most in my life were dead.

If I'd had half a minute to sit and reflect on the shitty hand I'd been dealt that year, I probably would have sunk into a pretty deep depression. But the reality was, there was too much to do. I didn't have *time* to sink.

Now here it was, four years later, and my Devils were serious contenders for The Holy Grail once more.

Once more, without *me*.

But I guess enough time had passed, because I managed to find a way to love the game again. I'd been obsessed with every second of this past season, rooting my boys on once more from the sidelines. Hell. I'd done it my whole life. All those years when the reality of playing for them was nothing more than a far-fetched dream. Could I really be anything other than excited about their success?

"That would be... phenomenal, Ave. Where do we start?"

She smiled slightly and took a sip from her drink. "I was hoping you'd be happy about it. Truth is, the guys are really looking forward to it."

"Well, of course they are. They're looking at three Cup wins within a decade. That doesn't happen every day."

"Yes, but they're also excited to see *you*, Zac."

I knew "the guys" wouldn't have said much about such a matter, but it was nice to know that at the very least, they hadn't completely forgotten their old teammate.

"Yeah. I guess I kinda... dropped out for a bit, huh?"

"You certainly did."

I caught a hint of bite in her comment, but there was no way I was going to open up *that* can of worms. Besides, we both knew where I'd been these past years. Which was more than I could say for her. I tried to meet her eyes as she picked at a stray thread on her cuff.

"I had my reasons, Ave." I cleared my throat. "But what about you? What have you been doing with yourself? Aside from looking fantastic while taking on the world, of course."

I offered her a sidelong smirk at that, which she managed to catch once she stopped the inspection of her sleeve. Her face met mine in the first genuine smile I'd seen since she stepped into my bar. Something stirred in my chest at the sight, and it was strange to realize that the mere sight of her unreserved grin could have such an effect on me.

I suppose I shouldn't have been so surprised. I mean, I was crazy about this girl back in the day. We used to have a blast together. She was smart and fun and she knew how to have a good time. She also had this great dimple that would appear in her right cheek whenever she laughed too hard. For some reason, I started to wonder if I'd ever get to see it again.

She looked at me for a moment longer than necessary, and then, just like that, the smile was gone.

She shot a skeptical, half-lidded stare in my direction before placing a palm on the folder and sliding it across the table. She was back in all-business mode as she said, "The preliminary contract is in here. Just your standard, non-disclosure kind of stuff. Look it over, or just send it off to your lawyer for review. I'll be in touch."

At that, she grabbed her briefcase, straightened her skirt, and walked out the door.

I watched the door close behind her, then sat there for a few extra minutes, trying to pull myself together. Too many questions had just been unloaded into my brain and I didn't like not having the answers.

Aside from the fact that Avery's mere reemergence into my life had thrown me for a loop, I now was faced with the possibility of having to see my old teammates again, too. I liked a lot of those guys, but it was pretty humiliating to think about seeing them again as an *ex*-player. Hell, if I hadn't torn up my knee four years ago, I'd probably *still* be knocking around the leagues. As it was, I hadn't returned to the ice even for fun. The day of my injury was the last day I'd ever put on a pair of skates. I could say it was because I'd been too busy running this place, but if I was going to be honest, I knew my avoidance was due to more than just a lack of free time.

I just couldn't bring myself to do it anymore.

I flipped open the folder but didn't give it more than a passing glance. I already knew I'd be giving the green light for the party.

Now all I needed to do was wait for my team to win.

Chapter Eleven

"Sonofa!"

I slammed my wrench against the side of the air-conditioning unit, a last resort to get the damned thing started again. Needless to say, it didn't do the trick. I'd been screwing around with the stupid thing for over an hour, trying to get it up and running. In the meantime, my bartenders were becoming overly cranky from the heat, and the few patrons that decided to brave it out were melting into puddles on their barstools.

I was going to have to call Barry.

Dammit. I was really hoping to avoid bringing in a pro for this. With some of my vendors and on-call guys, I could sometimes work out a bartering deal, but Barry was one of my few guys for hire that didn't accept "alternate payment" for his services. Plus, I could do without the lecture that he was sure to give me, telling me it was way past time to simply replace the unit with a newer model. Even if he didn't gouge me with the price—this time—the couple hundred bucks it was going to cost to *fix* it was money I didn't have to spend right now. Much less could I come up with the scratch necessary to spring for a brand new unit.

But one thing was for sure, if I didn't get some cool air flowing through this place soon, I'd be looking at an empty bar, and then *no* money would be coming in.

I went upstairs to my office and put the call in. *Yes, Barry. Just a fix. I know, I know. But just do whatever you can to get this thing working again, okay?*

I sat at my cluttered desk and ran my hands through my hair, dropping my head down on the mountain of paperwork that had gone unattended for much, much too long. It was depressing to try and tackle the pile of bills when the money simply wasn't there to pay any of them. I'd gotten pretty good at juggling and was able to keep the place afloat with a bare minimum of actual capital.

You'd be surprised how little it took to sustain an establishment like this. My wait and bar staff was paid less than minimum wage (their salaries were more dependent on tips), so their paychecks didn't put me in the poorhouse, thankfully. The kitchen crew wasn't breaking the bank with their hourly pay, as my restaurant manager was the only person to draw an actual salary (and a modest one at that). Our bands were only compensated with what they were able to bring in at the door, and with the piddly five-dollar cover charge, it was amazing that any of them ever bothered to come back. But thank fuck they did, because the money we made from the weekend crowds was pretty much the only thing that ever kept us in the black.

Barely.

I realized pretty early on that I'd never make millions managing some little hole-in-the-wall, but at least the money this place *did* manage to bring in was enough for me to survive. Hell. Even in its heyday, we weren't raking in the cash. But my brothers and I had never wanted for anything, and as long as we had a roof over our heads and food on the table, Mom and Dad were content with the life they'd made.

I, however, hadn't made my peace with living like a pauper. It's not as though you could blame me; NHL money was nothing to snub your nose at. But my original plan to retire with a buttload of cash in the bank was thwarted once I destroyed my knee. The money I *did* have socked away went toward my father's hospital bills, funeral expenses, and debts on the bar. In one single summer, all that cash just… disappeared. There wasn't much left to play with when all was said and done.

I just wish I were left with a *little* extra so I didn't have to constantly stress about it.

I flipped through that black folder once more, just like I had done about twenty times in the past weeks. The Devils were up two games to one in the series finals, having just won their latest match. Of course I wanted to see them win, but I was rooting for them to take the whole enchilada for more reasons than just my personal team pride. A high-profile victory party held at my bar would mean a certain boost in business for this place.

Ironically enough, it looked as though my livelihood would once again depend on hockey.

I peeked into the open door of my apartment and checked the score on the TV. It was still a scoreless game and we were already in the second period. Way too painful to watch alone.

I slammed down the rest of my water and decided to head back downstairs to the floor. The bar was busy enough tonight at least—most of our regulars had come to hang out as they usually did. But considering it was Game 4 of the finals, I would have expected to see this place a bit more crowded. With twelve televisions, great bar fare, and an endless supply of booze, The Westlake was the best place within a ten-mile radius to come and watch the games. As the suffocating heat radiated around me, I snickered in frustration, realizing how many more people must have come and gone before their asses even hit a stool. Most people didn't want to spend their evening in an oven, and God only knew how many potential customers had pulled a one-eighty once the heat smacked them in the face.

Speaking of ovens… I popped my head into the kitchen to see how the guys were faring. It was normally hot as hell back here as it was, but when the air wasn't working, it was unbearable.

The bar was separated from the restaurant by the large kitchen. Both halves of my establishment were designed to face the lake, but the view wasn't the only draw for my restaurant patrons. I might be biased, but I've gotta say, the food was fucking phenomenal.

Thankfully, I wasn't forced to spend much time dealing with the foodservice end of things. My skills were better utilized schmoozing with my bar patrons and dealing with the paperwork necessary to keep the entire establishment in business. That's why I let Felix run the show in regards to the restaurant and just stayed the hell out of his way. He was old as dirt, but he knew his stuff. I don't even know that my father actually hired him all those years ago. Rather, Felix appeared out of thin air to land on The Westlake's doorstep. Tuesday through Sunday, the guy started work at the crack and didn't leave until the last customer left the premises. Six to eleven, every day, without fail, without complaint.

A saint, I tell you.

I gave him an inquisitive nod which was returned with his customary, "Yes, yes. Everythin's fine, Zac. Now get out my kitchen." I smiled as usual, then gladly took him up on his offer to remove myself from the inferno.

Thankfully, Barry showed up just then. I gave him a wave (which he barely acknowledged) as he headed down into the boiler room. He didn't need me to escort him; he knew quite well where it was. But he didn't need to be so damn smug about it.

Despite the heat, I was happy to see that the stools weren't completely empty. Denny gave me an exhausted salute, and I figured it was best that I didn't bother to make eye contact with Alice. Her personality was pretty rough-around-the-edges to begin with, but add in the uncomfortable temperature and the inevitable loss of tips she'd incur because of it, and oh Jesus. This night would go easier for the both of us if I just stayed out of her way.

I noticed a cute little redhead sitting at the near end of the long bar, and took a moment to look her over in appreciation. We didn't normally get too many girls in this dive, much less cute ones, and almost never on a weeknight. I practically owed it to myself to go and chat her up.

"Don't bother, man," Denny said over my shoulder.

"What?" I asked on a snicker.

"She just got stood up and she's not looking for a replacement date. Trust me. I already tried."

I assessed her again, then turned toward Denny and waggled my eyebrows. "Watch and learn, my friend. Watch. And. Learn."

Denny grinned evilly, shaking his head and saying, "Your funeral, man."

I gave him the finger then made my way over to Red.

"'Evening," I offered on a grin. I noticed her drink was running low, so I moved behind the bar and asked, "Refill?"

She nodded. "Gin and tonic, extra splash of lime, two wedges."

Grabbing the Tanqueray in a *Cocktail* flip, I mixed up the drink to her specifications and placed it on her coaster. I didn't normally pull out the parlor tricks, but the ladies always seemed to like that move. She pushed her pile of money in my direction, but I waved her off. "On the house."

"Thanks."

"Came out to see the game?"

She gave a shrug and took a sip of her drink. "Yeah. I really like hockey."

Hmmm. Promising.

"Is that so?" I asked, sneaking a raised eyebrow at Denny and adding, "My name's Zac McAllister. I own the bar, but I used to own the ice."

She held out her hand, so I shook it. But instead of offering her name, she simply asked, "And?"

"*And*, you said you were a hockey fan."

"So?"

"You don't recognize me, do you."

"Should I?"

Jesus, this was just going nowhere fast. Had I become so irrelevant to the game in only four years of absence? "Well, it's been a few years, but I used to play for those guys right there." I gave a point to the TV, taking note of the score. Still not even on the board yet, dammit.

"Am I supposed to be impressed?"

"Most people are." *Is that smoke I smell? Because I'm pretty sure I just crashed and burned.* "I only played three seasons with them before I got shipped down south."

"Short career."

"Hey. That's better than most. We can't all be Gordie Howe."

"Who?"

I bring up the name of Mr. Hockey himself and she asks me 'who'? *Who?* Only the first player to ever score a thousand goals, the guy who holds the record for most consecutive games ever played, and one of the greatest athletes to ever play the game? Did she really not know who Gordie Howe was? Even a non-fan has at least heard of the guy!

103

Red hadn't been receptive to my advances throughout our entire exchange, but her complete lack of knowledge about a game she "really liked" was when *I* checked out of the equation.

I'm sure the shocked look of disgust must have been written all over my face when I answered, "Yeah. I think this conversation is over."

And at that, Red gave a shrug, gathered up her change, and left.

Relief flooded my bruised ego, but then a familiar bark of laughter filled my ears. "Wow. Does that 'owning-the-ice' line usually work?"

I turned to see Avery a few stools behind me. She must have slipped in while I was chatting with Red. "Usually."

"I thought you didn't use lines. Maybe you're losing your touch."

I came out to the floor and walked over to where she was sitting. Leaning an elbow against the bar and raising my eyebrows, I shot back, "Impossible."

That made her laugh. Good. I was hoping it would. I waved Alice over to hook Avery up with a drink, taking note of her order.

Attention, gentlemen: You can tell a lot about your odds with a girl from her chosen cocktail—at least according to what the old-timers have always told me. Let's pause here for a moment so that I may share their wisdom with you. You may want to grab a pen and some paper to take notes in case there's a test at the end:

THE COOL CHICK: A beer girl is laid-back, the kind of woman who's content to stay in for the night with a pizza and watch the games with you on your couch. She might be a friend of yours already. Maybe she used to date one of your buddies, but if it wasn't serious, she can be put on the Prospectives List. She can be found most often frequenting ball games, sports pubs, frat parties… and gives one hell of a blow job.

THE SURE THING: Shots of hard liquor indicate party girl, which can sometimes be a lot of fun, provided she doesn't do too many and turn into a crazy bitch. This is a special breed and must be handled with extreme care. Fun for an evening or two, but not necessarily the type you'd bring home to Mom. She can be found dancing on any random bartop, but tends to frequent loud establishments, normally when a rowdy band is on stage. Hell, she probably came with the bass player. She will fuck like nobody's business, and probably leave you sore the next morning.

THE NEWBIE: Piña Coladas and Daiquiris are for the young and inexperienced, so an I.D. check is suggested immediately before proceeding. Provided her license isn't a fake, she's fair game. And that's a good thing, because the Newbie is eager to please. She can normally be found in a darkened corner, making out with a random dude she just met five minutes prior. With any luck, he'll ditch her to seek out a girl who will be down for more than just kissing. In about twenty minutes, she'll be looking for her next hookup. Heartbroken and insecure, she's just waiting to prove her sexual prowess with the *next* guy she meets, and if you play your cards right, that guy can be you. A fake name is advised when encountering a Newbie, because she tends to be rather clingy after sex. The last thing you need is a starry-eyed stalker calling you at all hours for the next month because she hasn't yet learned the rules and can't take a hint.

THE BITCH: And if a woman's drinking something like a Mojito? Steer clear, my brothers. Any labor-intensive drink requiring more than two ingredients and a mashed *anything* means high-maintenance, entitled, and an all-around pain in the ass. This broad is looking for a sugar-daddy to fund her expensive tastes and you do *not* want to be that schmuck. She thinks she's way hotter than she actually is, so she's a lousy lay. She can normally be found at your local nightclub when she deigns to step foot into any establishment outside of a major city. But don't worry; if you're not wearing a designer suit, she won't be interested in you anyway.

THE GIRLS' NIGHT OUT: Any group of ladies that are drinking wine are normally married with children. They're finally out of the house with their friends and don't want anything to do with you, so back the fuck off. Besides, they'll all be wearing wedding rings, which is the first thing you should have checked for anyway. Shame on you for even trying.

There are exceptions to every rule of course, and since I'm only offering generalities here, I hope you ladies won't take it personally. And if repeating such assessments makes me seem like a misogynist, I apologize for giving you the wrong impression. I actually love women. They're smarter than we are, they're more sensitive than we are, and they generally smell a whole lot better. The fact of the matter is, however, that those old-timers may have known what they were talking about. I not only saw these stereotypes playing out every weekend at my bar, but experienced them firsthand back in my wilder days.

Therefore, I was pleasantly surprised when I saw Avery drinking a Loopy Seven. Booze plus soda meant low-maintenance, but with a touch of class. But Froot Loop-flavored vodka? And with a cherry? Not the usual request, and I found myself making adjustments to my list. Low maintenance, touch of class… knows how to have fun.

Alright then. Let's have some fun. "So, what are you doing here tonight?" I asked, flashing her one of my most irresistible grins.

"I don't see your beautiful face for four years and suddenly I'm graced with your presence twice in the same month."

Avery's mouth tightened into a repressed smile, but her eyes were bright as they met mine. She dismissed my compliment as if she hadn't even heard it, and instead answered, "I guess I was getting a little over-anxious."

Hmmm. I eyed her up and down, blatantly checking her out, and stepped closer to deliver, "Is that so?"

"Zac, you scoundrel," she spat out with a shaky laugh. "I meant I'm anxious about the party. It's torture trying to plan an event when I don't even know if it's going to happen. My mind hasn't stopped racing ever since I was assigned to this thing, but it's been in overdrive since their win last night. I kept trying to envision how I was going to set everything up, but didn't want to finalize any ideas until I could see how the flow of the room would work when packed with people."

I stepped out of her personal space at her monologue. Apparently, my close proximity was making her nervous enough to babble, and I wasn't looking to make her uncomfortable. Or maybe I backed off because being that near to her was having more of an effect on me than *I* was comfortable with. "Yeah, well, too bad you chose tonight. The air-conditioning is broken, so the place is hardly packed."

"I noticed." At that, she lifted the hair off her nape and fanned herself with her free hand. I watched as a bead of sweat made a leisurely trek from her hairline and carved a trail down her neck, just behind her ear. The sight made me want to run my tongue up the enticing wet line and bury my face in her hair. As I stared unrepentantly, I could almost taste the salt on my lips, smell the heat emanating from her skin, feel her hair tickling against my nose... so much so that I had to literally shake my head free of the vision. Where the hell did *that* come from?

I released a chuckle, which came out sounding nervous to my ears. Hopefully not to hers. "Well, no worries. I've got my main man Barry working on it as we speak. Before happy hour's through, this room will be colder than my ex's heart."

She giggled and shot back, "Nice, Zac. Whatever happened to... Julie, was it?"

I wasn't referring to anyone specifically; I was only trying to throw out a funny line. But now this can of worms was being opened, and hell. There was nothing funny about the situation.

And for the record? Julie was *not* my girlfriend.

"Yeah. Julie."

I didn't elaborate, hoping Avery wouldn't push too hard for any details. It was only now that I was older and wiser that I could look back and recognize what an asshole I actually was when it came to women. The injury turned me into a bitter dickhead for months, but even before that, I wasn't the easiest guy to deal with.

Back then, my life consisted of hockey and sex, in that order. I suppose that with all that blind ambition, the people in my orbit didn't get too much from me. Not that I had so much to give. It was only recently that I'd begun to try and figure out what kind of man I was going to be, what kind of life I was going to build for myself. And even now, this life was nothing to write home about.

I was still working on it.

Avery could tell I was being evasive, and thankfully, she opted against pressing the matter. Time for a change of subject. "So, yeah," I diverted. "I was just looking over that contract. Everything seems up to snuff."

"I told you it was pretty standard stuff." She gave a bite to her bottom lip before asking, "Does that mean your answer's going to be yes?"

Her eyes were hopeful and her trapped lips were trying to contain a smile. Simply adorable.

"Sure," I laughed out. "Actually, I already signed and faxed it over to your office about an hour ago. I guess we're a go. Now all we need is for the team to do *their* part."

Her smile broke out full-force as she smacked her hands together in excited applause. "Yeay! Oh, Zac. You don't know how much this means to me. My boss has really been watching over my events lately, and she is *not* a multi-tasker. I think the extra attention is because she may be looking to promote me, finally. A party as high-profile as this? It could really put me over the top."

Something about the way she said that made my heart sink. "So this is all about your career?"

She gave a stir to her drink as she answered, "Well, not *all*."

I was waiting for a sign, something to read in her expression that would clarify her statement. Something to let me know that despite the formality of our reunion, maybe there was a small part of her that had come back for *me*. I didn't need—or want—her to be the same, shy, starry-eyed girl she was back in the day. But the fact of the matter is, we used to get along really well back then. We were friends. I guess I was kind of hoping that maybe she missed us a little bit.

When she met my eyes, a spark of optimism ran through me as a hint of a smile played at her lips. "I was thinking it could mean big things for both of us."

Her mysterious smile shot right into my gut, and my heart started racing. I was caught off guard, intrigued by the playful look in her eyes. So intrigued that my brain shut off, and the question left my lips before I even had a chance to think about asking it.

"Why don't we take this conversation up to my place?"

Chapter Twelve

"Oh my God! Fuck me, Zac!"

I barely had Avery in my front door before the screaming started. There was really no controlling it, but the outbursts were actually making me uncomfortable, to say the least. Why, why, why did the screeching always have to be so goddamn *loud?* Was I supposed to play it cool at a moment like this?

I was trying to think of the correct way to handle the situation, but I was too stunned and embarrassed to do the right thing at that second. Plus, with Avery right there, I was kind of—you know—*distracted*. Maybe I should've just laughed and gone with the flow. You'd think after so many years, I would've come to expect such a reception by now. But it had been a while since the last time this happened, and I guess I'd just forgotten that there was a possibility that it could. I mean, who knew? Avery seemed so uptight. And yet, here was a string of obscenities flying around the room. If *I* was surprised by it, it must have shocked the hell out of her.

And yet, it continued.

"Love your cock! Oh my God! Fuck me, Zac!"

What the hell was I supposed to say? The truth is, I was caught off guard and actually feeling sort of mortified.

I turned to Avery, standing just inside my door, and registered her wide-eyed expression. She was staring at Magnum P.I., my twenty-two-year-old African Grey Macaw, wreaking social havoc from the confines of his cage in the corner of my dining room.

"Shut up, Magnum!" I yelled in his general direction, which had the effect of altering the chanting from obscene to self-deprecating as he repeated my words back to me.

"Shut up, Magnum! Shut up, Magnum!"

I ran a hand over my hair and offered an apology to Avery. "Sorry about him. He doesn't break out with that one too often, thank God. Apparently, only to embarrass me when I bring guests home." I went over to Magnum, ran my finger over his beak in a quick nuzzle, and then put the cover on his cage to clam him the hell up.

Avery hadn't moved beyond the doorway. "I'm going to do us both a favor and not ask for the details of how a bird would pick up such terminology."

The name Olivia ran through my head at that, even though I wasn't sure if that was her actual name. In any case, she was a former hockey groupie from way back when, a gorgeous hellcat whom I'd never met before nor since that one crazy night. She left me with a satisfied grin and my pet bird with an extended vocabulary. It was hard to forget a girl who could do that. What can I say? I like 'em spirited.

Without going into the details of such a dubious subject, I turned, faced her confidently, and answered, "I think it's pretty self-explanatory, don't you?"

Avery gave an exaggerated shiver. "Okay. Now I feel like I'm in a brothel. How many girls have you had up here?"

I shrugged. "Not many."

To tell you the truth, I saw more action in this apartment in the years before it became my home, and even then, it's not as though I was hooking up *all* the time. My brothers and I used to try and sneak up here on the rare occasions when one of us would meet a willing partner in the bar downstairs. But the kind of ladies that came here to drink weren't necessarily the type that you'd want to even touch, much less fuck. We'd only get lucky when the odd, unsuspecting sorority girl wandered in. Even then, my brothers and me would have to fight it out, not only over any pretty girls, but over who would get to call dibs on the apartment. Then after all that, we'd still have to make it past my father without getting caught, which wasn't often.

When Avery threw me a skeptical, sideways glare, I added, "I swear! What? You think I treat the bar like my own personal lady trap?" *Because I don't anymore*, I left unsaid.

"Can you blame me? The evidence suggests exactly that."

"Look," I started in, "Magnum picked that up from one wild night a long time ago. I've been trying to deprogram him ever since." I gestured to the sofa in the middle of my living room. "Please sit. I promise it's been sterilized."

That finally broke through her uptight demeanor as she flopped down onto the couch, laughing. "I'm going to pretend this slipcover is made of Kevlar, okay? Hopefully, it's acting as a barrier to contain any cooties within the defiled couch underneath it."

Her words had me doing a double-take, and when they registered, I found myself laughing right along with her. It wasn't even the same damn couch!

I was grateful that my apartment was fairly clean. I had to learn to be pretty self-reliant in the homemaker department ever since college. And trust me, when you grew up with a neat-freak mother like mine, you tended to pick up a cleaning tip or two. So, while my furniture was almost always in need of a good dusting and my floors would definitely benefit from a vacuuming more often than I implemented, for the most part, the place normally looked presentable.

It was upstairs from the bar, my home separated from my work by only the small, pass-through landing that served as my office space. I liked to think of that room as my sterile chamber, the limbo between work and life, where I could shake off the stresses of the day before entering my sanctuary.

The apartment was small, but the perfect size for just one person. For a short time back when my father first bought the bar, however, my whole family lived up here. I have fond memories of being crammed into the single bedroom with my three older brothers, even though I'm sure my parents weren't too happy about having to sleep in the dining room. But it was actually kind of fun, believe it or not, until we got too old to be sharing a single room. Thankfully, that arrangement only lasted a few years. It was pretty hard to get used to sleeping in my own bedroom in the new house, though.

Hell. I still didn't like to sleep alone. Not that I'd had much choice in the matter these days. Sure, I could pretend my dry spell was due to some sort of moral awakening, but the truth was, I simply didn't have *time* for a dating life.

The moral awakening came much later.

I tossed the black folder onto the coffee table and went to grab a bottle of water from my fridge. Avery was still working on her Vodka Seven, so I knew I had a few minutes before she'd need topping off. It was a little cooler up here, as my AC was reliant upon an old-fashioned window unit and not on the Kaiser down in the basement.

I was still sweating, though, but for an entirely different reason than the temperature in the room.

Avery was sitting on my couch, wearing yet another goddamned miniskirt, her legs crossed casually in spite of her stiff posture. I took a seat in the recliner, trying very hard not to stare at the lengths of exposed skin. We looked at each other then, a not-entirely-comfortable silence filling the space between us.

Avery broke the quiet first. "You look scruffy today."

"Oh yeah?" I laughed out, giving a rub to the dark stubble along my jaw. "It's been a couple days since I shaved. Scruff happens."

"You were scruffy the other day, too. Growing a playoff beard?"

I gave a snort. "Not hardly."

"So, just the Charlie Salinger, perpetual fuzz thing, then."

"The what?"

"*Party of Five.* The oldest brother was always rocking a five o'clock shadow. Do you have to shave at night or something to keep that look going?"

"I wouldn't know. I've never planned it out. I shave whenever I think to do it."

"And your hair is longer."

I wondered what the hell was up with her detailed scrutiny and instead offered, "Guess I'm overdue for a cut."

"No, I… I didn't mean that. You used to wear it much shorter when… It looks nice, I guess is what I'm trying to say."

"Oh. Thanks."

We each took a nip from our drinks, sipping leisurely, as though we both weren't thinking the same exact thing. Because the last time we were alone together, we weren't wearing this many clothes.

"Yours is shorter," I sputtered out, King of Conversation that I am.

"What?"

"Your hair. You cut it."

She tucked the right side over her ear and said, "Yeah. I thought it would look more professional. I chopped it off months ago and I'm still not used to it."

"I like it."

"Thank you."

"I kinda miss the ponytail, though."

Avery stopped inspecting the ends of her hair to look at me blankly. "What?"

That made me laugh. "The ponytail. Jesus, Ave. You don't remember? You always had your hair pulled back in the winter. Because of the static, remember? You always said it looked like you were being electrocuted when you took your hat off."

She stared at me, open-mouthed. "How do you remember that?"

"I don't know," I laughed. "You were always coming out with stuff like that."

Her eyes dropped as she ran a fingertip along the rim of her glass. "I didn't think you knew me well enough to determine whether I 'always' did anything."

"I knew you."

"We hardly ever talked to one another."

"I'd hardly say 'hardly,' Ave."

"I would."

I looked at her, stunned. It was pretty emasculating, finding out that she could so easily forget everything that had gone on between us. "How can you say that? You were always around. We hung out a lot back then. We practically considered you as one of the team."

"One of the *guys*, you mean."

"No way. You were way too pretty for any of us to think that."

She shifted uncomfortably at that, re-crossing her ankles and smoothing the fabric of her skirt over her thighs. I wished she would stop drawing attention to her legs. They were distracting enough as it was.

"There were *lots* of pretty girls back then, Zac. Lord knows you were aware of each and every one of them."

What the hell was that? I knew I'd seen my fair share of action back in the day, but just… what the hell was that?

"Was that a dig?"

"It's the truth."

I looked at Avery, just sitting there seething at me and shot back, "Well, I don't remember any complaints when I became 'aware' of *you*."

Her eyes tightened their focus as her mouth spat out, "Oh, am I supposed to be *grateful*?"

"Ha! Like you weren't."

She raised her brows and huffed, "I think I would have been more appreciative if you didn't pull a Houdini and disappear two seconds after I gave up the goods!"

Fuck this. She wanted to play? She had no idea who was holding the cards here. "Well, maybe if *your father* hadn't shit-canned me, I could've stuck around!"

She looked as though she wanted to rip my jugular out of my neck. "*What*? Are you actually trying to blame *me* for that?"

I sank back into my chair and tossed a flippant hand in her direction. "Why wouldn't I? It always seemed a little too conveniently timed that I was handed my walking papers the very day after we... After you and I..."

"You actually think I asked my father to trade you because we..."

"Well, why would I have any reason to believe otherwise?"

Her mouth was dropped open, glaring at me like I was an escaped patient from the mental ward. I felt like one. "*That* is the most insane thing I have ever heard. You think my father bases his career decisions on my hookups?"

I leaned forward for the kill shot, elbows on my knees, teeth clenched as I answered, "I think your father would do anything to make his precious daughter happy."

"You're a narcissist!"

"And you're full of shit!"

She gaped at me as if I'd just slapped her.

"Fine. I take it back," she said in a blood-curdling seethe. She stood up and slammed her drink down on the coffee table, the liquid sloshing over the sides of the glass. Her eyes were shooting daggers as her words dripped venom. "You're *not* a narcissist, Zac. You're just an *asshole*!"

She stomped out the door, slamming it behind her as I got to my feet and yelled, "A drunken handjob is hardly 'giving up the goods,' sweetheart!"

Magnum joined the conversation just then, piping in with, *"Asshole! You're just an asshole!"*

Tell me something I don't know.

I slumped back into my recliner as the screaming match played over in my mind. I downed the last of her drink, but it was too effing sweet and I found myself gagging on the mouthful I'd just swallowed. Grabbing the remote in disgust, I turned on the TV.

Fuck the Devils and their stupid, fucking Stanley Cup. I hope they lose. Then I won't have to see Avery Fucking Brooks ever again.

I looked over at the TV just in time to see the final score.

Ducks – 1. Devils – 0.

For those keeping score at home, that makes *two* games the home team lost tonight.

Chapter Thirteen

Game Seven of the finals was Saturday night.

The bar was normally pretty busy on the weekends, but tonight, it was completely out of control. We typically only managed to draw this many people whenever there was a big-name band on the schedule.

Or, I guess, a big game.

We were a sports pub year-round, but a hockey bar first and foremost. The fact that our boys were currently starring in the show created an atmosphere of apocalyptic proportions.

Every television set was on and tuned to NBC. Every stool was taken, every inch of floor space was occupied, and every glass was filled.

Just the way I liked it. If the bar did business like this every weekend, I'd have an easier time keeping out of the red.

I suppose our family was luckier than most, in that we actually were able to access the cash necessary to pay my father's hospital bills. But it wiped out my parents' small savings, and took almost every penny of the money I'd socked away from my cushy NHL days. At the age of twenty-three, after everything I'd worked for, I was back to Square One.

Now here it was four years later, and I hadn't yet advanced to Square Two.

Mom was living off Dad's life insurance, which was normally enough for her since the house had been paid off. But that didn't mean my brothers and I didn't slip her an extra bit of pocket money every now and again. They were supplementing her income way more than I was lately, because even though we didn't really discuss it, everyone knew I didn't have that much to give. Besides, I'd already paid more than my fair share. And because I'd done that, it freed my brothers up to get their lives started. They were all doing pretty well for themselves these days.

Though I guess you wouldn't be able to tell that from the state they were in tonight.

I looked over to the hightop table where my brothers set up shop hours ago. They wanted the best spot in the house, so Wyatt got here early this afternoon to stake his claim, and had downed about a hundred beers since. Bash met him a couple hours later and Finn didn't crawl in until a minute before face-off, but it looked as though they'd both made up for lost time. As evidenced by the sentinel of bottles crowding the table, I guessed they'd found a way to catch up to Wyatt.

Bash—we rarely called him Sebastian—was the oldest. He was thirty-six, but don't tell him I told you that. He liked to think he could still pass as a guy in his twenties, and none of us had the heart to burst his bubble. These days, he was a music teacher at a nearby high school, but back in '99, he was hauling lumber down at the docks while he worked on getting his teaching degree. Whenever one of us got pissed at him, "Al Bundy" was our preferred insult, as Bash used to be one hell of a football player back in his teen years, and we all knew he'd go back in time to his glory days if given the chance. It was kind of a jugular shot, though, so we tended to save it for only the most pressing circumstances.

Fact is, he tried to milk every ounce of fame out of his football persona way longer than he should have, and wound up riding it right into the ground. It got embarrassing there for a little while, so I was glad he cut that out finally. And hell, the guy was pushing forty and he was in better shape than the lot of us. I didn't go out of my way to piss him off too often. There was always the chance I could take him in a fight, but I wasn't looking to test that theory.

Finn was a decently successful stockbroker out in New York. He liked to think he was a real slick bastard, as evidenced by the fact that his nickname out there in the city was "The Shark." If you ask me, I think he's the one that came up with it, but seeing as how he didn't expect any of us to call him that, I couldn't give two shits what he went by when he wasn't here.

Finn had a model-hot girlfriend in New York… and another just-as-gorgeous girl right here in Norman. I didn't know if they knew about each other and I didn't *want* to know. It's not like I had to see either of them all too often, so I just kept my mouth shut when I did. Chances were, neither of them would be around too long anyway; *The Shark* had an image to uphold. Case in point: The dude was wearing a suit. On a Saturday. I didn't know who the hell he was trying to impress, but I couldn't imagine anyone here was thinking he just came from the office.

Rounding out the honor roll was Wyatt, whom everyone still referred to as "The Riot" even though his wild days were long over. He was making a pretty respectable living as manager of the sports complex one town over. The place was huge, with a full-size turf football field inside and another one outside, too, that doubled as a soccer field. Out back were three baseball diamonds with batting cages, and there was a driving range and mini-golf course adjacent to the domed hockey arena, where Wyatt and I used to spend practically every moment of our free time back in the day.

He'd been working there ever since he was a snot-nosed teenager. He was a hockey player like me, only he never had any intentions of going pro. After my knee healed, he used to badger me about getting back on the ice, but after a while, he just gave up. He knew I wasn't going back out there.

I knew he found it strange, because our lives had practically revolved around sports. My brothers and I were raised to be athletes, cheering each other on, excelling in our chosen games.

Me and Wyatt were the hockey players, and I didn't think my brother got his fair share of the credit for being as good as he was, being that I was the one who turned pro and all. I knew he was still playing the town leagues, still sleepwalking out of bed for those three AM ice times, still playing his heart out.

Finn was our baseball player, but he spent more of his energy making time with the ladies than working on his swing. Even still, he was a better-than-passable athlete.

Even Bash, with all his talent, never took his game to the next level. He only did the college football thing for a single semester before dropping off the team. He'd followed some girl out to Michigan when he knocked her up, and that move put an end to his university run. She lost the baby; he lost his scholarship. And man, was my father *pissed*.

After that, I think all their sports dreams were put onto me, and goddammit if it didn't kill me that I let them all down.

They'd all worked here at one time or another in their younger years, just like me. Unlike me, however, they'd grown up and moved on. I was essentially still slinging the drinks. Kind of fucked up to realize that the tables had turned. I don't even know when it happened. I went from being the hero of the family to being its biggest disappointment.

Just to be clear, I didn't begrudge them their success. They're my family, so of course I only wanted to see them accomplish great things, like they were already doing. I was actually proud that I was the one who was able to save us all those years ago, that I was able to step up, even if it led to the unenviable financial situation that I was in now. Any one of them would've done the same for me if I asked.

I just never asked, is all.

I headed over to their table and had to nudge some empties out of the way in order to deposit the full round of Buds. Rachel was normally pretty good at busing the hightops, but seeing as she had a few shots in her already, she was obviously less concerned with doing her job and more concerned about having a good time. She'd spent most of her night whooping it up with the rowdy group of hockey fans in the corner. On a night like this, I couldn't very well play the overbearing boss when I had a few drinks in me myself. It was the Stanley Cup finals, for godsakes, and she knew damn well I'd be letting her get away with it tonight.

Sebastian downed the last of his beer and grabbed for one of the new bottles. "To bringing home the motherfucking Cup!" he shouted at the top of his lungs. Everyone in the place went nuts, shouting back at him as he raised his beer and downed about half of it. I clinked mine against some nearby drinks then took a swig myself. Goddamn, it felt good to love this game again.

Felix had put together a couple of six-foot subs, and Wyatt had about half of one crammed in his maw when he said, "Holy shit. Can you imagine they actually win? Zac, you gotta get us into that party."

"Let's just see what happens, okay? No use talking about next week if we don't get through tonight."

"Don't be such a pessimist," he said. At least I thought that's what he said. It was hard to understand him when he was speaking through a mouthful of food.

"I'm not," I defended. "I'm just being realistic."

Finn shot a raised eyebrow in my direction. "*That* is half your problem."

"What the fuck is *that* supposed to mean?" I asked, shooting him a dirty look in the process.

I caught the silent exchange between Finn and Bash, their eyes meeting in a brief accord. I was waiting for one of them to speak up, but neither one of them did. At least not to explain Finn's comment.

Bash ran his palms across his forehead, his fingers spiking into his hair. "Holy shit. I think I'm drunk already."

"I think you're right, Chris Farley." Wyatt gestured to Bash's hair which was sticking straight out from his head.

We were cracking up already, but when Bash broke into "Fat Guy in a Little Coat," we absolutely lost our shit. Jesus. Growing up in a house with four boys was entertaining enough. But growing up in an *Irish* house with four boys was like living in a twenty-four-hour comedy club. No wonder my mother's laugh lines were etched so deep.

Finn pulled out a cigarette, enduring our groans of displeasure. I waved Rachel over to clear the table before my brother could use one of the empties for an ashtray. She grabbed him a replacement tray and gathered up the bottles, taking three trips before the table could be considered clean. She even delivered a fresh round—which was not her job—but I guess she figured she'd better step up her game before I gave her the ax.

Not that I ever would.

Maybe it wasn't the best business practice, but when I hired someone, it normally meant that I was stuck with them for life. Felix and Alice came with the place, but my full-time guy Denny and my Sunday guy Scott were my own personal finds. My cocktail waitress Farrah pulled double-duty for me; she worked the restaurant during the week, then served drinks in the bar on the weekends. And Rachel... Actually, I don't remember hiring Rachel. She was a tattooed-and-pierced little hellraiser who used to come in and drink pretty regularly. One day, she just up and started working here, and I eventually put her on the books.

But every last one of my employees was loyal to me in their own way, and for that, they received my enduring gratitude. I watched how my father handled his workers for all those years, and I guess I picked up a thing or two. The most essential of which was to always let your employees know how much you valued their contribution to your business. "I couldn't do this without you" went a long way, and more importantly, it was the truth. And when a person felt appreciated, they went above and beyond to try and please you, to pay that respect back. If they felt they were part of a team, then they had a vested interest in seeing that team win. That mentality held true whether the employee in question was a high-level executive at some Fortune 500 office building... or a degenerate working some two-bit bar.

I swear, this place was like The Island of Misfit Toys. My employees were a mixed breed, to say the least.

I couldn't have put together a better crew if I tried.

Chapter Fourteen

I woke up with a killer hangover, the likes of which I hadn't experienced in many, many months. My drinking the night before was three parts celebration and one part drowning my sorrows. In either case, it was hard not to join in with such an elated crowd last night.

The cheers were deafening at the final buzzer but that's when the real drinking started. I tried to forget that I was the only person in that room who had any reason to feel apprehensive about their victory. And even then, that apprehension wasn't enough for me to avoid getting lost in the moment. I forgot about the fact that I was merely an ex-player. I forgot about the fact that I'd been fired from the very team whose triumph I was toasting at that moment. I forgot about the consequences of having to see Avery again if they won. When it came right down to it, my boyhood idols—and onetime contemporaries—had just won their third championship inside of a decade. Do you have any idea how rare that is? It really was a spectacular victory.

My thinking was fuzzy, and there was a buzzing on the edges of my brain. I shook myself awake and realized the buzzing was actually a ringing, and reached over to grab the phone off its cradle.

I went to say hello, but it came out sounding more like, "Mrho?"

"Heck of a game last night, huh."

Avery.

I checked the clock on my nightstand, still half-asleep and wondering why she'd be calling at such an ungodly hour. Oh wait. It was after ten.

"Yeah. Heckuva game."

"Is it awful that a small part of me was rooting against them?"

In spite of my pounding head, I gave a chuckle. "No. I was doing the same thing. I'm glad they won, though."

"Me too," she sighed.

There was a pause in the exchange, our fight from the week before rolling around in both our minds. Neither one of us knew what to say about it. Thankfully, Avery launched in first. "Look. I'm really sorry about my outburst the other night. I said some not-so-nice things. Our fight never would have happened if I hadn't come up to your apartment with such a chip on my shoulder."

It was big of her to accept responsibility, but it's not as though I could let her take all the blame. "Yeah, me, too. I was being smug and conceited and I was doing everything I could to ruffle your feathers."

I thought I heard her smile on the other end of the line. No, seriously, I swear I could hear her grinning as she offered, "So... seeing as how we'll be stuck with each other all week... can we call a truce?"

"Yeah. Truce," I snickered.

"Do you mind if I stop in later? I have a vanload of hats and T-shirts to drop off. You do have somewhere we can start stockpiling all this stuff, right? Per our agreement in the contract?"

"Yeah, sure. I can close off the pool room this week. We can just put everything in there. Per our agreement in the contract."

That made her giggle. "Are you mocking me, Zac?"

"Just trying to keep everything on the up and up, Miss Brooks."

"Strictly business, you mean?"

I took a deep breath. "Yeah. I don't know. I think maybe it's for the best, right?"

There was a silent pause on her end, and I envisioned her twirling a lock of that auburn hair around her finger as she thought. "Yes. You're probably right, Zac. We have a pretty hectic week ahead of us, and there's no reason we can't get through it in one piece. Keeping things on a more professional level might be the best way to ensure that that happens."

"Sounds good." *If by good, I mean 'like shit.'*

"See you later?"

"See you later."

I rolled my sorry ass out of bed and started my morning routine. I took the cover off Magnum's cage which had him immediately squawking and chattering away, the happy, time-to-start-the-day yammering in which he always indulged. *"Good morning! Good morning! Rise and shine!"*

I was glad for his company most of the time, even if he rarely shut the fuck up. But Magnum was part of a package deal. He came with the apartment. Besides, we'd known each other since I was five. He was one of the few constants in my life.

I tossed a hunk of leftover Italian bread into the opened door of his cage and gave him a quick rub along his wings. I left the door open so he could escape if he so chose, and more often than not, he'd welcome the jail break. I normally let him free-roam around the apartment during the few hours I started my morning every day. So, it was as I was putting on a pot of coffee when I felt him nudging against my calf.

"Hey buddy. You may need to steer clear today. I'm not as surefooted as I normally am, and I don't want to see you get squished."

I must have sparked a memory, because Magnum started in with one his oldies, a rousing rendition of Bobby Darin's "Splish Splash."

In spite of my hangover, I found myself chuckling. "Yeah, buddy. You're right. Let's throw on some music."

I lifted him up onto my shoulder as I headed for the stereo and threw on a rock station. "Backyard" was the first song we heard, which was one hell of a way to start a day. The band that sings it used to play The Westlake back in the early nineties. They never forgot this place, though. Even after they became sort of famous, they'd still come back every now and again to play a night. One of the guys was a local, a cousin of my next door neighbors growing up. Bash and him used to jam together a little bit when they were teenagers.

I wondered if he was still in touch with him? If so, I thought maybe I could give the guy a call, see if I could get Thunderjug to book a few nights to come back here and play. They always drew a huge crowd. The bar could use that kind of excitement around here again.

I supposed it would be exciting around here soon enough.

The party was scheduled for the following Saturday, and from the chatter last night, I guessed the whole town already knew. In a town this small, nothing stayed secret for very long.

I put Magnum on his "tree" and hit the showers. The water helped to obliterate my headache, but I was definitely moving a little slower than usual.

Stepping out of the shower, I swiped the steam from the mirror in order to shave my face, assessing the damage staring back at me. My skin was looking a little pale (but that could've been due to the fact that I didn't spend my days lounging around in the sun), and my normally green eyes were surrounded with red. I didn't think my odds were too hot that I'd find some Visine in the medicine cabinet. Now that it wasn't covered in stubble, the scar on my chin was more pronounced; a souvenir from one wicked pissa of a game back in my BC days when I took a biscuit to the face. Kept all my teeth, at least. And I guessed my hair was looking okay.

Decent hair, a clean-shaven jaw… and teeth. That was about as good as it was going to get.

Sitting at my table with a bowl of French Toast Crunch, I attempted to slam down some breakfast. Magnum was perched on my shoulder, picking at the slices of apple next to my napkin when he wasn't bopping along with the stereo. He was uncharacteristically quiet until there was a knocking at my door.

"*Knock knock*! *Knick knack*! *Sharona*!" he screamed in my ear.

What the hell? The only way to my apartment was through the bar, and that was locked up until we opened for business. Felix must've been on fire or something, because he didn't normally bother me at home.

I answered the door to find Avery standing there, which pretty much knocked the wind right out of my gut. She took one look at me with my bird on my shoulder and busted up laughing. "Arrrrgggggh, matey! Where's your patch?"

"What are you doing here?" I managed to ask without much difficulty. Thankfully, her playful tone paved the way for an easy reunion, because I'd been a little worried about having to see her again.

"Helloooo. You get slammed into the wall one too many times? I just called to *tell* you I was coming over today."

131

"Yeah, but I thought you meant, like, *later* today."

"Sorry. I got anxious again."

"They have pills for that, you know."

* * *

Avery flipped the stopper and closed the door, locking it behind me as I carried in the last box from the van and plunked it on top of the bar. There were about a million more just like it stacked along two walls of my pool room, all the promotional stuff to give away at the event. I was going to have to go through them and put together a few care packages for my brothers as an apology. There was a good chance I wouldn't be able to get them into the party, and I wasn't looking forward to letting them down. I was thinking maybe some official NHL championship hats would serve as a peace offering.

We'd been screwing around all morning, busting chops and trying to one-up each other with the amount of stuff we could carry. Such a simple task shouldn't have been so entertaining, but it was.

Avery let out with a heavy breath and then bemoaned, "Oh my God! It's so hot out today! How are we supposed to focus on hockey when it's practically summer?"

You're telling me.

I swiped an arm across my forehead, wiping away the moisture that had materialized during our busywork in the scorching sun. At this rate, I was going to need a second shower. I took a look at Avery, who was flushed and out of breath from our box-transporting ordeal, her hairline damp with sweat. She looked hot. Maybe she needed a shower, too. Maybe we could take one together.

Apparently, I needed a cold one.

I shook the image from my brain as I made my way behind the bar. "How 'bout a drink? Water sound good?"

"Water sounds *perfect*. Thank you."

The bar wasn't set to open until twelve on Sundays, so I knew not to expect Scott for a few more minutes.

Which was good, because it gave me a little more time to be alone with Avery.

I'd have been grateful for the fact that she wasn't wearing one of those damned skirts again today, but she'd opted for a pair of stretchy pants instead. The frigging things outlined the perfect proportions of her sweet little ass, and I couldn't decide whether it was that or her legs that were causing me the greater agony.

Both. Definitely both.

Cut it out, Zac. Strictly professional, remember?

I grabbed us a couple bottles and took a seat on the stool next to hers. She cracked the cap and downed half her drink before letting out with a breathless, "Ahhh! Wow, I needed that."

I could use a bit of cooling down myself. I took a swig from my own drink, then rolled the bottle across my forehead, practically groaning with relief. When I opened my eyes, I saw Avery staring at me in a sidelong glance, her lips quirking in an almost imperceptible smirk.

"What?" I asked.

She shook her head and refocused her attentions on the bottle in her hands. "Nothing."

"What?" I asked again. "What's that look?"

"I said it was nothing."

"Ave, I know when there's something going on in that overactive brain of yours. You were definitely thinking more than 'nothing.' C'mon, spill it."

She huffed out a laugh. "Noooo. No, I'm not going there. Drop it, Zac."

"No."

"No?"

I gave out a sigh. "Look, Ave. I think today was a good turning point for us. I had fun working with you. You made *unloading boxes* fun. I know I said we should keep things strictly business, but… I'd like us to be friends again. And we can't really do that when you've got this wall up between us. I know we didn't really end things so great all those years ago, but—"

"No. You're right. *We* didn't."

I was caught off guard by the tone of her voice. "What do you mean?"

"You know exactly what I mean. *We* didn't end things at all. *You* did. On that note, you can't really end something that never actually started."

I took a big inhale. Apparently, it was time to straighten some shit out. "We doing this?"

She was flipping the cap around her fingertips as she answered, "No."

That made me chuckle. "Look, Ave… I wasn't exactly… *boyfriend material* back then. I hope I never led you to believe otherwise." That was a lie. The truth was, I was more than ready to stop all the running around. Back then, sex in mass quantity was as much a part of my life as breathing. One night with her, and suddenly, I could give it all up. I *wanted* to.

"You didn't. I mean, not at first. I saw the way you were with those girls."

"I was an ass."

"Yeah, you were. But only because…"

"What?"

She chucked the cap over the bar and into the garbage pail. "Two points!"

She was trying to avoid the topic but there was no way I was letting this go. "Stop changing the subject, Ave. It might be good for us to get all this out. You know, so we can start fresh."

The tension had been brewing between us since the first day she came walking back into my bar. We'd avoided talking about it, and all that served to do was blow up into a huge fight. The screaming match in my apartment the other night was every unsaid thing between us coming back to bite us in the ass. If we had any hope of moving forward, we had to first clear up the past.

She hesitated as she thought about it, staring out the wall of windows to the beach. Some families were already out there, setting up for the relaxing day ahead, not a care in the world. I kept quiet, letting Avery come to a resolution on her own. She must have arrived at one, because her posture straightened as she cleared her throat.

"Fine." She twisted sideways on her stool and bent her legs up to her chest, wrapping her arms around her shins. Her stubborn chin was resting on her knees, but her eyes seemed to be having some trouble meeting mine. "The thing is, I liked you a lot back then, okay? You were like a double-fudge sundae with arsenic sauce. Tempting, but dangerous."

"Also delicious."

"Zac, shut up and let me get through this."

I turned my stool to face her and rested an elbow on the bar. All ears.

"I know we only hooked up that night because I was drunk enough to instigate it and you were drunk enough not to protest."

That one kind of threw me. "You think that's why we finally hooked up?"

"Isn't it?"

"Sort of." All the drinking that night was *how* it happened, not *why*. "But it's not like I never wanted to before."

"You thought about it?" she asked, incredulously.

"All the fucking time." I huffed out a laugh at that. If she only knew *how much* I'd thought about it, she probably wouldn't believe me. "I just always thought *you* didn't want to, you know, friendzoning me and all."

She was silent for a moment before admitting, "I *didn't* want to. I made a huge point to keep you at arms' length because I didn't want to just be another..." She shook her head before meeting my eyes. "I just thought it was safer not to get involved."

"Me too," I busted, raising my brows and shooting her a smirk.

She finally unclenched her pose and sat normally, facing me. "But I guess I couldn't stay away any longer. I finally caved. I was kind of crazy about you back then."

My mind started spinning. All these years, I always just assumed it was a one night thing. Yes, we were friends. Yes, we flirted incessantly. But the way things were left between us... I never allowed myself to believe she felt anything more for me. "You were? But you never said anything."

"It was hard to get a word in edgewise with all those other girls in your face all the time."

It was easy to avoid having to confront how much I really liked her while I was so busy whoring around. I guess I couldn't really blame her for not seeing it. Hell, I didn't *want* her to see it.

I didn't want to see it.

"They didn't mean anything to me. You—" I stopped myself, afraid to admit how much she meant to me, how my whole world changed in an instant all those many years ago... how I was forced to forget it only hours later. It wasn't too hard to move on once I was in a new place, Avery thousands of miles away. It wasn't too hard to convince myself that I'd been mistaken about how hard I'd fallen, that I was drunker than I actually was.

But having her sitting right there next to me, I couldn't lie to myself anymore. I couldn't lie to *her*. It would have been so much easier to say nothing, but instead, I went ahead and spilled my guts anyway. "You could've been the one to change that. You *were* the one to change that. That one night we had... I really fell hard for you. Hell. I'd fallen for you long before that, but I never wanted to admit it to myself."

Her eyes went wide. Hopeful. Gorgeous. "You did?"

"Hell yeah."

"But it was only one night."

"It was more than one night, Ave." I shot her a knowing smirk at that. Our love affair had gone on for years before it ever got physical. "You gonna tell me you didn't feel it, too?"

"No. I did. I just admitted as much, didn't I?" She broke her gaze to pick at her nails. "But when you told me that night, I thought it was all a lie. Because then you left."

"I didn't leave. I got traded. The very next day."

"Right. I knew that. I guess I just figured you were in on the decision." She shrugged her shoulders and met my eyes again. The smile was back as she said, "You know, a simple explanation could have cleared everything up years ago. There were phones back then, right?"

"Yes, which I would have used if I wasn't so angry with you."

"Huh?"

I sighed heavily, running a hand over my hair. "I told you the other night. I thought you went running to Daddy and got me traded off the team."

Her mouth dropped open in shock. "You were *serious* about that? Why would I do such a thing?"

"I just figured you were having some fun with me. Once the fun was over, you realized what a mistake you'd made and had to get rid of me."

"Which you now realize is insane, yes?"

It wasn't easy to talk about, but seeing as I was the one who instigated this conversation, I knew it would be unfair to hold anything back. "Yes. But you have to remember, I wasn't used to girls liking me for anything more than…" I let out a heavy breath and then just laid it out there. "But then when you… I actually thought there was a chance you wanted more. When I 'figured out' you didn't, I was crushed, Ave. Honestly, I was genuinely… hurt."

"I'm sorry."

"It's not your fault, obviously. But even beyond that, getting traded turned out to be the worst thing that could've ever happened to me."

"You were a hockey player. It happens."

"No, I know. I'm not pouting about it. Players get traded all the time; I get that. It's just that in *my* case, it created this crazy domino effect. I was let go from my dream team, then a few months after I got shipped off to Texas, I busted up my knee. Career over."

I paused for a moment, letting my failed life hang in the space between us.

"I guess I blamed your father for all of it, and by association, you. Like, if I'd still been here in Jersey, the injury would never have happened."

Avery gnawed on her bottom lip, mulling over my revelation. "I can see why you'd feel that way. But Zac, you know he's not to blame, right? Or me, for that matter."

"I know it *now*."

We were silent as the conversation rolled around in our minds.

Avery repressed a smile as she said, "So much for strictly business."

I chuckled, then used her own words against her. "Phones work both ways, you know."

"Oh, right," she huffed. "Like I was going to be the one to call you. I didn't think a womanizer like you would even remember my name the next day, a fact which was confirmed when I never heard from you again."

I looked at her in astonishment. I'd seen her angry, but that was the first time I'd ever seen her be *cruel*. Jesus. She really fucking hated me.

"Jesus. You really fucking hate me."

"I don't hate you. I feel sorry for you."

"*You what?*" Her comment hit me worse than a high stick to the face; my blood immediately started boiling. Of all the words she could have chosen, she had to go and pick the only ones that were like a knife to the jugular. "You *feel sorry* for me? What the fuck, Avery?" I stood up abruptly, scraping the stool across the wood floor. "Oh, I'm some pathetic loser who runs some two-bit bar in some nothing town—"

"I didn't say that!"

"Some useless hockey player who can't even put on a pair of skates anymore? You think I don't already know I'm a failure?"

139

"You're not—"

"You think I want your *pity?*"

I was completely riled up and out of control. I could feel my pulse racing and the ache in my forehead where my brows were drawn together too tightly. Avery had gotten to her feet, and I could see she'd taken a few steps back as I advanced.

Seeing her fearful retreat out of my wrath snapped me out of my tirade and forced me to realize what I'd just revealed. I was immediately embarrassed by my outburst, by the emotions I wasn't even fully aware that I possessed. Rage, humiliation, disappointment... regret. I had no idea why those feelings chose this moment to come bubbling up to the surface, but there was no stopping them now that they'd been released.

My chest tightened and there was an actual stinging behind my eyes. I was on the verge of losing it and needed to get the hell out of there before I did. "You can show yourself out."

I knew I was being a rude asshole, and I hadn't even processed exactly why. No one wants to be pitied, for godsakes, but as I ascended the stairwell to my apartment, I started to realize that maybe that's not at all what Avery was trying to do.

Chapter Fifteen

The day of the Stanley Cup party, people were coming and going all day, disrupting my regulars who were trying to get their last moments of boozing in before they got kicked out for the private party. They weren't too happy about the situation, but thankfully, they were pretty understanding regardless.

I'd avoided coming downstairs any more than necessary because I figured the best way to apologize to Avery would be to simply stay out of her way. I'd done so all week, only communicating with her through answering machines and hand-written notes stuck on the register. Simple requests from her; stupid responses from me. I'd leave her jokes or drawings, anything I could think of to try and apologize.

Except, you know, actually saying I was sorry.

Up until now, we were able to keep our distance, as she'd only stop in whenever I wasn't around. (I swore, when I found out which one of my bartenders was tipping her off, I was going to tear them a new asshole.) But now that it was party day, there was no avoiding one another. There was too much hands-on stuff to do that required us to be in the same room at the same time. Well, too much for *her* to do. I was just an extra body in the way. As evidenced by the fact that we eventually bumped into each other.

Literally.

I was carrying three cases of wine at the time, so my vision was limited. I managed to plow right into her as she came around the corner.

"Sorry," I said, automatically.

"Ha!"

I put the cases down on the nearest hightop, and diverted her before she could scurry away. "Ave, wait! Can we talk for a minute?"

She lowered her clipboard and turned to face me. She was wearing light blue velour sweatpants with a matching hoodie, unzipped to reveal her *Punk'd* T-shirt underneath. She looked soft, like a favorite stuffed animal you'd want to curl up with in your bed.

She wasn't *acting* soft, though.

"Why? What do you want?" she asked, clearly exasperated by more than just the hectic pace of the past hours.

"I know you're busy, but..." I scanned my eyes around the room, taking note of everyone scurrying around, the customers sitting at the bar. I knew she was due an apology, but it was awkward to execute with so many people around, and I just couldn't find the words. "I wanted to talk to you. About the other day."

She could see I wasn't going to tell her what she deserved to hear. "Maybe it will be best if we just avoid one another today, okay, Zac?"

I was a little put off that she was treating me like a disease in my own bar, but I figured I'd let her call the shots right now. I owed her at least that much. "Yeah. Okay."

Since my attentions weren't required downstairs, and since I was trying to avoid Avery anyway, I went back up to my apartment to lie down and try to take a nap. I lay there for a full thirty minutes, but it was no use. I was feeling too guilty about my fight with Avery, and too edgy about the fact that I was going to be in the same room with my old teammates again. The last time we'd all been here together, I was a player. And now... Now I was going to be the guy serving their drinks.

Running this place was an honest way to make a living, so I shouldn't have been embarrassed about the fact that I was doing it. But let's be fucking real, here. It was decidedly a step down from the adulation and glory of being a sports star. Most things were.

And yet...

I suddenly realized I cared more about what Avery thought of me than the opinion of my old teammates. And I was being unnecessarily stubborn at not offering up an apology. Why was it so hard for me to accept when I was wrong?

Maybe because the only *other* girl who stuck around long enough for me to hurt her eventually split because of it. Not that I can blame her. A person can only deal with such jackassery for so long. Julie hung in there longer than I ever expected, though, gave me more credit for being human than I deserved. Until finally, she got tired of my bullshit and moved on.

She never expected an apology whenever I screwed up. Maybe she just didn't hold me to a high enough standard. Or maybe she just realized I was incapable of admitting when I was wrong. Maybe she never cared about me enough to bother. And why would she? I only hurt her, over and over, until she finally realized she'd had enough.

And then she left.

* * *

143

Later that evening, I came down to join the circus. There was a more formal reception planned for the fall, but for now, this was just the *party*, and it looked as though everyone was more than ready to get it started.

Avery had hired a phenomenal band, and they were playing Iron Maiden's "Number of the Beast," kicking some serious ass in the process. The place was already rocking, and I got caught up in the energy and excitement as I said hello and shook some hands. A few of the old-timers had been invited, and it was pretty frigging awesome to meet some of my childhood idols. They were living legends, for chrissakes, guys I'd watched on my television back when my head was filled with dreams. And now here they were, right here in my bar.

Most of my former teammates were congregating over at the long wall, signing the collectors' sweaters and photos that were slated to be auctioned off for charity. They signed all the gear, then posed for pictures in front of the customized backdrop while the photographers snapped away. We'd let the press in willingly, but only gave them an hour to take any publicity shots before kicking them out the door.

That's when the real party began.

Avery had spent the week transforming my bar into a New Jersey Devils paradise. There were red tablecloths over every hightop table and new spotlights installed over every booth. Even my regular high hats were replaced with red bulbs, tossing a fiery glow onto every surface in the room.

Every TV was playing the same highlight reel, all the most stellar moments from this year's playoffs, along with some classic footage of the old guard's athletic feats.

She'd brought in a mobile cooking station and set it up in the corner, and hired a chef to fry up some Taylor Ham and cheese sandwiches. The entire room smelled fucking mouth-watering. She'd had some tables set up near the square bar, and the things were just covered with platters upon platters of Felix's party fare. Sandwiches, french fries, cheesesteaks... lots of boardwalk food. There was also an entire dessert table set up with a candy buffet, cranberry salad, and pastries from *Calandra's*. She'd commissioned a cake from a place called *Carlo's* down in Hoboken, baked in the shape of the New Jersey Devil himself. It was the coolest thing I'd ever seen. Who knew you could make a statue out of cake?

Avery had resurrected our old drink menu, and had a bunch of hockey-themed cocktails printed onto the chalkboard before hanging it on the wall. Reading them made me snicker. I'd forgotten about Game Misconduct. That drink was a killer. Seeing it sent a shock of nostalgia straight into my brain.

My father would have loved this.

I checked in with my bartending staff to make sure they were okay, then detoured into the kitchen to see if Felix had everything under control. Of course he did.

I came back out to the bar just as Avery stepped up to the platform. She looked incredible. Her sweatpants-and-T-shirt combo had been replaced with a skintight red dress that showed off every luscious curve. Black-and-red fuck-me heels accentuated her toned calves. Her auburn hair fell around her face in messy curls, the kind of hair that looked like she'd just rolled out of bed. Or wanted to be invited *into* one.

She was simply stunning, and I found it hard to draw air into my lungs, much less form a cohesive sentence.

Thankfully, I wasn't the one doing the talking.

She took over the small stage and welcomed everyone for coming before handing the mic off to the commissioner. There was a lot of back-patting and shoulder-clapping as he introduced the money behind the team, and everyone in the room tried to seem enraptured as they politely suffered through the boring speeches. It was all a bunch of bull, but a necessary evil during an event like this.

Because everyone was focused on the stage, and because Avery was walking right by me at the time, I took the shot while I could. I didn't say a word as I grabbed her around her waist and pulled her with me through the nearest doorway, which just happened to be the ladies' bathroom.

She gave out a quick yelp, but by the time the door closed behind us, she'd regained her composure. "What the hell, Zac?"

She stood there smoothing out her dress, then dipped her face toward the mirror to check on her hair.

Cut it out. You look gorgeous.

I met her reflection in the mirror, put my hands on her shoulders and said, "I feel really bad about screaming in your face the other day. You didn't deserve that."

Her eyes met mine in a hesitant sigh. "I was trying to be playful. I swear I wasn't pitying you. I was only trying to bust your chops and my words came out all wrong." She didn't owe me an explanation, but I was happy to hear one all the same.

"I know. I know that now. I just… I'm sorry." There. Was that so damned hard? "You unknowingly struck a nerve. I just got overly defensive, I guess."

She turned to face me, saying, "I thought you were an *off*ensive player."

I did a double-take at her words, and caught the smirk on her face. "Damn straight," I chuckled, glad that we were apparently friends again.

"Did you see it yet?" she asked.

146

I knew exactly what she was talking about, so I didn't bother with the dirty comeback and simply grabbed her hand to lead her out the door.

We walked together to the end of the long bar where the guys had been taking pictures earlier. Next to the backdrop, on a marble pedestal… was The Fucking Stanley Cup.

There it was. The frigging Holy Grail, right there at my fingertips. I knew the thing was in for a continued life of debauchery, and was curious to see what fate it held for the night ahead.

The Stars won it the year I was with them, but as I was dealing with bigger things that summer, I didn't share in the celebration. Besides, I was only on the team for four months, most of which was spent riding the pines. I didn't feel a part of the win.

But it still had my name carved into the side.

I found it easily enough, and ran my fingers over the engraved letters: *Z. McAllister*.

Jesus. My name was on the goddamn Stanley cup. The fucking Cup! I couldn't believe my eyes, but there it was.

And it sure looked pretty sitting in my bar.

* * *

Avery was a whirlwind. It was amazing to see her floating around the room, playing hostess, taking care of every little detail, so confident, so self-assured. I couldn't take my eyes off her.

She was so different from my memories. Back then, I thought she was just a sweet, shy girl who gave a whole new dimension to the term 'puck bunny.' She loved hockey but was scared as a rabbit. I didn't realize how wrong I was until that one night when we—

"Maniac! How the hell are you?"

I turned at the unmistakable voice of Guillaume, clapping me on the shoulder with one hand, a drink spilling over in the other.

"Guy! You old son of a bitch. How are you?" I asked as we took a seat at one of the hightops. Damn. I really missed this dude.

"Oh, fine, fine. Finally have a drink in my hand, so all is good."

"Who are you kidding, 'finally'? You never stop drinking."

"Well, if I never stop drinking, I don't have to be hungover."

We both had a laugh over that one. The two of us made small talk for a little while until some of the other guys decided to join us, and we instantly found ourselves reminiscing about the old days. Soon enough, we had the rowdiest table in the place.

Especially once my brothers got involved.

They'd snuck in through the kitchen, but I wasn't exactly surprised. I knew they'd find a way to crash this party. I supposed it was easier to break into a place when you had the key.

The band was killer, and it wasn't too hard to sense a theme with their music. They were in the middle of The Stones' "Sympathy for the Devil," but they'd already played "Devil Went Down to Georgia," "Devil in a Blue Dress," fucking Cliff Richard's "Devil Woman," a couple of Judas Priest tunes, something from *Spinal Tap* for godsakes…

Jesus, there were a lot of Devil songs.

When they broke into Van Halen's "Running with the Devil," we all pretty much lost our shit. It was our unofficial fight song, and the walls shook as every last one of us screamed the lyrics back at the band. Yes, we were drunk. But goddamn if it wasn't one hell of a good time.

Avery's father shot a warning look in our direction before realizing that he didn't need to play babysitter—at least for a few more months, anyway. His grimace relaxed as his face met mine in a genuine smile, which was surprising, to say the least.

Aside from a handshake and quick hello, I hadn't gone out of my way to talk with the guy. Avery and I had been able to clear the air about *our* misunderstandings, but I hadn't cleared up *anything* with *him*. The fact remained that the man tossed me out like trash.

But even though I still carried a huge chip on my shoulder about it, it was actually kind of nice to see him enjoying himself.

It was nice to see *everyone* enjoying themselves. Especially me.

Alice came by to take our drink orders, which was odd, because she normally wouldn't deign to emerge from behind the bar. Taking orders was for the cocktail waitresses, not my head bartender. As I mentioned previously, she wasn't the most pleasant person, but thankfully, she was all smiles as she asked, "Now what would you boys like?"

Travis leered back, announcing, "I think I'd rather not say in the presence of a lady, darlin'."

Alice pressed a hand to the hightop and placed her face within inches of Trav's. "Let me know when you find one." With that, she reached across Guillaume and downed one of his awaiting shots.

The guys all howled as Travis put an arm around Alice's waist, pulling her between his knees. I figured he was about to get a fist between his eyes for that, but instead, Alice smiled and said, "You're cute. We don't get too many cowboys around here."

Travis amped up his twang to reply, "Darlin', that's because I'm the only cowboy this town *needs*."

We all groaned and rolled our eyes, Guillaume going so far as to throw a crumpled napkin at Travis's head.

He didn't let that affect his game, however, because he gave Alice another quick squeeze and asked, "What time do you get off, Blondie?"

Alice was in rare form. She smirked and answered, "I guess whatever time you show up to my apartment."

There was a collective "Ooooooh!" like we were the goddamn canned sound effects from an episode of *Married with Children*. We were all laughing through our jeers, until Travis finally released my employee and Guillaume complained, "*This* guy. He makes it look so easy."

I was having fun with my old friends, but I found my eyes wandering involuntarily any time I'd catch a flash of red in my peripheral vision.

Avery was a sight to behold. I knew that brain of hers must have been going a mile a minute, but outwardly, she appeared calm, cool, and collected. I couldn't look away.

The band started in with The Beatles' "Devil in her Heart," and I used that as a good enough excuse to get my hands on her.

I excused myself from the table and walked up behind Avery. "Dance with me."

She turned, startled to see me there. My expression must have been both wolfish and convincing, because her eyes went a bit wider as she stammered out an "Okay."

I slipped my arms around her and spun her out to the floor. It was the first sustained contact I'd made with her delectable body in all these weeks of being near her, and my senses became all too aware of that fact. The dress at her waist was silky but I slid my hand up a few inches to rest on the exposed skin of her back. Her flesh was warm and smooth, and her neck smelled like fresh air and... cinnamon? Jesus Christ, she smelled like fucking cookies. Was that her perfume? Do they make cookie-scented perfume? They really should.

For the record, I'll mention that I'm also a proponent for a bacon-scented fragrance, just in case anyone out there has the power to make that happen.

"You smell like cookies."

That made her giggle. "Thank you?"

I spun us around in a full turn before settling back into an easy two-step. "Nice party. Whoever planned this thing did one helluva job."

She pulled back so I could see her grateful smile. "She had a lot of help."

"Nah. I was just the grunt you ordered around all week with your little notes. That didn't take a heck of a lot of skill. You, on the other hand, made all this happen. Not only that, but you made it look easy. Seriously, Ave. Just take a second and look around. Look what you did."

I watched her eyes scan around the room, a shy grin eeking its way across her face. She'd been planning like crazy for this night, so I was glad that she was allowing herself the few minutes to drink it all in. Which was even better for me, getting this chance to drink *her* in.

Avery seemed to melt into me with every step we took. I took a shot and dipped my head next to hers, hoping she wouldn't push me away. She didn't. I ran my nose along her ear, could feel her shiver as I whispered, "This is nice. You and me, being nice to one another. Don't you think?"

She let out with a shaky sigh before answering, "I do."

151

Her voice was barely audible, and I could tell she must have been feeling the same pent-up agony as me. At least if her hand at my shoulder was any indication. She'd slid it closer to my neck, her thumb brushing a light caress under my ear. There was lava in my veins from her touch, and I found myself mentally warning my impending hard-on to keep itself in check. Jesus. I was getting more worked up than that time Gina Mentozzi's C-cups were rubbing against my chest during "Sister Christian" at the eighth grade prom.

I pulled back to gauge the expression on her face, surprised when her eyes met mine. There was a similar fire brimming in their depths, a smoldering, half-lidded capitulation that told me this night was headed in a very interesting direction.

I slanted my palm across her lower back to her hip, drawing her tightly against my body, my face buried against her hair. I took a huge inhale and then just went for it. "I think maybe we should get out of here."

"Oh shit!"

Not exactly the reaction I was hoping for, and my heart sank straight away. But it soon became apparent that Avery wasn't responding to my insinuation, as her comment was directed toward the door.

"What the heck is he doing here?" she asked.

I turned in the direction of Avery's wide eyes, but didn't see anyone particularly threatening.

"Who?" I asked, drawing her attention back to the confused look on my face.

She stepped out of my arms and bit her lip.

"My husband."

Chapter Sixteen

Avery is married.

It was the first thought that entered my mind when I woke up this morning and hadn't stopped running through my brain since she'd uttered those words twelve hours ago.

My husband.

How was this possible? She never wore a ring, for godsakes, and she sure as hell never mentioned it. Until last night. She just blurted out the offending information then left me with half a boner in the middle of the dance floor.

I went through my Sunday routine in a daze, trying to rid my brain of the unwanted memories from the night before. I was trying so hard *not* to think about it that it was impossible to think about anything else. I was so distracted that I almost forgot to call in a bartender for the day. Scott had called in sick, and I barely remembered to call Alice to fill the shift. Thank fuck I did, though, because I would have been *completely* useless behind the bar.

Alice was the one who reminded me that it was Sopranos Sunday, a little weekly event that we'd had going on for a couple of years now. Because of the stupid writer's strike, we didn't have any new episodes to look forward to, but we watched Season Four all over again while we waited for Season Five.

Felix would whip up a bunch of Italian food and a lot of the guys would show up wearing a bathrobe over their clothes. We always kept a stack of *Star Ledgers* on the end of the bar, but this week, almost everyone had their own copy.

The Westlake made the front page of the Sports section and there was a four page story in the centerfold about the party the night before. I'd fooled myself into thinking I'd been distracted from obsessing about the Avery situation until I came across her picture. Well, not *her* picture. She was in the background of a shot. But she was still there in my fucking face, dammit.

I folded up the damn paper without even finishing the article and just tried to concentrate on my customers. But they had a million questions about the party, and I found myself editing the story of my evening considerably before it was suitable for public consumption.

Speaking of consumption… I kept the drink board up on the wall. I figured the guys would like a taste of the party from the night before, even if they didn't get to attend it. It was a little early in the season to change the menu over to our football drinks anyhow. We'd be back to serving First Downs and Blindsiders soon enough.

In the meantime, there was nothing to do but wait.

* * *

I didn't have a locked-in schedule for all the shit that needed doing around here, but Monday mornings were always slated for inventory. Denny and I were at the square bar as usual to make the weekly liquor assessment. Even with all the extra booze we'd brought in for the party, my stock was wearing pretty thin.

Damn. My old teammates really cleaned us out.

The bar was typically dead for the first hour after opening, so it was as good a time as any to take care of any behind-the-scenes stuff. We didn't normally see too many other humans until the lunch crowd rolled in. And by crowd, I mean Richie Rum-N-Coke.

So, because there were no customers sitting at my bar, and because Denny and I had just finished up our list... there was nothing to distract me when Avery walked in.

I watched as she shot an apprehensive glance in my direction and then took a seat at the end of the long bar. "Denny. Take a lunch."

He looked at me in confusion, probably wondering just exactly when it was that the aliens had invaded his boss's body. "I don't ever take a—"

"Just... Do me a favor and head next door for an hour, okay? I got this."

Denny gave a shrug. "Okay, man. But any tips you make while I'm gone are *mine*."

I rolled my eyes. "Fine, fine. Just get the fuck out of here already."

He shot a look down the bar and then aimed a knowing smirk at me. But thankfully, he didn't offer any commentary on the obvious reason behind my sudden benevolence. He simply threw his towel in the sink, untied his apron, and started whistling.

"One hour, Den. I mean it."

"No problem, man." He raised his hands in defense as he backed his way out of the bar. "See you in an hour."

I looked across the room to Avery, who was slumped in her seat, staring out at the beach. Taking a deep breath, I headed over toward her. "Hey. What's up?"

She wouldn't meet my eyes as she brought her fingers to her temples. "Zac, let me just start by saying I'm so sorry."

As casually as possible, I asked, "For what?"

She wasn't buying it. Not that I was selling it very well.

"I know I dropped a bomb on you the other night about Mike, and you must really be thrown for a loop because of how we… how you and I were…"

"Flirting like crazy?"

"Yes. That."

I shouldn't have cared, but it was nice to know that at least we'd been on the same page. "Well, I can't say that I'm happy about it. Is he… Is he good to you? I mean, he's your husband." It seemed insane that that would be something I could be concerned about at that moment. But for some reason, I was.

"He is."

Well, that was that. I felt my stomach sink, but what the hell could I do about it? She was married. Happily, apparently.

I brushed a hand through my hair and fell back into default mode. "Hey. Let me get you a drink. What'll ya have?" I hopped behind the bar, figuring it would put some much-needed distance between us.

Avery had her elbows on the bar, her head hanging in her hands. "He was."

"What?"

"He was… I mean… Grrr!" She flipped her hands palms-side-up on the bar and raised her head. "He *is* very good to me, but he *isn't* my husband anymore. Well, he won't be once the papers are finally signed, that is."

A rush of hope washed through me. "He's your ex?"

"Yes. Well, no. But he will be soon. A couple months, in fact, if all goes according to schedule."

My own concerns evaporated as I saw the conflict on Avery's face. "I'm sorry. This can't be an easy time for you." I held up a bottle of Chardonnay, and she shook her head yes.

"It is and it isn't," she continued. "I never really believed it when I heard about someone going through an 'amicable divorce.' But that's exactly what this is. He's a good guy, and I'm… well… I'm just not the right girl for him."

The guy must've been crazy. Avery would be the right girl for any lucky bastard fortunate enough to catch her eye. "So, he instigated the breakup, you mean?"

"Sort of." I slid the glass of wine in front of her, but she didn't take a sip. She just wrapped her fingers around it and peered into its contents as if the liquid inside could conjure up the right answers. I guessed her attempts at clairvoyance weren't working, because she raised her eyes to mine and sighed out, "We probably should never have gone through with it in the first place. I mean, obviously, we weren't meant to be each other's *forever*, you know?"

I watched her face as she spoke, her expression turning from frustrated to longing. The wistful way she mentioned 'forever' as if it were a tangible thing, a possession to behold, an object to grasp in one's hand.

She tried to lighten the moment, and said in an upbeat tone, "At least I won't have to change my name."

The abrupt change of topic threw me, but I rolled with it. "You never changed it?"

"I kept Brooks for work. I never changed it to Sargento."

Good thing. *Avery Sargento* didn't exactly have a great ring to it.

Regardless of her marital status—even as it would be only a few short months from now—I knew I had to back off. I'd be a world class asshole if I were to press my advantage with everything Avery was going through. She seemed heartbroken about the demise of her marriage, and if she still had a chance to work things out with the guy, as bad as it sucked, I'd have to give her the space to do that.

I may have loved the ladies, but I did *not* move in on a girl when she was already buried under a ton of baggage. Dating me was problematic enough on its own.

"So, yeah. My marriage is falling apart and my career is in the shitter."

That knocked me out of my personal pity party. "Your career? What do you mean? What happened?"

"Well, here I am on a Monday morning, sitting in your bar. I just quit my job."

"Holy shit!"

"Yeah. They gave my promotion to Kendra."

Idiots. How could those people not recognize how incredible she was? "Aww, Ave. I'm so sorry to hear that."

She swirled the wine around in her glass. "I couldn't believe it. I mean, I really gave that job everything I had. Then to just be dismissed after all that? After the kickass party I just threw? I didn't even think about it. I just up and quit. I don't normally do *anything* without planning it out first." She looked up at me, a slight upturn at the corner of her mouth. "I'm a planner."

"I've noticed." I offered a warm smile which she returned easily enough.

"Maybe this will be a good thing. The Summer of Avery, you know? Maybe I can take my time to find a *good* job this time." She took a sip of her drink then tipped her head back to face the ceiling. "Oh, God! What was I thinking? *This* is why I'm not impulsive. I hate this feeling of *not knowing*. Quitting my job? Probably pretty stupid of me, huh?"

I gave a wipe to the bar and offered, "You couldn't be stupid if you tried."

She gave me a shy smile for that, then promptly changed the subject. "Let me ask you. How cliché is it that I'm spilling my problems to a bartender?

"Not cliché at all. Because I'm not a bartender. I'm the owner."

"Good. So then, you're the guy I should ask about getting a job?"

I knew she was only kidding around. She was way too good for this place. But the fact that she was finally trying to lighten the mood gave me the opening to play along. "I can't have someone as unfriendly as you waiting on my customers."

Her mouth gaped open. "Unfriendly? Are you kidding? *Nice* is practically the only thing on my resume. I've spent my life being 'nice.'"

"Well, you sure as hell didn't go out of your way to be 'nice' to *me* at first." I raised my eyebrow at her, which just made her purse her lips in a repressed smile.

"*But*," I went on, "you've got a great ass. And since most of my customers are men, they may overlook the personality problem."

She gave me a dirty look for that, but didn't dwell on it. "Does that mean I'm hired?"

"Does this mean you'll plaster a smile on your face during your shifts?"

"I can do that."

"Then yes. You're hired."

The curtain closed on our performance, and she dropped her head onto her arms again, moaning, "Oh, God. Why isn't it this easy to get a *good* job?"

"Hey! Don't knock this place. With that body and your lack of a resume, it's either this or *Hooters*."

"I'm sorry! I didn't mean—"

"I know what you meant. It's good that you realize you're better than this place. I'm not offended. You have bigger things ahead of you than this dead-end dive."

"It's an amazing bar, Zac. Don't sell yourself short."

I snickered, "Oh it's amazing all right. An amazing money pit."

"It doesn't have to be. Why are you holding back?"

Holding back? I lowered my brows and huffed, "I'm not."

She shot me a skeptical glance at that, but didn't elaborate. "With a little creativity, a little push, this bar can be a goldmine."

"Goldmine might be stretching it."

She looked at me as if I were crazy. "Zac. You own the largest commercial establishment within one of the most affluent neighborhoods in the whole town. You should use that."

I was well aware of the moneyed citizens that made up the town of Norman, and hell, if Norman Hills was its palace, Lenape Lake was its crown jewel. But the people in this town tolerated this broken-down pub at best… and would like to see it met with a bulldozer at worst.

"Those people aren't coming in here."

"They're not coming in here because they think it's a shithole."

"It is!"

"It doesn't have to be."

I saw the gears turning as she scanned her eyes around the room, the steam virtually shooting out of her ears. I leaned across the bar and asked, "What are you thinking about over there, Brooks?"

She was excited, hopping off her stool and grabbing her purse, all but bouncing toward the door. "Just give me forty-eight hours. I might have a plan."

"Whoa, whoa. Hang on there a minute, Sparky." I came around to her side of the bar and held out her forgotten car keys. She took the two steps back in my direction to retrieve them as I asked, "What's this plan of yours?"

Her lips scrunched into a pretty pout as her eyes lowered into pensive slits. "I'm not sure yet, but I might have a great idea for an event for your bar."

"I can't pay you—"

"Just give me a small cut of the take and a fabulous letter of recommendation. That's all I ask."

"That doesn't seem very fair to you."

"Fair schmair. I'm unemployed for godsakes. I've got all the time in the world to work on this stuff. It will give me some good material to pad my resume. So, no worries, okay?"

She was the one who was out of a job, yet she was telling *me* not to worry? This girl was something else. "I'm not the one risking anything here."

She dismissed my concerns with a flippant wave of her hand. "No risk. My father said he'd help me out for a little bit until I can get back on my feet."

Benny? Jesus. Maybe the guy wasn't such a douchebucket after all.

"And you know what?" she started in. "I'm *glad* I didn't get that promotion. That firm was so stifling. This way, I'm forced to get a better position somewhere else."

"Why go to another firm at all?"

Her smile dropped as she glared at me in confusion. "What do you mean?"

161

I leaned against one of the stools and offered, "I mean you're smart, you're ambitious, and you know your stuff. Why wouldn't you just start your *own* business?"

Her brows were furrowed as she blinked at me. "My own event-planning firm? I guess I never... How could I...?" The switch took an extra minute to flip in that beautiful brain of hers, trying to make sense of my words. Suddenly, her eyes went bright as her mouth fell into a surprised smile. It was as if I could actually see the lightbulb going off over her head.

"You never thought to strike out on your own?" I asked.

"Well, no. Not exactly. I mean, I dreamed about it, but..."

"There's no reason why you can't. You said yourself that this was going to be The Summer of Avery. If not now, then when?"

"Are you going all Kennedy on me?"

"Er, a, I'll have the clam chowda."

She ignored my dead-on JFK impersonation and instead chewed on her bottom lip, mulling over her revelation. "I'd get to make my own rules."

"You already do."

"I could work right out of my house. I wouldn't even have to rent out a space right away."

"Or ever."

"I could do this. I mean, I could really do this, right?"

"Sure could."

"Holy shit, Zac! You're brilliant! Thank you!"

Before I could even get out the laugh that was threatening to erupt, Avery threw her arms around my neck and squeezed the ever-loving hell out of me. I was surprised, but I hugged her back, wrapping my arms around her middle and pulling her closely against the length of my body.

It was just a friendly hug.

At least, it was supposed to be.

Her body was pressed against mine, her arms squeezing a bit tighter around my neck. I suddenly had the unquenchable urge to back her right up against the damned bar and slam my mouth against hers.

I could do it. I could kiss her right now. I could just grab her by the back of her hair and lower my lips to hers. Who would stop us?

I buried my face in the hair at her ear and breathed her in, letting my hands slide ever-so-slowly up her spine. Before I could get lost in the scent of her, she pulled back, and I reluctantly released her from my grasp.

Her face was flushed and she wouldn't look me in the eye, instead swiping a hand over her hair and grabbing her purse, stuttering her goodbyes as she made her retreat for the door.

And then I exhaled.

Chapter Seventeen

The Westlake Pub has the distinction of being the very first communal establishment constructed in this town. Before the courthouse, before the school, before the hospital. Hell. The bar had been built before the man-made lake was even finished being dug out of the ground. It was practically as much of a historic landmark as Norman Rock out front of the municipal building.

Prior to the Rock's infamy, the town was informally referred to as Lenape (pronounced LEN-a-pee), named after the Native Americans who used to populate the area before they were— according to my elementary school textbooks—*asked very nicely* to share their neighborhood with the extraordinarily non-violent white people who spilled over from New York City.

Anyhoo.

A hundred or so years later, the story goes that when the founders first decided to build their courthouse, they had a ton of Lenape forest to clear out first. This was back in the 1800s, before power tools and backhoes, so you can imagine what an undertaking it must have been. As they went to level the hill at the edge of the site, they encountered a huge boulder underneath the ground, and they soon came to the realization that there was just no way to remove the thing efficiently. Some of the townspeople voted to relocate the prospective site of the courthouse, but no one wanted all that hard work of clearing the forest to go to waste. Some voted to just blast the boulder out of the way with dynamite, but bringing in an explosives crew was going to cost a lot more money than our resident architect had budgeted for.

Ultimately, it was ten-year-old Norman Lasser who suggested just building around the big rock, shaking his head in discouragement, and explaining, "It's just common sense." Everyone else was quick to agree. The rock was left in its place, the ground was dug out around it, and new plans were drawn up for a C-shaped courthouse to surround it.

The staying power of "Norman's Rock" soon came to embody the spirit of this entire town, eventually becoming its claim to fame and the most outstanding feature of its landscape. Before long, the area of Lenape came to be known as the town of Norman, all because of some stupid, stubborn rock named for some outspoken kid with all that common sense.

Basically, we got a new name for our town, and the peace-loving Lenape got the shaft once again.

After the courthouse was built, people from all over would stop in to see our weirdly-shaped building framing the house-sized boulder that refused to be moved.

A few years later, a brass plaque was attached to the stone. It's still there to this day, and it reads:

Here stands the rock of Norman.
It's just common sense.

And if there was anything the people of this town liked to think they were full of, it's common sense. I mean, *obviously*, the first brainiac to suggest building the town pub before anything else must have been *full* of common sense. A school? A hospital? A post office? Who needed any of that stuff? So long as the people of Norman had their watering hole, nothing else mattered.

So, yeah. Common sense abounds.

The completed construction of the courthouse gave Norman its town center. An entire municipal complex has since been added to that original structure, including a police station, jail, and numerous council offices.

One such council office was occupied by The Norman Society, a group that started out as a few old cultured biddies who were practiced in the fine art of planning tea parties. The group had since evolved into the premier social club of our entire town. Almost every month, there was one event or another scheduled for this community, mostly held at the beach or the ball fields or the clubhouse next door to my bar. There was the St. Patrick's Day party and Octoberfest for the grown-ups or the Junior Olympics and Sock Hops for the kids. There were block parties, bonfires on the beach, parades, barbecues… and a ton of other social events for the people of this town to get together and talk about how rich they were.

Every September, the town held their annual "Norman Days." You'd think from the way the people here looked forward to it that The Norman Society's sole purpose in life was to plan the weekend-long event. Our new mayor had been touting this year's Norman Days as "A Very Special Celebration" almost since the first day after *last* year's celebration. 2003 would mark the one-hundred and fiftieth year since the town was founded, and by God, The Norman Society had been hard at work ensuring that this was going to be the party to rival them all.

As a member of Norman's Chamber of Commerce, I had of course been asked to contribute something of value to this year's festivities. Most businesses would set up a canopy tent along Main, and spend the day handing out freebies and coupons to any event attendees. Some would have carnival-type games set up, and the idea was that the more interesting tent you had, the more people would come and check out your operation. It was a great way to get your name out in front of the citizens of the town, especially if you were the owner of a new business.

But The Westlake didn't have that problem. Everyone who lived here was well aware of my pub. They chose to ignore its existence, however, because a broken-down building on the edge of their precious lake was a thorn in the side of all these fine upstanding people who had such common sense.

Unlike my new event planner.

Because, as it turned out, Avery's first order of business was to weasel my bar into a highlighted feature of Norman Days.

"You're nuts," I said to her when she first proposed the idea. "There's no way those people want anything to do with this place."

"They send you an invitation every year," she shot back. "You said so yourself."

"It's not an invitation. It's a reminder that they'll expect me to close up shop for the weekend."

That was the truth. It was an "unspoken agreement" that Norman Days would take over my parking lot for the two nights of their celebration. Ever since the clubhouse was erected next door, we'd been forced to share the parking lot. But whenever the town was having one of their larger events, they'd rope off the blacktop, knowing the party would spill out of the clubhouse and into the lot. With no place to park, it was stupid to schedule a band and piss off anyone that tried to come and see them. The out-of-towners would simply skip the night at their favorite watering hole, and with only a handful of regulars to fill the stools, my bar was a ghost town. More often than not, it made more sense to simply shut down for the weekend, knowing I wasn't going to have any customers. It only happened one or two other nights throughout the year, but *always* for the two nights of Norman Days.

"You close because you don't want to fight them. And that's the right move; you don't want them to have any further reason to give this place a hard time. But don't you see what a perfect opportunity this is? It can be your chance to let this place shine."

"Yeah, Ave? This place hasn't 'shined' in a hundred years." I ran my hand along the top of the nearest TV, holding up my fingers to show her the layer of dust.

Avery rolled her eyes. "That's why I brought the cleaning crew."

The aforementioned cleaning crew had been tearing my place up all morning. Under Avery's supervision—and my chagrin—they attacked every inch of my grimy pub. They vacuumed all the stalagmites of dust hanging from the ceiling, pulled every bottle off the shelves, and scrubbed down every corner.

Avery had me walk through the bar with her, pointing out which of the dusty, old decorations could go. Most of the stuff I couldn't care less about, but when we got to the Notre Dame banner, I put my foot down. "Nuh uh. No way. The Fighting Irish stays. It's been here since the bar was built, for godsakes!"

"It looks like it."

When she could see I wasn't going to budge, she capitulated. "Fine. But at least let's get it professionally cleaned."

That, I could agree with.

The rest of our seek-and-destroy mission went much the same way. All the old beer posters and promotional banners were taken down, all the blow-up race cars, the cracked mirrors, the broken neon. Even the stuff we decided to keep was removed temporarily, allowing access to parts of the walls that hadn't seen daylight in decades. My poor bar looked so empty.

But clean. I had to admit that it looked clean.

Avery had gone to some fabric place and picked up a huge roll of dark green vinyl, and was planning to unscrew the cushions from all six booths, under the impression that she'd be able to reupholster them without too much trouble. She suggested we leave the tables exactly as they were however, explaining that the numerous names carved into their tops held too much history to simply dispose of. "Once you have some brand new cushions on here anyway, the booths will look more shabby-chic than simply crappy."

I didn't know what the hell she was talking about, but I figured she knew more about that kind of stuff than me.

With a budget of five hundred dollars—which Avery assured me we wouldn't exceed—and a timeline of two weeks, she'd managed to transform my dingy bar into an inviting pub. Sure, the floors could use refinishing and the bar tops had seen better days, but ultimately, I couldn't believe it. The place looked a hundred times better than it had only fourteen days ago.

There was new paint on the walls, the windows had been squeegeed, and every burned-out lightbulb had been replaced. The booths and the stools had new vinyl on their cushions, and all the pictures on The Wall of Fame had gotten an upgrade with some dollar-store black frames. She'd also gotten my old Devils jersey framed without telling me. As much as I wanted to protest, I just couldn't refuse her gift. She was really excited about it, and after it went up, I allowed myself to be proud of my accomplishment, however short-lived.

We re-hung some of the nicer mirrors and banners, all of which had been scrubbed to the point of gleaming, and I had to admit that having everything new and clean and matching really made a huge difference.

All that, and the bar still managed to be the casual place that it was before. My regulars had watched the transformation, nervously wondering if I was going to go high-class with the joint. Despite my assurances, they were finally able to see for themselves that their repeated pleas to "not get rid of the dank" hadn't gone unheeded. I was really happy with the middle ground Avery had struck; the place was clean and classy, but still relaxed and welcoming.

Aside from Martha Stewarting my entire establishment, Avery was busy planning for the part The Westlake would play during Norman Days.

It was unfathomable that we had spent practically every minute of the past weeks together without a single fight. It was nice, actually. I guess once we made the decision to keep things platonic between us, there was nothing to fight about. At least with each other.

I'd been mentally warring with *myself* all week.

There were the times when Avery would be up on a ladder and her cute little ass would be taunting me from under her stretch pants, and I'd have to physically remove myself from the room in order to keep from grabbing it.

There were the times when she'd joke with me, her comments and fluttering lashes verging right on the edge of flirting, and I'd have to bypass the dirty comebacks in favor of a straight answer.

And the time she showed up for painting day in her little pink short-shorts and white knee socks? Jesus. I had to excuse myself to the bathroom and splash cold water on my face. We got the walls finished in no time flat, mostly due to the fact that I kept a blinders-on focus on the job at hand.

Now here it was, Friday evening, the night we'd been working toward.

Norman Days was scheduled to kick off the festivities with a huge party at the clubhouse. Twenty-four hours later, they'd be trying to outdo themselves for Night Two. In the daylight hours in between, there was the parade, carnival, and business tents planned for some family-friendly entertainment.

No one ever acknowledged that such innocent fun was bookended by two solid nights of debauchery.

Avery had arranged for a stage to be erected on our end of the parking lot, and hired one of our more popular bands to play. The plan with the outdoor stage was to draw people out of the clubhouse into the parking lot, and hopefully, into the pub. It was my call to keep Alice out from behind the bar—after all, we were trying to make a good impression on our potential clientele—so instead, she and Travis were assigned to stage duty. I figured no one would pull any crap with those two babysitting, but just in case, Alice's personality was better suited to yell at people should the need arise.

Avery borrowed the T-shirt gun from the arena, and I gave her a dozen boxes of leftover promotional tees from the liquor distributors that I'd hoarded over the years to load it up. She advertised that there'd be a special prize for anyone who caught the *Zima* one. Her scheme worked. There were tons of people who rushed the stage at Alice's announcement, and Travis shot that thing into the crowd like he was warding off a zombie apocalypse. It was pretty funny, watching all those people clamoring for every crappy tee Travis blew out at them.

Denny and Scott were behind the long bar, serving up one-dollar beers and reduced-price booze. Avery had devised a contest over the course of the week, letting people vote on which shots should be featured. When our very own Penalty Shot concoction won (basically a double shot of chilled vodka poured over a frozen slice of sugared orange) she contacted *Absolut* about sending over some spokesmodels. They stood near the entrance and manned the ice luge at the square bar, posing for pictures and handing out promotional shot glasses all night.

She thought a hot dog cart would be a big hit (she was right), and suggested we serve some just-as-convenient sandwiches. Felix had made platter upon platter of gourmet wraps which were stacked three shelves deep in the walk-in fridge. Anytime anyone would notice a tray running low, all we had to do was grab a new one to replace it. With all the people crowding the place, it was the easiest fare to offer, but with Felix's special touch, one of the best tasting, too.

But the best idea Avery had... the truest stroke of genius to lure in the most influential fish of this town... She spread the word *everywhere* that a huge portion of the night's proceeds were going to be donated to Norman's little league team.

Brilliant.

Norman's pee wees had made it all the way to the regionals before being eliminated, which was a pretty big frigging accomplishment. You couldn't go anywhere in this town without seeing the banners on the streetlights or the posters in the shop windows, and Avery thought it would soften The Westlake's image to be the most vocal supporters in town.

Everything from the free food, T-shirts, and shot glasses to the dart tournament and pool challenges advertised a sign requesting a donation be made to "our little winners," encouraging everyone to help the team with my father's favorite pronouncement that "We'll get 'em next time." She'd hung their picture all over the walls at every station and on a line of mason jars along the bar.

I took her cue and bolted a locked, wooden box to the wall of the pool room, and hung a posterboard sign stating: $1 DONATION REQUIRED TO PLAY. It was something my father used to do just to keep everyone from gambling. Too many fights erupted after too many drunks tried to "make it interesting."

He'd pick a different cause every month or so, and hand over whatever cash was brought in during their run. When people knew they had the option of donating a couple bucks to a worthy cause, they were less inclined to try to win some for themselves. Psychology. Go figure.

Dad would have loved that I was doing this. He was the one that taught me how to play pool in the first place. Kicked my ass so many times that I was forced to learn the game well enough to beat him. My father was never one of those guys that let his kids win to make them feel better. Every board game, every sport… he made sure to give it his all. It's why my brothers and I excelled in our athletic endeavors: Because we loved that feeling of having truly earned the win.

I figured whatever money we brought in could go to the American Cancer Society in his honor, and as it turned out, I had to empty the box twice before the evening was through.

Friday night was packed, a smashing success.

But once the word spread, Saturday night was positively insane.

Chapter Eighteen

When the clubhouse saw how effective it was to move the band outside, they decided to follow suit. We let them set their band up on our stage, figuring we could wait the extra day to break it down. It was just good business.

My bar was packed wall to wall with warm bodies, and it was almost impossible to get from one end of the room to the other. As I sliced my way through the crowd, I felt a hand clasp my shoulder and a familiar voice yelling over the noise. "Hey Maniac! What's the deal? I can't even get to my stool!" A good-natured Jerry Winters was standing with Roy Bread, Richie Rum-N-Coke, and The Incredible Hank.

I gave my regulars a round of handshakes and asked, "You guys having a good time?"

Hank shot back, "One dollar beers? You better believe it!"

The guys all laughed and toasted one another as I excused myself and made my way to the square bar. The shot girls were such a hit with my male patrons the night before that we asked them to come back and do it again. They readily agreed. And why wouldn't they? They'd made a shit-ton in tips.

The rest of my *real* drinkers were at the long bar. I went over to check out the action. "How's it going, Den?"

Denny looked about ready to pass out, but he was smiling, so I took that as a good sign. "Oh man. They haven't stopped! You may have to send Alice back here to help us out for a few."

"Not a chance. We're trying to bring in new customers, not drive them away."

With that, I hopped behind the bar to get my guys out of the weeds. The crowd was positively electric, and as nerve-wracking as it was to keep up with the drink orders, I understood why Denny still managed to have a smile on his face. Working a busy mob was grueling, but man, was it *fun*. I fell back into the natural rhythm of it all, crossing behind Scott and ducking under Denny, tossing a coaster on the bar here, scraping foam off a pint there. It was a choreographed dance that could only be carried out by three guys who were as familiar with the workings of a bar as they were with each other.

Wow, I missed this.

I missed the energy of a packed bar. I missed the raucous laughter, the booming sound of a crowd singing along with the band, the offensive smell of a cloud of cigarette smoke, the squish of my beer-soaked sneakers.

I. Love. This. Bar.

It was a welcome revelation, which was the main reason why I was smiling ear-to-ear as I looked up and saw Avery.

"You're happy!" she yelled at my sappy self.

"I am. And you're brilliant."

"I can't argue that."

We both laughed as I asked her, "What'll you have?"

"Loopy Seven. With a cherry."

I shook my head at her weird drink choice, but served it up to her anyway. On busy weekends, we bypassed actual glassware and just used plastic cups. They were safer, and with such a huge crowd, easier to clean up at the end of the night. We hadn't had to break out the cups in quite some time. "And if you even think about paying, I'll have you kicked out of here."

175

"I wouldn't dream of it. Thanks!" She raised her cup in a toast and turned to head back to the party. Something about watching her retreating form turned my insides cold.

"Avery! Wait!" I called out, jumping over the bar before I could lose her in the crowd. She stopped in a near-panic before she realized nothing was wrong. Well, nothing except the fact that I just didn't want her to leave. I turned back to Denny and asked, "Den? You guys got this?" He gave me an affirmative salute, so I reached behind the bar for a bottle of wine and two glasses before putting my hand at Avery's back and ushering her outside. I needed air.

"You scared me back there!" she said once we were finally outside.

"Sorry. I wanted to hit the beach and didn't want to go alone."

"We're going to the beach? Don't they close that off at night?"

"Like that's going to stop me?"

"Rebel."

We walked together around the side of my building, trying to shield our ears from the blasting sound of the band going at it on the stage. The lot was filled with people dancing, smoking, talking... hundreds of Normanites gathered in and between the clubhouse and The Westlake. Avery's instincts had turned out to be right; the people of this town would accept my invitation and be drawn to check out my bar. All I needed to do was amp up the hype and open my doors.

If you build it, they will come.

We reached the chain-link fence that enclosed the beach. It was after hours, so sure enough, the gate was bolted shut. I handed the wine and glasses to Avery, then gripped my fingers through the chain link, giving it a good shake.

"What are you doing?"

"Testing to see how sturdy this old fence is. I haven't hopped it in a few years, and wanted to make sure it would hold."

"Wait. You expect me to hop that fence?"

"Don't be such a girl."

"Girls wear *skirts*, Zac!"

I looked over my shoulder at Avery, fidgeting in discomfort in her tiny, flouncy mini skirt. I gave her a wicked eyebrow wiggle, which I guarantee would've had her slugging me if her hands weren't otherwise occupied.

"I promise not to look. Scout's honor," I added, crossing two fingers over my heart then holding them up in a boy scout salute.

Avery snorted. "Oh, now I'm supposed to believe you were a boy scout? That's rich."

I ignored her as I pulled a nearby park bench over to the fence and hopped up. "Here. See? I'll go over first, you can hand me the stuff, then I'll turn my back while you climb over. It's not that high. You'll only need to figure out how to get over the top on your own; that's the hardest part. Then you can just drop down into the sand. No problem."

"Fine. But how are we supposed to get back *out*?"

"We'll cross that bridge when we come to it."

She tightened her eyes into slits and glared at me.

"C'mon. You're gonna tell me you never climbed a fence before?"

"Not since I was about ten, and definitely not while wearing a skirt."

"Chicken."

"Dick."

I loved this new side to our relationship. It was as if all our fighting had suddenly turned amusing once we both decided to smile through our jabs. I shot her a final grin before grabbing the top of the fence, sticking the toe of my sneaker into the chain-link, then hoisting myself up and over to land in the sand.

"Perfect dismount!" I exclaimed once I was on the other side.

Avery was biting her lip as she passed the bottle and glasses over to me. She downed the rest of her Loopy Seven, ditched the cup into a nearby trashcan, then stood there for an extra second with her hands on her hips, assessing the situation.

"Come on," I said. "You can do this."

"Did you have to make it look so darn easy?"

"I make everything look easy."

She rolled her eyes then ordered me to turn around. I did, like the gentleman I am, even covering my face with my free hand for added insurance.

I heard the rattle of the chain link... then the scream from Avery.

I lowered my hand, but didn't turn around. "You alright?"

"No! Ow!"

"Do you need my help?"

"No!" I heard the fence rattle again, along with her growl. "Oh God. I lied. I need help. But I swear, I'll kill you if you laugh."

I turned around to see Avery folded over the top of the fence, her hands in a death grip on the chain link, her skirt around her waist, her ass and legs dangling down the side.

You better believe I cracked right the hell up.

"Zac! It's not funny!"

I caught my breath and shot back, "It's *extremely* funny!"

"Shut up and get me down from here! My skirt is caught on the damned fence!"

I pulled myself together and went to play superhero. I tried my best to ignore the sight of Avery's little panties staring me in the face, and simply grabbed hold of her legs to lift her up. The slack allowed her to free a hand and unhook her skirt from the top of the fence, and I lowered her onto firmer ground. The first thing she did as her feet hit the sand was to smack me, and I cracked up, ducking for cover from her attack.

"You planned that!" she laughed out.

"How could I plan *that*? Hell, it worked out better than I could've ever hoped, but…"

"Shut up!"

"Aww. C'mon, Ave. I hardly saw anything."

"Liar."

"I'm not lying, Stripey."

"Oh my God. Just kill me now."

"Why? It's not like it's anything I haven't seen before."

Her laughter stopped instantaneously, and that's when I realized what I'd just said. I gave a sheepish rub to the back of my hair and said, "I wasn't talking about you specifically."

She smoothed a hand over her sore midsection, not meeting my eyes when she said, "Just forget it."

I led her over to the strip of sand that separated my bar from the lake. At night, we could see everybody inside through the windows, but they couldn't see us. During the daytime, the opposite held true, but for now, I was grateful for the privacy. I pulled a couple towels from the covered cart and laid them out near the edge of the water so we could sit.

We got ourselves situated and I pulled out my keychain to crack open the bottle. I poured our wine and handed a glass to Avery, who smiled and clinked my own before taking a sip. "We lucked out with the weather, huh?"

I kinda liked hearing her refer to us as "we." *We'd* been quite the team over the past weeks, and *we'd* gotten along really well throughout all the planning. I was smiling as I took a swig from my glass and answered, "Yeah. It's perfect."

She met my eyes just then, and from the pink that was flushing her cheeks, I knew she was aware I was talking about more than just the weather. We'd shared a handful of private moments over the past weeks, and as much as I tried to keep things aboveboard, sometimes, I couldn't help myself.

"So, what's the deal with the lake?" she asked, trying to lighten the moment. "Why do they keep it under lock and key?"

"Well, they don't. Not for their members anyway."

"So, if you got a membership, you'd be allowed to use it?"

"Yes. But my family never bothered." I pointed to the deck off of my restaurant. "We always had our *own* beach access."

That made her chuckle as she nudged against my arm. "Wow. You really *are* a rebel, huh?"

"Without a cause, baby."

She cracked up at that as I stood and held out my hand. "You wanna take a walk on the wild side, Ave?"

She shot a suspicious glare in my direction as she reached out her hand. "Probably not…"

I hauled her to her feet, then pulled off my shirt.

She took a step back with a hand over her mouth, clearly flustered as she stammered out, "I don't… What are you *doing*?"

"Going swimming. Why, what did you *think* I was doing?" I teased as I whipped off my shoes.

She stood there blinking at me for a moment, clearly taken aback. I wish I could say I was sorry for freaking her out, but her shock was just too much damned fun.

I slammed down the rest of my wine and started to unbutton my shorts.

"Whoa! Okay. Hold on there a minute," she sputtered, holding a hand over her eyes. "I don't have nearly the amount of alcohol in me necessary to deal with this."

She took another sip from her glass.

Then she took another.

"Relax, Ave. What's the big deal? We've been sweating our asses off all night. Doesn't a swim sound perfect right now?"

I could tell she was mulling it over as she bit her lip and stared out at the water. Seemingly out of nowhere, her stance changed. She put a hand to her hip, tightened her eyes, and met my challenge. "Okay. You know what? You're right. I'm being a total baby about it. Hell, you've already seen my undies."

She polished off her drink before tossing her empty glass onto the towel. She stripped off her skirt, threw her shirt at my face, and before I could take another breath, she was running into the lake.

"Holy shit, that's cold!" she shrieked before plunging under the water. Her head broke the surface, laughing. "But oh my God, it feels great! What are you waiting for?"

I'd been frozen in place since the first second she agreed to a swim. But my heart had pretty much stopped once I watched her strip off her clothes. Fuck. There was no way I was going to be able to get these shorts off while keeping things PG-13.

"Come on, you jerk! You're the one that talked me into this!"

Screw it. I ran toward the edge and dove into the water, shorts and all. The chill hit me immediately, washing over my entire body from head to toe. That R rating I was so concerned about only a minute before was now indisputably a G.

"Fuck, that's cold!" I shouted once I came up for air.

"Told ya."

After a minute of treading water, the temperature went from freezing to refreshing. I planted my feet on the sandy bottom, enough for my chest and shoulders to break the surface. I ran my hands over my hair, slicking it back out of my eyes, and I couldn't help but notice Avery sneaking a look at me.

She used to do that all the time. Back in the day, I used to always catch her looking at me. It was kind of nice, actually, to see her checking me out like that.

Hands off, McAllister. Remember?

"So," I started in, trying to change the subject. "We've been so crazy with this thing that I haven't asked you about your life. How's it going?"

"My life?" she asked, scrunching her face up in confusion.

"Yeah. You know, with work and… everything else."

Obviously, I wanted to know more about her divorce, but there was no way to come right out and ask her about it.

Avery seemed to pick up my hint anyway. "Well, *work* is at a standstill. I'm still trying to figure out my plan of attack. As for 'everything else,' it is what it is."

I hadn't gotten any insight into the details of her separation, and it wasn't my place to press for them, so I let it drop. I leaned back in the water and let my body float, staring up at the sky and trying to forget that I had an almost-naked Avery only a few feet away.

"I think we were both in love with the *idea* of love, if that makes any sense."

I stood back up and asked, "What?"

"Mike and me," she answered. Obviously, the subject hadn't been as closed as I thought.

"Are you two still… at odds about this whole thing?"

Smooth, Zac.

She gave a shrug and swirled her hand along the surface. "Most likely not. I mean, we both realized that we were probably never destined to be husband and wife. Lifelong friends, to be sure, but friends nonetheless. We should have recognized that sooner, but... I don't know. It's not like either of us had so much experience with marriage before we got married, you know?"

"Experience is only something you gain after the fact."

"Exactly. But it wasn't really a surprise. We were pretty much doomed from the start. Things had happened really fast for us. Well, the second time anyway. We'd dated while I was in college, then broke it off after a few months. A couple years went by, we ran into one another, moved in together, then pulled a Vegas quickie only six months later." She gave a shy smile and added, "Being impulsive usually only leads to disaster for me, but... it worked for Casey and Simon. I just figured…"

"You figured you'd go for it."

"Yeah. Even knowing my track record, I guess I just wanted to do something crazy for once. I mean, I normally plan every detail of my life. But I should have known better. The only times I allowed myself to just go for it, I got burned. Vegas quickie marriage, hooking up with *you*..."

Her eyes went wide as she realized what she'd just said. "I'm sorry," she stammered uncomfortably. "I didn't mean to say that out loud."

I wasn't insulted; I knew what she meant. Things between us had gone from awesome to convoluted within a matter of hours. Of course she would have regrets.

I had them, too.

I regretted not calling her to straighten everything out years ago. I regretted ever making her feel second-rate. I regretted wasting a single day being angry at her when in all honesty, she made me happier than any person I'd ever known in my life.

"It's okay. Ave. I know what you were trying to say."

Her eyes met mine in gratitude, and at that moment, the only thing I wanted to do was to kiss her. Out there, in the water, under the stars. Every urge in my body told me I should just grab her and plant my mouth on hers… but I fought it.

Because she was still married.

Even though she was separated, it wasn't up to me to make the first move.

She had to come to me.

I met her eyes just then, before lowering my gaze to her perfect mouth, inviting her to close the gap between us. When she tucked her bottom lip between her teeth, I took it as a good sign. I moved half a step in her direction, fully expecting her to meet me the rest of the way, let me wrap my arms around her bare middle, pull her delectable body against my own, feel her sweet, wet skin pressed against mine, when…

"You should do pizza," she sputtered out nervously. "There're no good pizza places around."

Shit.

I shook myself out of the moment, trying to play it cool as I fired back, "There are a hundred good pizza places around! This is New Jersey, in case you forgot."

She let out with a huff. "No, I know that. But there are no good pizza places *right here* in the lake."

Goddammit. I had a barely-clothed Avery two feet away from me out here in this secluded lake, and we were talking about pizza, for godsakes?

I tried not to grumble as I responded, "There used to be. Right there, as a matter of fact." I pointed behind us to my bar. "But the ovens broke down a few years back and I guess I just decided not to bother with it anymore."

She gave a flippant shrug and replied, "You should remedy that."

As let down as I was, the conviction in her voice actually lightened my mood. I reluctantly admitted to myself that she was adorable when she was trying to be evasive, and I was surprised to find myself smiling. "Alright, Brooks. You may just be on to something. I'll think about it."

Chapter Nineteen

It was crazy-late by the time we closed up shop last night, so I was a little slow-moving as I got my day started. It was Sunday, so I cleaned out Magnum's cage and straightened my apartment before heading downstairs.

Scott was already there, setting up for the afternoon. He'd hooked up with the town's Barbeque Club years ago, and arranged to let those guys bring in their creations every week during football season. It was an indoor tailgate for them and a no-brainer for us. The customers knew Sundays were BYOF until the four o' clock games, so we didn't make any money from the restaurant until the evening. But that was fine, because we sold beers like crazy to make up for it. Ten dollar buckets. You couldn't beat that.

I helped Scott with the folding tables, then checked in with my kitchen. Sunday mornings were always hectic back here, because Felix used that day to prep all the food for the week ahead. A couple of the guys had sauces brewing on the range, a few others were chopping endless piles of vegetables along the counters, and Felix was busy trimming a mountain of chicken breasts on the large island.

"Hey Felix. Let me ask you. How do you feel about pizza?"

He looked up from his work and answered, "It taste good?"

"No, I mean, about us adding pizza back on the menu."

Felix gave a scratch to his chin with the back of his gloved hand. "Well, I s'pose we could. But it have to be gourmet pizza. No pepperoni."

"I think we'd have to have pepperoni."

"I don't like pepperoni."

I shook my head and snickered, "Well, then you don't have to eat it. But a lot of other people like it, so, I don't know what to tell you."

"My brother do pizza."

"What?"

Felix proceeded to wiggle his hands above his face, miming as if he were spinning a circle of dough. "Pizza. My brother. He do it."

"Like, makes it?"

"Yes. I call him for you."

"Wait. Hold on. I don't even know if—"

"I call him for you."

Well, there we go. I guessed we were going to be serving pizza again at The Westlake.

I put in the call to The Incredible Hank to see if he'd be interested in handling the repairs, and he showed up almost before the phone hit the cradle.

He was crouched down on the floor, trying to find the correct angle to check out what was doing behind the ovens. "Hey, thanks for thinking of me for this, Maniac."

"No problem. Barry would never get his lazy ass over here on a Sunday and I figured you'd be coming in today anyway."

"Well, I could sure use the work. Thanks."

He started tinkering with the lines as I stood there watching. An idea entered my brain, and I was blown away that it hadn't occurred to me before. "Hey, look, Hank. Would you maybe be interested in making this a regular thing?"

Hank stopped what he was doing, looked up at me, and asked, "What do you mean?"

"Well, I need someone to run maintenance around here, because Barry's prices are murdering me. And let's face it, the guy's a dick. If I have the excuse to get rid of him, you'd actually be doing *me* the favor. Fix the AC when it goes bust, clean the bathrooms and the floors every day, stuff like that. It's not glamorous and I can't pay you a lot, but..."

"No, I'll take it." The guy actually had tears in his eyes. "Thank you Zac. Thank you. I didn't know how the hell I was going to make rent this month. There're no jobs out there for an old codger like me. I swear, I've been looking. I'm ashamed to go home most days; it's why I spend so much time here. Thank you."

The hope in his eyes almost broke me right then and there. I knew the guy was struggling, but I didn't realize things were going *that* badly for him. Why didn't I see it before? My chest tightened, and I had some trouble getting the words out. "No, really. Thank *you*. I can really use the help."

I had to get out of there. I was *thisclose* to turning into a bawling sap.

I excused myself, quietly instructing Felix to load Hank up with a bag of takeout whenever he was through.

I headed right for the walk-in fridge and shut the door behind me. Taking a deep breath, I ran my fingers into my hair and stared up at the ceiling. My fists were still gripped on top of my head as I exhaled, trying to get a handle on my emotions.

Pussy.

By the time I finally pulled myself together, it was kickoff, and thank fuck for that, because I could sure use the distraction. The place was already hopping with my regulars, but I saw a bunch of new faces, too. Nice.

I sat down at the bar next to Avery, who was indulging in a plate of ribs. She was a mess, and the sight of her sitting there covered in barbeque sauce was enough to banish the last of my mood and have me chuckling.

I relayed my earlier conversation with Felix, and filled her in on my recent decisions. "Hank's on the repairs as we speak," I said, swiping some sauce off her cheek with a bar napkin.

"That's great! Wow, you work fast."

"So I've been told." I shot her a raised eyebrow, which had her shaking her head and seizing the napkin from my hand, taking over the cleanup job for herself.

"And Felix's brother can make the pies? That's perfect."

I reached over the bar and grabbed a roll of paper towels. Looked like she was going to need them. "I don't know, Ave. A Portuguese pizza chef? Shouldn't I hire someone Italian?"

"Don't be so close-minded," she fired back. "The Portuguese make an excellent pie. Haven't you ever seen *Mystic Pizza*?"

"No."

"Well, you should. It's a great movie. Besides, Felix swears by him, and you know he loves this place almost as much as you. He wouldn't steer you wrong."

* * *

We decided to let the little league team be the guinea pigs for our new pizza menu. It was my idea to invite them in for a private party one Sunday morning in order to present them with a check for all the money we'd raised.

I'd already tested Horatio's various concoctions for myself days ago, and had given him the green light—and the job— immediately after. Portuguese pizza. Who knew?

189

The kids filled every stool of the long bar, bellying up like old pros.

My future customers, ladies and gentlemen.

They thought they were doing something forbidden, hanging out in a bar where grown-ups came to "drink beer."

"Not just beer," I shot back. When I caught the warning looks from a few parents, I pulled out the soda gun. "Stick 'em up," I advised Number 7, pointing the thing at his chest.

He put his hands up as I gave a quick squirt of club soda to his shirt anyway, which just had all the kids cracking up. My attack was followed by their enthusiastic, pleading requests to let them try it out, so I invited a handful of them behind the bar to teach them how to use it.

They thought it was pretty damn cool.

I served up some Roy Rogers and plain old sodas as Farrah brought out the pies, placing them on pedestals stationed along the entire bar. The kids dove in like they hadn't eaten in days, which just made me laugh. I remembered all too well what it was like to be a ravenous, rapidly-growing ten-year-old.

The parents feasted on some pizza, too, but a few of them opted to order off the menu. No problem. We aimed to please.

Number 12's mother polished off her Cobb, saying, "I can't believe we've never been here before. I didn't think it was this nice. And the food is fantastic!"

I thanked her, along with everyone else, for the numerous compliments that followed.

The coach was so taken with the place that he asked if I'd like to be their sponsor for next season, and of course, I agreed. And that was even before I presented him with the check! When I did, the dude's eyes went wide, but he hadn't seen every trick up my sleeve just yet.

I'd gone to the local sporting goods store to load up the team with some new equipment, and proudly handed over the large canvas bag stuffed to the gills. Finn helped me put together a good selection of bats and helmets, plus we'd thrown in a whole new set of catcher's pads. *Norman Sports* gave me a huge discount on everything, and made sure every kid got one, too. I passed out the 20% off coupons, then had everyone put their names into a hat to raffle off the fifty-dollar gift card.

The nearby *Old Barn Milk Bar* supplied us with tubs of ice cream for the occasion, and *Give Me Candy* insisted that I shouldn't pay for the five-pound bag of assorted treats. Both places were so excited to have been asked to be a part of things that they gave me some gift cards to use at our *next* event.

I guessed those business-owners already knew what it had taken me this long to figure out for myself: It felt good to give back every once in a while.

I mean, hell. I originally thought selling one-dollar beers during Norman Days was going to put me under. But as it turned out, people donated a whole lot more than they normally would because of all the money they weren't spending on booze. It may seem stupid that we'd gone through all that trouble to raise so much money only to give it all away, but doing so gained me the favor of not only the little leaguers and their families, but numerous other citizens of this town as well.

Those same citizens had turned into new customers. A lot of them had been coming in pretty regularly since that maiden night, either hanging out at my bar or eating at my restaurant. I guessed Felix's food had drawn them in, drug-dealer style. They'd gotten a taste, and now they were hooked.

My bottom line had improved with all those Normanites seeking their regular fix. I'd already broken even from that

191

weekend. It had only been a couple weeks since Norman Days went down and the crowd was still going strong.

The customers weren't the only ones with generous wallets. It seemed every business Avery or I approached was more than happy to load us up with gift certificates to their establishments, and I accepted them gratefully, socking them away for future events. Sometimes, I gave them away just for the hell of it.

Like the time one happy hour that I saw Chuckie Fabulous sitting at the end of my bar. He was a trivia fanatic, our resident Cliff Clavin, constantly spouting his wisdom about the most inconsequential topics. He'd been driving around in the same beat-up old Monte Carlo forever. The crack across the windshield showed it wasn't because he was a classic car collector, although he'd be able to tell you everything you'd ever want to know about the subject.

A few weeks before, he'd chewed my ear off about *Mythbusters*. He was so enthusiastic about the damn show that I ended up watching an episode and got hooked myself.

Inspiration struck.

I gave a ring to the triangle hanging over the taps. People took notice when that thing was sounded, because normally, it meant someone was buying the house a round.

Everyone cheered, but I told them to calm down as I rifled through my donations envelope. "Don't get too excited, people! I'm not giving away any free drinks."

There was a collective groan as I snickered and continued, "But, I *am* giving away a *one hundred dollar* gift certificate to Lou's Auto Body."

I hopped up onto the bar and held it up to show the crowd, most of whom were appropriately intrigued.

"Alright. The first person who can tell me the correct answer takes home the prize." I stood there for a pause, trying to think of a question that would be skewed in Chuckie's favor. It had to be something obscure, but something I knew that he knew. The natives started to get restless.

"Okay. Got it. Alright, who can tell me what would happen if you dropped a penny on someone from the Empire State building?"

A few people yelled out, "It would kill them!" But when I didn't confirm it, everyone looked at each other in confusion, consulting one another about the possible answer.

C'mon, Chuck. Please know this.

Sure enough, he popped up from his stool and announced, "Nothing! Because of the air currents!"

Everyone looked to me for confirmation.

"You are correct, sir!" The place erupted in applause as I jumped down and handed over the gift certificate, saying, "Here's your prize. Thanks for playing."

The guys all gave Chuckie a pat on his back, and he was smiling ear to ear as he eyed the thing proudly. He continued his answer, excitedly explaining, "Maybe it would hurt, but the air currents wouldn't allow it to build up enough speed to even break the skin!"

It wasn't every day that Chuck got to steal the show, so I was as happy to put him in the spotlight as I was about helping to get his car fixed.

It felt good.

I felt good.

Chapter Twenty

Avery came bounding into the bar early one night. I'd gotten pretty used to her hanging around with all the events she was always planning for the place.

We'd held a dart tournament for the town's softball league and Avery got *Norman Sports* to sponsor it. We raised a couple hundred bucks and a whole new crew of customers. She planned a poker night for them the following week, and though we could only let them gamble for prizes, the night was a smashing success.

We actually ran out of Budweiser that night, and I had to send Alice out to the local *Bottle King* to grab some more. Avery contacted Anheuser-Busch, and they were so impressed that we'd managed to sell out of their product that they offered to sponsor our pool tournament a few weeks later. They had one of their reps deliver a bunch of customized banners with the specifics, and Avery pasted them all over the bar and around town.

A few weeks later, she devised a contest to come up with a new drink for the menu board. The deal was, you had to drink it before nominating it. We sold a *lot* of liquor that night. I had to call for a few cabs for the handful of guys who were too drunk to drive home, so yeah. It was a good night.

We brought a ton of new customers into the bar with that one, and Avery made some good business connections.

Even on days when we didn't have an event scheduled, it wasn't so out of the ordinary for her to come by just to hang out. Tonight, she was here to hang out.

The happy hour crew was going strong, and every stool at the long bar was filled. So, I mixed her a cocktail, cracked myself a beer, and set us up in one of the booths. She turned her body sideways, leaning her back against the wall and letting her feet hang over the edge of the seat. She flipped her sandals at the ends of her toes as she said, "Let me ask you… Give me the pros and cons of being self-employed."

She'd been focusing so much attention on my bar that she hadn't spent too much time getting her own business off the ground. I guessed she was finally ready to dive in. Good for her.

"Well, you pretty much already know. Being self-employed just means that *everything's* on you, and I'll tell you, it's not for everybody. There are nights when I'm so dog-tired and I still have to close out the numbers from the day's take. There's no use in putting it off; it'll just be waiting for me tomorrow. I both love and hate a busy night. Love it, because I know the money's rolling in, but hate it because that always means more paperwork for me. More numbers to tally, more credit cards to approve, more booze to order for the following weekend. Juggling the cash in order to make sure everyone gets paid isn't any fun, either."

"Like, your employees?"

"My employees are the least of my concerns. They get paid first, so the money's always there. It's the vendors that I have to be a bit more creative with."

I couldn't hide the proud smile that was threatening to slip into a full-blown grin.

Avery saw my battle and shook my arm. "Like how? What do you do?"

"Well," I started in, still trying not to bust, "You know Ralph? My linen service guy?"

"Yeah?"

195

"Well, let's just say he's a bit of a sports fan."

Her forehead scrunched as she asked, "Yeah, so?"

"Ralph works for memorabilia, is what I'm trying to say."

"Oh my God! Really?"

"Yep. And the guy will take anything that's seen the inside of an arena: Used ticket stubs, signed programs, socks worn during the games…"

"Zac, shut up!"

Her reaction made me laugh. "Very convenient when I don't have the cash."

She was appropriately impressed, but then her brows furrowed as she gnawed at her bottom lip. "But where do you get all that stuff? You're not giving away all your private stash, are you?"

"Ah. Very astute, young Grasshopper. I'm still in touch with the infamous Johnny."

"*Johnny's* Johnny?"

"Yep. Aside from the Devils who are always hanging around, he throws private parties for lots of other guys in the NHL. Some NFL players, too. I don't know about you, but most party guests like to eat food."

Her eyes widened as she got where I was going. "Which you provide."

"Correct."

"At cost to you."

"And them. My only out-of-pocket expense is my kitchen staff's wages, and I'd be paying that anyway because they're already here. The way I figure it, I'm getting my bar towels and tablecloths essentially for free, Ralph's getting some collectibles to clog up his man-cave, Johnny's throwing his party on the cheap… everybody wins."

She was mulling over the new information as I added, "You should hear what I do for my liquor suppliers!"

I'd always made a point to make my credit card payment on time so that I could *charge* my bill from the liquor distributor, who was brothers with the guy who supplied our paper products, and who would discount his price if we supplemented it with booze. A crazier full-circle there never was.

Damn. That was as recently as a month ago. It was nice to have some steady money coming in these days.

I'd already given all my employees a raise, and was well on my way to paying off the few debts this place still had hanging over it.

It had been years, but it sure as hell felt good to breathe again.

Until I looked at Avery too hard. Because then I'd forget to.

I shook my head straight and asked, "What's with the curiosity? You finally ready to get your business going?"

"Yeah. I had cards made up and started putting the word out. Too bad no one's hired me yet." She shot me a sly smile and added, "Except you, of course. But you pay shit."

We both shared a chuckle over that one. I'd tried a few times to toss a couple bucks her way, but she wouldn't accept it. She said she hadn't done anything worth being paid for yet, and considering all the money I'd been dumping into various charities, felt too guilty taking any piece away for herself. Whenever I tried to explain that I wouldn't have been able to give *any*thing if it weren't for the business she drummed up in this place, she always dismissed my claims and changed the subject.

"What about Travis and Alice?" I asked.

"What about them?"

"Well, they're trying to plan a wedding for January, and neither one of them has any clue what they're doing. I mean, case in point, they're having it *here*, for godsakes."

After only three months, Travis and Alice had gotten engaged, and God help them, they wanted to have the wedding at the place where they'd met. Of course I was going to do everything I could to help, but arranging a wedding was a little out of my wheelhouse. With all the new business, it would be easier for me to delegate the planning to Avery. I finally had some extra money coming in and could actually pay her to plan the thing. It could be my wedding present to them, and a great new event for Avery to showcase her talents.

"Ooh! A wedding! I haven't planned one of those in over a year." Her brain was already buzzing; I could see the ideas taking shape before her eyes. "I'll have to talk to the happy couple first, but I'm already thinking we'll need lights. And maybe some potted trees. And lots and lots of tulle."

"I have tools. You can just use mine."

"*Tulle*, not 'tools,' you tool." She giggled to herself before asking, "Is it okay if I stockpile some stuff here?"

"Yeah, of course." I pulled my keychain out of my pocket, wiggled off one of the spares, and handed it over. "Here. It's to the front door. This way, you can haul your own damn boxes," I teased.

She busted me right back. "I don't know, Zac. A key to your place? This is pretty serious."

I shot her a sham dirty look. "I trust you. Just don't steal anything. I know people. They'll find you."

I locked up over thirty minutes ago, but the party was still going strong.

The party of two, that is.

Avery and I had been going drink-for drink all night, and now she was insistent that she help me close up shop. We were presently in the process of flipping the stools onto the bar so Hank could do the floors in the morning. We both had one hell of a buzz going, and she almost wiped out more than once during our task.

"You," I finally admonished, putting my hands at her shoulders and directing her to stand against the long bar. "You stay right here before you hurt yourself."

She snapped her teeth at my hand and slurred, "I only hurt the ones I love, baby."

She giggled at her own joke, and I just shook my head as I flipped the last of the stools. Then I headed over to her. "I'm afraid to ask this, but do you want a drink?"

To tell you the truth, I would have much rather spent the end of our evening in my nice, comfy bed instead of hanging around my abandoned pub.

Barring that, there was always booze.

I let the bar hold me upright as I took a swig from my beer. I smiled to myself as I watched her perk up from her slouched position next to me.

"Yes! In fact, I wanna buy the round a house. Wait. Yes! Shots of house for the round, baby!"

Damn. She was drunker than I thought. I pointed a finger at her half-filled glass, realizing it was nothing more than melted ice at this point. "How 'bout some water instead?"

She took another air-chomp at me and said, "My teeth keep trying to bite you. Sorry."

"Yeah, well, your *mouth* keeps calling me baby."

"Sorry."

"No, don't apologize. I like it."

"The biting or the baby?"

"Both."

I stared down at my beer and cleared my throat. "So, what's with your sudden predilection toward alcohol tonight? I don't think I've ever seen you this drunk before."

Well, there was that one time, but I'd been trying really hard to forget about the details of that night.

She sighed, then dropped her head onto her arms. "He contested the divorce! Can you believe that? We were all set and ready to go, but then... I don't know. He said he was having second thoughts."

Shit. "Are *you*?"

"Noooo. Well, I'm sad to see the marriage end and all, but not sad enough to halt the proceedings. Now it's like we're starting from Square One, and it will be months before the judge signs off on it."

"*If* your husband can agree to go through with it this time." I started to feel sick. What if the guy decided he wanted to work things out? What if *Avery* did?

"He will. We had a looooong talk about it yesterday. We both know it's for the best. He just needed some closure."

She was drunk, but that was the first solid indication I'd ever gotten that told me maybe she wasn't sitting around pining for the guy. I had to know for sure. "What about you?"

"What about me what?"

"What's it going to take for you to get *your* closure?"

"I'm already closed, thanks."

Even though it was exactly what I wanted to hear, I wasn't entirely buying it. She seemed hesitant, like there was something she was fighting to say. "There's something you're not telling me, Ave."

She gave a *pffffft* to the hair across her forehead and leaned her torso against the bar, twisting a straw into knots. "Alright. Fine. I just... I just hate the feeling that I *failed* at something, you know? I'm not used to failing. And the thing is, I was *good* at being married. It just... I guess it just always felt like I was playing house, though, you know? I was a good homemaker, but I wasn't a good *wife*. We both deserved better than that."

I breathed an involuntary sigh of relief. I was half expecting her to tell me that she still loved the guy, but thank fuck that's not what was bothering her.

She looked stressed about it though. Maybe I shouldn't have been celebrating just yet.

Maybe I should've been trying to cure her hurt in the best way I knew how.

"If it makes you feel any better," I said, holding my hand over her glass. "I won't pull away if you want to try and bite me again."

She stared at me blankly for a second until my words registered... and then she busted out laughing. "Did you just say 'bite me'? Well, screw you, too!"

The dimple in her cheek made a welcome appearance, and I was almost knocked out by the sight.

She'd been invading my life for months, torturing me every day with her killer legs and her topaz eyes and her gorgeous smile. I couldn't take it anymore.

Her lips settled into a tiny grin, the devilish look in her eyes shooting straight into my gut. I didn't know if it was the booze finally giving me the proper balls or what, but I knew what I had to do.

I reached an arm around her waist, slanted my hand up her spine to her neck, and gave a light squeeze. Before she could even react to that, I spun her around until her back was against the bar, my body trapping her along her front.

I was only able to catch her stunned expression for a second before my face came closer to hers, moving in for the kill. It wasn't even a kiss, just a slight brushing of my mouth against hers, our lips barely touching. It was taking all my restraint not to slam myself against her, but I wanted the decision to be hers. *She* had to want this. She had to come to me.

My heart was beating an unfamiliar rhythm behind my ribcage, the sweet smell of fresh air and cinnamon invading my nostrils, the taste of pure ecstasy hinting from her lips. Just the slightest give here and I could take us both away. Make her forget there was any other guy on the planet.

"Zac…" she breathed out cautiously, her hands in fists against my biceps, her heavy-lidded eyes trained on my mouth, wondering and wanting.

But still, I waited. I waited for what seemed like an eternity, her enticing mouth and her delectable body just a breath away, my fingers sweeping against the smooth skin of her nape. Barely touching her when all I wanted was to bury myself inside her, feel her give what I so wanted to take.

But I waited.

C'mon, Avery. Give me a sign. Give me anything to let me know you want this too.

I felt her chest rise as she took a deep inhale, and her mouth pressed just a bit firmer to mine. When I brushed my lips back in answer, her eyes widened in acknowledgement as the smallest whimper escaped from her throat.

Fuck it. Good enough.

"Don't look so surprised," I whispered against her lips. "You knew this was inevitable."

And with that, I tightened my arms around her and pressed our mouths together.

My God.

She didn't resist. I felt the muscles of her shoulders relax, her fists unclenching to wind into the back of my hair. I kept my hand on the back of her neck, pulling her face closer to mine, opening my mouth slightly, begging to be let in.

And when her lips parted, I knew I was royally fucked.

My tongue swept inside to tangle with hers, and I heard the first gasp between us. To tell you the truth, I didn't know if it was coming from her or me. I touched and I tasted, my senses completely consumed by this woman in my arms. I thought I remembered what kissing Avery felt like, but I was wrong. This, what was happening now, was infinitely better.

I groaned into her mouth and shoved my hips against hers, my cock already on the verge of pain, my restraint overwhelmed by this vixen within my grasp. I knew I was a lost cause. I was insane over this girl. She'd broken me years ago; I was hers. I knew she was too good for me, knew I could never be enough for her. And still, I wanted her anyway.

I slid my hands down her luscious curves and wrapped them around her backside, pulling her into intimate contact with the insistent hard-on behind my jeans. I rolled myself against her, trying to make her lose it, but the added friction was almost *my* undoing. I was way too worked up to even think of staying in control, and I knew if I didn't get a handle on my body's reactions, this night would be over before it even began. And I had much bigger plans for us.

But when Avery pressed *back*, I almost lost my mind. I felt the length of her incredible body against every inch of mine. A moan stirred in the back of her throat as her hands knotted into my hair.

And that was it.

I was gone.

My tongue was buried in her sweet mouth, my cock was grinding against her shorts... and oh fuck. I was going to explode.

I pulled back just enough to take a breath. *"Jesus, Ave,"* I whispered, tightening my fist into the back of her hair, my words feathering over her lips. "Is this okay? Is it okay to want you this bad?"

She shivered against me as her heated stare met mine. There was a fire blazing in her eyes, and I wanted to show her just how hot I could *really* get her if she'd only let me.

She was going to let me. I could tell that she would.

I went to lower my mouth to hers again, but then I caught a hint of something else in her expression. Fear? Remorse?

A wave of guilt washed over me, and goddammit, I immediately knew I shouldn't have taken things this far. I was probably scaring the hell out of her by moving so fast. We had to slow down. She was drunk, for fucksakes.

And I sure as hell wanted to be more than just her rebound guy.

I released my hold on her and grabbed my beer.

She didn't even bother to try and look me in my eyes as she said, "I'm sorry, Zac."

I took a swig from my drink and shot back flatly, "It's okay. Don't worry about it."

"I don't want this to change things between us."

Too late. "It won't."

"Good," she punctuated, inspecting her nails and flipping her shoe off her toes. She averted her face and scanned her eyes around the room, those gears in her inebriated brain cranking away.

Out of nowhere, she sputtered out an idea. "You know something? We should do a Casino Night. I think we should take advantage of the fact that we have an enthusiastic new audience, strike while the iron's hot."

I knew she was attempting to bring us back to friendly banter, but I was still trying to get my hard-on under control and feeling a little cranky over our halted kiss. So, my words came out a bit pissier than I intended. "Yeah. Sounds great."

She bit her lip and swiped a hand through her hair. "Are you mad?"

"I'm not mad."

"Then why do you have that little line between your eyebrows? That's your game face."

"I'm not playing a game, here." I shot her a warning look at that. She knew damn well what I was talking about.

"What?"

I wished she would just stop pushing me for once. Why couldn't she just let things happen the way they were supposed to? Between us, with my bar… Why couldn't she just let things be what they were so obviously meant to be? "It's not a game for me, okay? It's do or die. Literally. I've been living hand-to-mouth for the past four years, and what? You think I'm hanging around here as a hobby? Oh sure. I could make a successful business too if I had Daddy's money to keep me afloat while I played entrepreneur."

She looked at me as if I'd kicked her in the teeth. I may as well have. We'd been getting along so well for weeks. One little setback and I immediately turned into a defensive dickhead, springing a surprise attack. How quickly I reverted back into asshole-mode.

It's what I do.

I realized instantly how shitty my words were, and braced myself for the storm that was surely coming. The wrath I deserved.

Only it didn't come.

Her mouth was dropped open, but no sound came out of it. My shoulders slumped, the guilt of my words weighing down on me heavier than a truckload of concrete.

The dead air between us gave me the chance to jump in, hat in hand. "Oh, Jesus, Ave. I'm sorry. I don't know where the hell I get off. You've only been trying to help me out from Day One. I don't even know why I'm fighting you on this."

"I do."

Her voice was soft, those two simple words a tiny pocket of air, bubbling their way through the surface of a raging river. Yes, I was angrier than I'd let on about our broken liplock, but my outburst was due to more than just that. If she had some insight

206

into my fucked-up rant, I'd sure as hell be open to hearing about it. "What?"

She crossed her arms over her chest—in defense?—as her eyes met mine. "You won't be disrespecting your father by making this place successful. He'd want to see you doing well." I was stunned by her words, and could only stand and gape at her as she continued, "You've been living 'hand-to-mouth' because you never *tried* to turn this place around. When I first came back here, I really wondered what happened to that aggressive guy who used to dominate the ice. Where did that killer spirit go? I knew it was still in you, and I'd like to think I helped bring it back out. And now you're tapping into that killer spirit to fight me instead of using it to see how far you can really go. It's like you don't even *care* how well things have been going, Zac."

I was expecting a rebuttal to my rant, not a helpful insight, and her words sank in. Had I subconsciously been trying to keep this place from being a success all those years? Like, if it did better under my management than my father's, that that would somehow show him up?

Maybe that was the case prior to this year, and it was an interesting thought to ponder. But I'd been *overjoyed* about all the new business Avery had brought in recently. I thought I'd made that obvious. Why would she think I didn't care?

My brain was in overdrive, trying to register all the events of the past minutes, and I couldn't come up with the right thing to say. Too much shit had just gone down for me to make any sense of this night. One second, she was putty in my arms. The next, she was playing psychologist with my head.

And then, suddenly, it came to me. And it was so fucking obvious, I was ashamed of myself.

I never thanked her.

Of course she would be led to believe I didn't give a shit. Of course she would come up with her cockamamie conclusion that it was some type of fear-of-success thing. Since I never offered any gratitude, she mistook it for lack of enthusiasm. I needed to fix that.

She stood in a determined stance, jutting out her stubborn chin, waiting on my response.

So, I gave her one.

"I couldn't be any happier about what you've done with this place, Ave. And I'm in this, I swear. I can't *wait* to see how far we can take it. I'm grateful as all hell for all your hard work." I ran a hand through my hair and met her eyes. "I should have thanked you long before now, and I'm sorry that I didn't. *Thank you.*"

Her shoulders relaxed as she let out a sigh. "I'm enjoying the work, Zac. Truly. And it's nice to know it's not being done in vain."

She started to move toward me, coming in for a hug. I froze as her arms wrapped around my neck as I just barely allowed my hands to rest on her back.

Too dangerous.

I should have never kissed her; it was my mistake. *An exhilarating, heartbreaking mistake.*

Stepping out of her grasp, I aimed my comment to the floor. "I'm also sorry about before. I won't let it happen again."

Chapter Twenty-One

Hockey season had started again.

It used to be my favorite time of year, but over the past half-decade, all it did was serve as a reminder of my failed plans. This year, though, I didn't sink into my annual melancholy. I was excited for my Devils to kick some ass. I was glad they were coming back to the ice as champs.

My rookie year was like that. We'd taken The Cup that summer; I started playing with them in the fall. There was a certain arrogance the players displayed, which would have been off-putting if it hadn't been so rightly earned.

You'd think that coming off a championship season would only keep the winning streak going. But what normally happened is that players from a winning team were suddenly in high demand, and it made more financial sense for a franchise to bring in some new blood at a cheaper price rather than try and match the offers for their top performers... making a defense of a previous championship a near impossibility.

Some of the same players stuck around, most of the same coaches. But the momentum was gone by the time a new season rolled around.

It was that situation that usually brought some new faces to the ice. Just-drafted rookies and guys who had spent most of the previous games riding the pines. Players who were still hungry enough to want to claim a win for their own.

A player like Pat Giordano, who was currently filling in my old spot on the front lines.

Giordano was a kickass athlete, and I didn't know whether it made me feel better or worse to see my doppelganger dominating the game. He was already proving himself a formidable force to be reckoned with on the ice, and a frequent visitor to the penalty box when he was kicked off of it.

Like I said, the guy reminded me of me.

We had the game playing on every TV and customers drinking at every stool. Lately, a crowded bar was a common occurrence, but seeing as it was Halloween, it was a funnier-than-usual one tonight.

A bunch of the guys were wearing costumes—Hell, I'd even thrown on a fedora—but Joey Bricks' was the best. He was dressed up as a red-and-green-faced superfan, channeling Puddy from The Face Painter episode of *Seinfeld*. It was fucking hysterical. Every time anyone looked his way, he'd put on his game face and scream, "The *Devilllls*! We're number one! We beat anybody!" then stick out his tongue Gene-Simmons-style and put up the horns.

Had me laughing every time.

A bunch of kids came in trick-or-treating, which was nice, but really kind of screwed up. That had never happened before. We used to only get the random teenager every year who'd sneak in on a dare from his buddies. But tonight, they were filing in pretty regularly.

I was grateful that I'd picked up a few bags of candy for my customers, who griped that I was now giving it all away to the kids.

I recognized a few of the little leaguers who came in with their parents, and every time I announced their presence, the guys all passed the hat. The kids made out like bandits, and their parents all thanked me and shook my hand. It was fairly awesome to finally be considered a part of this community, whom I'd started to realize weren't the snobby, uptight people I'd originally believed them to be. The ones I'd gotten to know were pretty damn cool.

The ones I *didn't* know made a huge point to introduce themselves. They raved about the Norman Days party the month before, letting me know what a good time they'd had.

"Heck. It's a party every weekend. You should come in more often," I'd say.

It was the same line I offered to anyone who inquired about the place over the past weeks, and more often than not, the simple invitation was all it took. Because come they did. The past month had seen a steady stream of new customers, and I couldn't have been happier about it.

After the latest group of kids left the bar, I'd had it up to here with my customers' grumbling. I mean, Jesus. I could just get them some replacement candy tomorrow.

"Chill out, assholes," I finally said. "I'll buy the house a round if you'll all just shut up already." I gave a ring to the triangle which had everyone cheering and appropriately won over.

But apparently, I'd reprogrammed them all too well. Like a Pavlovian response, once that bell was rung, a few guys started cheering, "Give-a-way! Give-a-way!"

Crap. I'd done this to myself. The random giveaways had become a regular feature at The Westlake, and it seemed I couldn't go more than a few days without being called out for slacking.

"Alright, alright, fine," I laughed out.

I rifled through my prize box until I came across a gift certificate for *Give Me Candy*. I figured it would shut everyone up if they could buy their own damn chocolate bars.

"Okay. Now for a question," I said as I jumped up onto the bar. Scratching the back of my hair as I thought, I searched my memory for something to ask. I'd signed up for a daily email service that sent me trivia every day just for such occasions, figuring I sure as hell could use the help. "Got it. Okay, for a twenty-five dollar gift card to *Give Me Candy*, who can tell me whose face is on the five-thousand dollar bill?"

At first, a few of the guys thought it was a trick question, but once I assured them the bill actually existed, they started yelling out names of presidents with abandon.

Jerry Winters took a shot in the dark when he shouted, "James Madison!"

"Hold up, we have a winner! Mr. Liverwurst is correct!"

There were grumbles and cheers as I hopped off the bar and handed him the gift card. "Here's your prize. Thanks for playing."

"Well, thank you, Maniac," he said proudly. "Looks like someone's got something for *you*."

Jerry nodded his head in the direction of the kitchen. Avery was standing there with a sheet cake, surrounded by my mother, brothers, and the entire kitchen staff. As they marched over toward me, the whole place broke into "Happy Birthday."

Felix took the cake from Avery, placing it on the end of the bar with a "Happy birthday, Meester Zaaa-aaac!" as I stood there with my arms crossed, trying to hide my smile.

"You thought we forgot, didn't you?" my mother asked, all cat-who-ate-the-canary.

"I thought it was a little weird that you didn't say anything when you called before."

"Like I could forget my baby's birthday."

There was a collective "*Awww*" from my customers, every last one of them busting my chops.

Mom shuffled a hand at me. "Well, go on. Blow out your candles!"

I started to bend over the flames when Avery added, "Don't forget to make a wish."

I paused in my action and looked at her. She was wearing a long blond wig and dressed in a pink, velour sweatsuit, her makeup completely overdone. She had the hourglass figure of Anna Nicole Smith, only without all the extra girth. She looked like the Anna Nicole from her modeling days.

In other words, *hot*.

My eyes lowered down her body and back up to her face in a half-lidded stare, envisioning every dirty thing I wished I could do to her. Our kiss from the other day had been playing across my mind almost every minute since it happened. We'd come to an unspoken agreement not to discuss it, but I had to imagine she found it just as hard to forget as me. I'd been really good about remaining hands off since then, but fuck it. It was my birthday. I could fantasize if I wanted to. "Hmmm. Just one?" I asked. Without breaking contact with her eyes, I blew out the candles.

Avery's mouth dropped open slightly, and a beautiful pink flush colored her cheeks. She started pulling off the candles and dumping them in a nearby ashtray, and I could see that her hands were shaking. *Heh heh.*

She actually stuttered when she said, "O-okay. I need to bring this in the back to cut it up."

She went to grab the cake, but thankfully, my mother stepped in. "Why don't you let Felix take care of that. I don't think you should be handling any knives right now." She gave a knowing pat to Avery's shoulder and then made off with my cake.

Avery sank down onto my stool at the end of the bar, letting out with a huge sigh. "Even your mother knows when you're being a cad."

"She should," I smiled back. "She raised four of them."

* * *

While everyone was busy loading up on my birthday cake, my family and I took over a quiet, unoccupied corner of the square bar so I could open my presents. It wouldn't be quiet for long. In about an hour, this entire place was going to be packed. It was Friday night, after all.

"Here you go, dickwad," Bash said as he placed two wrapped boxes on the bar.

"Sebastian!" my mother admonished. "Don't call your baby brother a dickwad."

We all stopped dead in our tracks at that, staring at our mother in a disbelieving pause. We weren't used to hearing her talk like that.

Wyatt broke the silence when he busted out with, "Yeah, Bash. *Finn's* the dickwad."

We all lost our minds cracking up as Mom put her arms around Finn and laughed, "Oh, you know that's not true, sweetheart," giving him a big kiss on his head. She was still chuckling as she explained, "The bottom box is from me; the littler one on top is from your brothers."

"And Avery," Wyatt added.

Avery went in on a present with my brothers? I lowered an eyebrow at her. "Really?"

She swallowed her mouthful of cake and tried to sound impassive as she explained, "I only put in the phone call to the right people. It was your brothers' idea."

"Well, now I'm intrigued."

I tore off the wrapping and opened the box to find... "Holy shit!" I pulled out the Wayne Gretsky sweater and held it up in front of me. "No fucking way!"

My mother bypassed the reprimand and just shot me a scowl.

"Sorry, Mom, but... holy shit!"

My brothers laughed as Avery said, "It's signed. Look." She bent the front corner of the jersey up to show me, and I immediately turned it over in my hand so I could check it out. My fingers ran over the signature, right there in front of my face. I couldn't even find the words.

"Thank you, guys!" I flipped the thing over my shoulder and gave each of them a hug. Then I grabbed Avery's face between my hands and kissed her cheek. "This is the coolest thing ever. How did you...?"

"Well, you may not be too happy to hear it, but *my father* was the one with the necessary connections."

I didn't even care that such awesomeness had come by way of a man I loathed. "Wow. Please be sure to thank him for me."

Avery's lips pursed together. She seemed happy that I was okay with it. How could I *not* be? "Will do," she answered.

"I'm going to get it framed. I'll hang it up right there on the wall next to mine."

"That's a little blasphemous, don't ya think?" asked Finn, like a complete wiseass.

Before I could shoot him down properly, my mother piped in on a wary grin. "Shoot. That's a nice gift. I hope you like mine as much."

"Well, let's find out!" I said through a chuckle. I was in unusually good spirits on my twenty-eighth birthday. Normally, I couldn't care less about it.

The box was about the same size as my cake, and because of that, I didn't have any clue as to what else could be inside. But I couldn't imagine my mother had wrapped up a cake, for godsakes.

I unwrapped it carefully just in case. Lifting the lid, I peeked inside. My head and shoulders immediately dropped, and I closed my eyes to stop the threatening tears. Once I could unclamp my jaw, I said, "Wow, Mom."

I pulled the large, wooden sign out of the box, holding it up by its gold chain. The surface was stained in a dark brown, and the words were carved into its grain, but painted with a metallic gold:

The Rudy McAllister
Memorial Billiard Room

My brothers went uncharacteristically silent at the sight, and Avery clamped a hand over her mouth. Mom tried to sound unaffected, but there were tears in her eyes as she explained, "You're doing such a good thing with that pool room. I just thought it was deserving of something that showed its significance."

"It's perfect, Mom. Thank you." I put an arm around her and gave her a huge squeeze. "I'm going to hang it up right now."

I shook my head to get my brain straight and then held up the sign, announcing, "Hey, check it out, guys!"

They all turned on their stools and expressed their approval, some even going so far as to offer applause. I dragged a bar stool over to the pool room's entrance and stepped up to reach the hooks over the door. I straightened the sign, gave my fingers a kiss, and tapped it before climbing down, watching as it slowed its swinging, settling into its new home.

Perfect.

Chapter Twenty-Two

Thanksgiving was always spent with family at the restaurant. Since we always closed for holidays, it normally allowed for a nice, private tradition.

But this year, Felix and Horatio were joining us. They weren't able to get back home to visit as they usually did over Thanksgiving week, and had I known ahead of time, I would have bought the damn plane tickets myself.

We knew it must've sucked for them living so far away from their family, so we invited them to come and join ours for the day.

My mother kept shuffling them out of the kitchen, insisting that she didn't need any help putting our holiday dinner together.

Felix was none too pleased about the situation. "Your mother kick me out of my kitchen!"

Wyatt clapped a sympathetic hand on his shoulder. "I know. Sorry, dude. She always wants complete control on Thanksgiving."

"She told me I need to get out or I won' get any supper!"

Finn piped up from behind the bar, "You'd better listen to her, Felix. She means it. That is *not* your kitchen today."

He waved his hand in dismissal, letting out with a grumpy, "Bah!"

I had Finn grab him a beer and told him to enjoy the day off. I don't think Felix knew what a 'day off' was.

Horatio was certainly enjoying himself. He was lounged out on one of the three sofas that we'd hauled into the bar from the restaurant's waiting lounge. We did that every year so we could pass out while we watched the football games.

Bash started twirling the remote around his fingers. "Hey, Zac. You sure you want to watch football? There's a Jeff Dunham special on instead."

I knew there was no way he'd turn off the game, but fuck him for even bringing it up. "Fuck you, Bash. Don't even joke about it."

He had his finger poised over the button, threatening to change the channel. "Aww, you sure? I hear he's got some new puppets."

"Bash... I'm this close to kicking your ass right now. Cut it out."

My dick of an older brother gave a chuckle and put down the remote.

Okay. Let me explain.

The thing is, *I do not like ventriloquist dummies.*

When I was little, I had a Charlie McCarthy, and Bash convinced me that it came alive every night while I slept. I'd wake up every morning and find him in my chair at the breakfast table, or sitting on the toilet. It freaked me out, but I had to pretend like it didn't bother me, otherwise Bash would use it against me my whole life. You know, kind of like how he was doing now. So, one night, I snuck up into the attic and hid Charlie in the rafters, figuring my days of torture were over.

And then, a few days later, I woke up to find him *hanging from a noose* in my bedroom. I sat up in bed and screamed my head off.

Bash had his bike taken away for a week, but the trauma for *me* lasted a lifetime.

So, yeah. I don't like ventriloquist dummies.

I hadn't had to confront my old childhood phobia until this new ass clown Dunham came on the scene with his stupid, fucking "comedy" show. Bash had found out about the guy when he caught a special on Comedy Central over the summer, and had been torturing me with its existence ever since.

"Hey," he called out, changing the subject. "Anyone up for a game of pool?"

I immediately got to my feet and shot back, "Oh, you are so on, you tubby bastard."

Bash hauled himself off the couch. "Okay, yeah, I'll kick your ass in a minute. Lemme just get another drink first."

He walked away as I stood there, taunting, "What the fuck? You don't come into my dojo, drop a challenge, and leave, old man."

Wyatt just about spit his beer through his nose.

* * *

Once the Christmas season rolled around, Avery came up with the idea to do a Giving Tree. We dragged the fake tree out of storage and set it up in the corner of the bar, decorating it with about twenty hanging tags of kids' names she'd gotten from the nearby women's shelter.

I swear, my customers were the absolute best. The tree was stripped of names within a few days, forcing Avery to go back to the shelter and get more. It was my idea to get the other local businesses involved, and when they did... holy shit.

We had stacks of donations piled up in the booths, and when they started spilling over onto the square bar, we decided to move everything into the pool room to get ourselves organized. *Sneaker Hut* had donated *fifty* boxes of shoes, so Avery paired them with the coats and sweaters from *Clothing Town*, giving every kid on our tree a winter wardrobe along with their new toys.

In the end, each kid wound up with a *stack* of presents, which Avery wrapped and tied together with wide, red ribbons. The entire pool room looked like Santa's fucking workshop. Tied to every stack of gifts was an envelope that contained numerous vouchers from all the local businesses. We had gift cards to everything from supermarkets and restaurants to book stores and hair salons. Thousands and thousands of dollars that the people of this town donated in the spirit of Christmas once they heard what we were doing.

The local choir came to sing Christmas carols one evening, and the reception was so well received, I scheduled them to come during a Friday night happy hour. Denny made Hot Toddies and I made sure to stock up on the egg nog. Avery filled some red and green tin cups with candy canes and scattered them all over the bars.

Scott kept a stock of white paper and scissors under the bar so my customers could cut out paper snowflakes—which was a huge hit—and Rachel and Farrah hung them on strings from the ceiling. Denny hung some lights, and Alice… planned her wedding. She was spending more time at the bar beyond her usual shifts, and thanks to a Christmas miracle in the form of a fiancé who kept her in good spirits, she was actually pretty pleasant to be around these days.

Avery and she had become fast friends during the planning, and that only served to prove how skilled she was at her job. I mean, hell. She made *Alice* happy. It was magic.

She made *everything* magic.

On the Monday before Christmas, Avery took over the restaurant's kitchen to bake cookies. She'd been signing up the local ladies to partake in a cookie exchange that evening, which I guess required her to turn into a Keebler elf.

I popped into the kitchen to see how she was doing. She'd been in here for hours, and I wanted to check out her handiwork. Plus, my entire bar was filled with the most tempting smell; I had to check out the source.

"Chocolate chocolate-chip mint. Want one?" she asked, pointing to the work island. "I guarantee it'll be the greatest thing you ever put in your mouth."

I raised an eyebrow but bypassed the dirty remark. Too easy.

Grabbing a cookie, I took a bite… and holy shit.

"Holy shit! These are amazing!"

I went to grab another but she slapped my hand away. "They're for the cookie exchange!"

Scowling at her reprimand, I shot back, "Give me a break. You have about a million of them here." I really needed another cookie. When you think about it, it was actually kind of mean of her to make me taste something so delicious when she wasn't going to let me have any more.

Jesus. *That* sounded way too familiar.

"Zac. There are no less than thirty women coming to this thing. I need to bag a half-dozen for each and every one of them, plus plate a dozen for the party. You can have whatever's left over."

"What if their cookies suck?" I pouted. "You'll be giving away fifteen dozen perfectly good cookies just to get their crappy ones."

She rolled her eyes and tried to appease me. "I'll make you your own batch, okay? It'll be payment for letting me use your ovens."

"Fair enough," I said, as I grinned and swiped another cookie on my way out to the bar.

* * *

Once the ladies showed up, it was a regular hen house in my restaurant. I let Avery schedule the event for a Monday, knowing the restaurant would be closed, allowing for a private party that night. I had Felix whip up a bunch of little sandwiches for them and donated a couple cases of wine, so they all thought I was Superman.

Their average age was probably somewhere close to a hundred, but that didn't stop them from fawning all over me. I took their flirting in stride, told everyone how lovely they looked, and flashed each and every one of them a charming grin at every opportunity. All that special attention got me in good with the clubhouse biddies, and charmed the fucking girdles off the ladies from The Norman Society. At one point, Mrs. Grady actually gave a pat to my ass, and I looked over to see Avery practically choking at the sight.

I made my escape and sat down on one of the couches with my fingers at my temple, watching the whole scene go down. It was a relief to finally remove myself from center stage, blend into the background, and just check everything out from afar.

To check out Avery.

She was totally in her element whenever an event was going down. I found it strange that a girl who had spent most of her life shying from parties was now the one planning them. And doing it well.

My eyelids lowered into a lazy, half-lidded glare as I watched her, mentally transmitting all the dirty thoughts that were racing around my brain. The theme of the evening was "Ugly Holiday Sweaters," and even in the stupid elf getup she was sporting, Avery managed to look irresistible.

She was busy playing hostess, but she must have felt my stare, and raised her eyes my way. I didn't bother to break my focus. I was envisioning getting her out of that stupid sweater, running my hands along every inch of her bare skin, devouring those perfect lips with my mouth.

By the way Avery flushed and turned away, I knew she could tell exactly what I'd been thinking. She was visibly flustered, but I could still see her sneaking the occasional glance in my direction.

I could also see she was fighting it.

* * *

After the party, Avery and I found ourselves alone in the restaurant. I knew I should probably have checked in over at the bar side of things, but any minute I had her all to myself was too tempting a prospect to pass up.

We took a seat at one of the candlelit tables near the glass wall to catch our breath and polish off the leftover food. In the warmer months, we opened all the doors for indoor/outdoor dining. On this side of my building, there was a large deck that jutted into the lake that offered ten extra tables for al fresco seating. I was excited to think that they'd be put to good use this spring.

It was empty now, though, affording an unobstructed view of the lake outside. Even when it was dark, you could see the outline of its shape from the glow of the houses that bordered it, and when there was a full moon, the entire surface of the water was an illuminated mirror. It had frozen solid in the past days, and I knew it wouldn't be long before the ice was swarming with people.

I'd have to come up with a plan to serve free hot chocolates off the deck. It would be a cheap and easy way to keep all this goodwill going.

Avery had helped to turn The Westlake into a staple of the community, and even though I told her all the time, I didn't think there would ever be a way to properly thank her. Even more than that, she'd helped me to recognize how angry I've been these past years. Between my father's death and the death of my career, I didn't feel there was anything to look forward to other than frustration.

She helped me to see there was more to life than that.

Even when your dreams don't pan out, even when you can't rub two nickels together, even when it seems all hope is lost... There's always something to look forward to.

I leaned back in my seat, popped a mini sandwich in my mouth, and shot a smile at Avery as I chewed.

"Well, I think tonight was a smashing success, don't you?" she asked, twirling a spoon in her coffee.

"Sure was. Although, I think I'd steer clear of Mrs. Grady's almond crescents if I were you."

"Why's that?"

"They're purple."

That had her sputtering out a laugh. "Hey," she started in once she caught her breath. "I want to thank you for letting me take over your place tonight. I want to pay you back for whatever money you put out for this thing."

"Like that's going to happen."

"No, really, Zac. I'm viewing this as a work thing. Let me pay you something."

I didn't like the idea of her shelling out any cash from her own pocket, considering that tonight was just as much a 'work thing' for me as it was for her. But I knew how stubborn she could be about such things. It would be easier just to cave and let her think she got her way.

I shot her a sham dirty look. "Fine. Fifty bucks."

"Sold!" she giggled. "That's one helluva bargain, thank you."

"You're welcome."

"And I'll be able to pay you back sooner rather than later. I'm pretty sure I've already drummed up some new business."

"Oh yeah?" I asked. "The biddies planning a kegger or something?"

That made her laugh. "No, you dork. The ladies from The Norman Society think I should join their committee."

I raised an eyebrow at her. "You're not going to start wearing muumuus and rolling your pantyhose down to your ankles, are you?"

She cracked up and explained, "No! That was exactly their point. They think it's time to bring some younger blood into their club. There'd even be some money in it for me."

"Wow, Ave. That would be great for you. Jesus. I'm glad this stupid bar turned out to be good for something."

She tightened her eyes as she scrutinized my face, mulling over my comment. "Zac, don't you see? This 'stupid bar' brings people together. You're helping them in your own little way. You bring happiness to others. Don't you know how hard that is? How many people can say that about their jobs?"

I eyed her in admiration as a stunned smile tugged at the corner of my lips. The thing was, she was right. And I knew it. I'd spent so many years just looking out for myself, and now, I couldn't believe how incredible it's felt to help others. Selfish, though, because doing something good always made *me* feel good. It's like I was doing it for me.

"What am I doing to make *you* happy, Ave?" I asked, not trying to hide the hope in my voice.

Her mouth dropped open slightly as her cheeks turned pink. I caught the spark in her eyes in the brief second it took for her to look away. She picked something off her plate and held it up between us, smiling as she said, "Keeping Felix on the payroll."

She shot a wicked grin at me as she took a bite from her sandwich.

The tease.

Chapter Twenty-Three

New Year's Eve was one part newcomers, one part old friends, and all parts insane.

The restaurant was still seating people at eleven o'clock, and my bar was packed wall to wall. Aside from my regulars, there were a ton of other faces filling the room, every last one of them drinking their faces off. My brothers had all popped in at some point for a quick shot before heading out for bigger plans, but it was nice that they'd all thought to at least stop by.

Casey was practically drooling over Finn. "Avery. You have access to *that* and you're hanging around with *this*? What is wrong with you, girl?"

"Look who's talking," I shot back. "I'm not the one who hooked up with Toothless Wonder over there."

First Rule of Getting Your Balls Busted: *Deflect*.

"Now that hurts, baby," Simon guilted his wife, "You know damn well I'm ten times hotter than that guy. Even without the teeth." We were cracking up already, but when Simon pulled out his spacer, Avery almost fell off her stool.

It was pretty fuckawesome that the four of us were all together in the same room again. It had been years since that happened. Right before I tore up my knee, Simon got traded down to Philly. Seeing them tonight had me feeling ashamed that I hadn't kept in better touch. But I cut ties soon after coming home from Texas. Being around Simon only reminded me of everything that I had lost.

At least it used to. I didn't feel that way all the time anymore.

Which was good, because what use is *Auld Lang Syne* without some old friends around?

New Year's wasn't the only reason Casey was in town to celebrate. Last week, as it turned out, Avery's divorce was finalized.

The two of them had spent almost every minute of the past few days together, going to movies, shopping, naked pillow fights... whatever the hell girls did when they got together.

Simon and I spent most of that time drinking.

He lifted his shot above the table. "To healthy gums!" he shouted as we all raised our glasses in a toast.

We downed our booze as Avery laughed out a grunt. "Blech! How many of those have we done?"

"Who knows?" I asked. "I lost count hours ago."

* * *

I didn't even know what time it was when I finally threw the lock on the door. I'd switched to water sometime after midnight, but the damage had already been done. My skull was already slipping into a hangover and it hadn't even hit a pillow yet.

I crossed my arms over the bar and dropped my head. "Jesus. I'm beat."

When I looked up at Avery, she was just sitting on the stool next to me, grinning like a lunatic.

"Why are you smiling at me like that?"

"No reason. I'm just smiling. Smiling's my favorite."

"Well, cut it out. You're giving me the creeps."

"Ooh. You're an *angry* elf!"

I didn't know what the fuck she was talking about, but she sure was finding herself hilarious, holding her sides and busting up in a fit of giggles.

"Franciscoooo!"

I ignored her babbling and looked out at the view. It was such a clear night and the frozen lake looked so inviting. I felt a familiar ache grip my chest as I stared longingly out the windows.

Suddenly, I had the urge to get on that ice.

No. You know what? More than an urge. I *had* to get out there. It was now or never.

I brought my hand down onto the bar, snapping Avery to attention. "We're going ice skating."

The noise startled her, and she had her hand over her heart as she asked, "*Now?*"

"C'mon. Where's your sense of adventure?"

"I don't know, Zac. Isn't it illegal or something?"

"Who's going to arrest us? The park ranger? He's a twenty-two year old kid in a golf cart who happens to drink at my pub. I think we're covered if we get caught."

"It's not just that. I'm—"

"Drunk?"

"Sort of, but… I don't know how to skate very well even when I'm sober."

She said that last part shyly, and my mouth dropped as I took in the information. "You're kidding! You've grown up around hockey your whole life and you never learned how to skate? I find that pretty hard to believe."

"Well, my father was too interested in making sure his *players* could skate. Not his daughter."

That was pretty much the saddest thing I ever heard. I told you her father was a dick.

Avery must have seen my face fall at her revelation, and quickly covered, "What am I saying? You actually want to go skating and I'm debating you about it? Oh my God, Zac. I'm so sorry. I forgot you haven't…"

She trailed off, probably realizing that she was dancing too close to pity.

I think we've all learned how well I handle being pitied.

"Alright. That's it. No more arguments, no more excuses. You and I are getting out on that ice *now*. Move it, Brooks!"

I shuffled her to her feet and grabbed her scarf. She groaned in protest as I wrapped it around her neck, tying it into a loose knot at her throat. It may have been the booze, but I found myself staring at the little spot of exposed skin, wondering what she would do if I just lowered my head and pressed my lips to the sweet, soft, inviting hollow of her throat.

I raised my eyes as her brows lifted, looking at me blankly. Her lips pressed into a tight line as she swallowed hard.

Then she let out with a nervous giggle as she grabbed her coat, breaking the moment.

I directed her into the alcove that separated the restaurant from the bar. Pulling open the closet door, I rifled through the wooden box of skates on the floor until I came up with my old practice blades. They were filthy and frayed, stiff from misuse after so many years. But they'd be able to get the job done.

"Here," I said, handing them over to Avery. "These are from when I was twelve. They should fit good enough."

She inspected them in her hands before holding them next to her feet as I plucked my skates off the hook on the wall. I had a quick moment of apprehension as I ran my fingers over the patterned leather in my hands. I almost changed my mind.

But there was Avery, standing there all proud and excited. I didn't want to let her down.

We escaped out the alcove door, onto the deck, the cold smacking us in the face as we tied on our skates. When I was finished, I looked over at Avery.

She was sitting on the bench seat next to me, biting her lip to keep from grinning. "They look good on you."

I shot her a smirk and replied, "Everything looks good on me, baby."

She rolled her eyes as I laughed.

The lake had frozen over days ago, and thankfully, it hadn't snowed. So, there was no shoveling required before we could head out onto the ice, take advantage of the endless sheet of glass.

I left Avery on the safety of the deck while I stood at the bottom of the stairs and took a huge inhale, looking over the expanse of my surroundings, psyching myself up to make my next move.

And then, for the first time in almost five years… I stepped out onto the ice.

From the first clink of my blades, my feet moved on their own. I ventured out aways in a large circle, testing the surface, which I soon discovered had to be at least a foot thick.

I was overwhelmed as a rush of memories flooded my brain and filled my entire being. I immediately felt my father out there with me, saw visions of him teaching me how to skate when I was little, cheering me on as a teenager. I took a moment to breathe in, to appreciate the pure nostalgia that my mind had conjured.

By the time I came back to Avery, I was smiling. "You ready?"

She responded with a hesitant grin and a nod of her head. I held my arms out for her and she took them as I helped her down the steps. Once on the ice, she seized my jacket in a death-grip as I skated backwards, letting her get the feel of it. She almost wiped out a couple times, but I always caught her.

Her ankles kept turning in and I tried not to laugh. "Easy, Drunky," I busted.

It took a while, but once she seemed a bit more surefooted, I said, "I'm going to let go, okay? I'll stay right here, so if you feel like you're going to fall, just grab hold."

Very tentatively, I released my grip on her, keeping my arms stretched out toward her just in case. She was unsteady at first, but holy hell, she was getting it! A rush of pride washed through me as I thought, *I did this. I taught her how to skate.* I was more than a little proud of myself.

And her.

"Holy shit, Ave! You're doing it! Look at you!"

She started to pick up a little speed, and I was about to tell her not to get so cocky when...

"Race ya!" she called out, leaving me standing there staring at thin air, at the spot she just occupied.

I watched her take off down the lake, her little skirt flying around her legs, her sweater-tights a receding gray blur.

"Oh you lying, faking phony!"

I chased after her; she had one hell of a head start but she was no match for me. I gave her scarf a tug as I zoomed by, and once I was on open ground, picked up even more speed.

My legs moved on their own as I kicked off and pushed myself to go as fast as my aching knee would allow. The chill was slashing against my face, my nose was leaking, my eyes were tearing up from the cold… and I felt fucking phenomenal.

How could I have denied myself this part of me for all those years? Because that's what this was: A part of me. The air, the ice. The skates at my feet were an extension of my body, two limbs I'd cut off years ago.

Once I neared the bridge, I skidded out, kicking up a spray of mist against the moonlight. I watched it settle as I tried to catch my breath. The cold filled my lungs in a soothing chill only to be exhaled in a cloudy haze. It was quiet, and the calm allowed me to realize *I was at peace*.

I wasn't a very spiritual guy, but for the first time in my life, I was suddenly one with everything around me. The fog rising off the lake, the smell of the winter crisp in the air, the distant sound of animals in the trees, the scrape of blades against the ice…

Avery skating in my direction.

She slowed her pace and did a full circle around me, eyeing me up cautiously, seemingly tuned in to my epiphany. Her breath came out in a smoky cloud as she smiled and said, "You're happy."

She'd said that to me once before, five years ago on this very night. And I *was* happy. I was then, and I was now. How did she always know?

"Yes. I'm happy. Happier than I've ever been in my life."

Happy? I was practically manic. My goddamn heart was nearly beating out of my chest to see her standing there smiling, proud that she was able to share this moment with me.

The look in her eyes was almost as elated as mine, and in my euphoria, I found my blades sliding closer toward her. I let my vision drop to her lips, clearly offering an invitation, even though I wasn't exactly sure she'd accept.

She hadn't come to me over all these past months, why would she do it now? Would the fact that her divorce was finally official change that? Would a signed piece of paper make any difference between us?

I sure as hell hoped so.

I mean, Christ. She'd essentially been "single" since the spring. And yet, I gave her the space to let her figure everything out on her own. Gave her the time to decide not only to come to me, but come to me for more than just a distraction from her troubles.

And here I was, still waiting.

Our eyes were locked together as our heated breaths fogged the space between us, caught in a standoff, each waiting for the other to come to some sort of resolve. But as much as I was dying to get my lips on her at that second, I didn't move in for the kill.

The decision was still hers to make.

She took a deep breath as her eyelids lowered to my mouth, and then before I could register what was happening… she was gone.

Apparently, her decision was to skate back toward the bar.

* * *

After we'd shaken off the cold and stripped down to a single layer of clothing, we pulled a couch over to the fire and tried to thaw out. I loaned her a pair of my slippers which looked like cinderblocks on her tiny feet, and I watched in amusement as she wiggled them from the ends of her toes, her feet stretched out toward the flames.

"That was fun," she let out on a sigh.

"Of course it was. You and I always have fun on New Year's Eve." Her mouth dipped open as I shot her a wicked smirk.

That's right. I went there.

"I thought it was *Christmas* Eve," she said, trying to sound unaffected.

"It was New Year's. Trust me."

She stared into the fire, saying, "I'm surprised you remember."

"I'm surprised you don't."

Her eyes dropped to her hands as she picked at a fingernail and said softly, "I did. I do. Of course I do."

There was an awkward silence between us as our one night rolled around in our minds. I started to think that that's all we would ever have. Isn't there some sort of point of no return? Can two people be friends for so long that they simply skip over their window of opportunity? Does another one ever open?

Avery's voice broke my train of thought. "It's kind of dangerous for me to be here alone with you."

I shifted my focus away from the fireplace and asked, "Why's that?" even though I already knew the answer. I was trying to psych myself up for the Big Letdown, the speech where she told me what a great friend I was, but that I really needed to back the hell off.

But she didn't elaborate. Instead, she took a deep breath and changed the subject.

"Cute shoes," she busted, nodding at my slippered feet. I gave a chuckle and wiggled my toes at her comment. Her eyes met mine as her lips curled into a mischievous grin. "Wanna fuck?"

Chapter Twenty-Four

We tore at each other on our way up the stairs, never breaking contact with our lips as we ripped off our clothes. A scarf here, a sock there; leaving a trail of debauchery all the way up to my apartment.

Once we reached the landing, I almost tripped on a stack of boxes in my blinders-on focus on Avery's body, her lips. I guided her over a pile of papers before sweeping my apartment door open and backing her into my living room.

The bed was about twenty feet too far away, so I drew us both down to lie on the couch, Avery's body under mine. I pulled off her sweater, she unbuttoned my jeans. Our mouths were a sloppy tangle of tongue, teeth, lips, gasping breaths, and... giggles? Holy shit. We were both laughing. Both of us reveling in the pure joy that we were giving one another. I didn't think there was ever a time when I laughed during sex before.

Avery wriggled out from underneath me, and I sat up on the couch, feeling a physical ache from the loss of her body under my hands. She stood facing me with a sly smile, and I swear, looking at her standing there wearing just a bra, mini skirt, and that dirty grin, I almost came. She was so gorgeous, so playful and sexy, she pretty much broke my heart.

She feathered a hand down her chest to her stomach and back up to her neck again, her eyes never leaving mine until she turned her back to me. She reached up to undo her bra... then held it out to her side before casually dropping it to the floor. Fuck.

She shot me a sly look over her shoulder, and my mouth went dry. That devilish grin was still playing at her lips when she suggested, "You should really be more naked right now."

She didn't need to ask me twice. I stripped off my T-shirt as she unzipped her skirt, but then my body became paralyzed in the act of pulling off my jeans, my hands frozen at my waist as I watched her slide that little skirt and her knit tights down her legs. Slowly.

Holy shit, she was trying to kill me. The luscious round curves of her ass came into view, her little white thong taunting me. I ran a tongue over my lips in anticipation, dying to get my mouth on her once again.

Avery turned toward me just then, and goddammit, hooked her thumbs into the strings at her hips, lowering her panties to the floor.

A lot of girls are self-conscious about their bodies, and most of the time, they really don't need to be. Men love women's bodies, especially when they're naked. We're just so grateful that you're letting us see you without any clothes on that we don't think to analyze all those imperfections you've convinced yourself you have. To us, you're beautiful. And the most attractive thing about a woman is when she knows she's beautiful, too.

So, I didn't know if the booze was having a calming effect on Avery or if she'd just grown confident in recent years, but she stood there for an extra minute to let me get a good look at her. My eyes ran down the length of her body then back up again, taking in every inch of her creamy skin, the pink tips of her perfect-handful breasts, the landing strip between her legs.

She was so fucking beautiful. Her body, yes, of course. But her mind, her heart. And even though every inch of her delectable flesh was within my grasp, I found myself mesmerized most of all by those topaz eyes staring into my soul.

She let me have my fill before kneeling on the floor between my legs, running a hand up my chest and pulling at my neck, lowering my face closer to hers. For all her sexy display, the kiss was soft, sweet, unhurried, and I marveled at how with a beautiful naked woman on her knees before me, the most prevalent emotion I was feeling wasn't lust, but... Nope. Not going there.

"You're so beautiful," I said before becoming conscious I was even speaking at all.

She raised an eyebrow and shot back, "I bet you say that to every girl that gets naked in your apartment."

"Well, I figure it's only common courtesy."

She laughed and gave my chest a smack. "Jerk. And why are your pants still on?"

I remedied that issue in about one-point-five seconds.

Avery's hand slipped down my front before she followed her touch with her eyes. It was strange and disconcerting to give up my usual control, sitting there sprawled across the couch at her mercy. My brain was hesitant, but another body part wasn't feeling quite so apprehensive. Either that, or it was scared stiff. She ran her palm over its length, then shot me another one of those evil grins.

Fuck.

She flicked out her tongue to taste just the very tip of me, and holy shit, I almost exploded right then and there. I stretched my arms along the back of the couch and let her explore me with her mouth, trying not to lose it from the feel of her wet lips wrapping around me. She licked and she sucked and she drove me insane, my breath coming out in an unsteady exhale, my hands clenched in fists on the sofa cushion.

Holy hell did it feel good.

She swirled her tongue around me and closed her lips over my head, sliding her mouth down until I hit the back of her throat, then sucked me hard on the way back up. Then she did it again. And again. And—oh fuck. It was all I could do not to grab the back of her hair and fuck her sweet mouth. But I kept my iron-clad hold on the couch, my fingers in a white-knuckle grip against the fabric as it twisted in my fists. *"You're killing me."*

I flinched a little when her teeth scraped lightly along my head, the sensation so enticing, I felt myself tightening way too soon. I was afraid I wouldn't be able to hold out much longer, but I talked myself down. There was no way I was coming anywhere else than between those gorgeous legs.

I put a hand at her jaw and gave a nudge, with the intention of pulling her face up to mine for a kiss. Avery took the cue and slid her mouth off me, but instead of meeting my lips, her teeth bit into my inner thigh.

"Shit!" I yelped through a laugh.

She was playing me, her eyes meeting mine in a teasing grin as she peppered my skin with wet kisses, along the scar at my knee, up my leg, across my stomach, my chest…

"God, Zac. It's like I can't get enough of you."

Smirking, I shot back, "I haven't gotten anything of *you* yet."

I finally grabbed her arms and pulled her to me, slamming her mouth to mine, tasting myself on her lips. Avery straddled her knees on either side of my hips and kissed me back. She pressed herself against me; I could feel the wet warmth of her against my bare cock, and oh Jesus. I didn't know how much longer I could do this. I was already out of my mind, but by some miracle, I managed to hold it together.

I grasped her breasts in my hands and flicked my tongue against one, hearing her gasp as she arched her back, offering herself to me. I took the invitation and wrapped my lips around one sweet, pink tip, sucking at it until it hardened against my tongue. Avery rested her head on top of mine and her hair fell across my face, her tits smashed against my mouth, the palm of my free hand sliding across her luscious ass. I massaged the flesh at my fingertips, pushing her toward me and thrusting my hips upward, letting her feel just how badly I wanted her.

She let out a groan and pushed back, her thighs grasping my hips, her ass tightening against my palm. Jesus, I was going to die before this was over.

I hardened beyond belief, my hands gripping her ass and my mouth and tongue against her tits, her wetness rubbing against my hard cock... *Ah fuck. I need to be inside.*

"You ready for me?" I asked.

"Yes."

"I'm going to fuck you so fucking hard."

"Yes."

"I'm going to ram my cock in you so deep. You want it?"

"Yes."

"Ask me. Tell me you want it."

"Fuck me, Zac," she said on a gasping exhale. "Please fuck me."

Her words shot a jolt of electricity right through me, hearing her dirty mouth begging for me. I reluctantly released my hold on her to grab a condom out of the side table drawer, when...

"Fuck me, Zac!"

Jesus. Not now.

"Fuck me, Zac!"

"Shut the fuck up, Magnum!"

"Fuck up, Magnum!"

I tore my lips away from Avery's skin, planted her naked ass on the couch, and growled, "Hang on."

In the most obscene three-legged race in history, I shuffled a few steps with my pants around my ankles until I could kick them off and walk like a man. I pulled the room divider across the doorway and threw on the radio, blasting The White Stripes to drown out my stupid bird.

That oughtta do it.

When I turned around, I found Avery lying gorgeously across my couch. Damn, my furniture never looked so good. She was aiming that playful smile at me as she purred, "I always said McAllister's got the best ass in the business. Wow. It's even better without the hockey shorts."

I grinned back as I covered her body with my own. She was just the right fit under me, skin to skin, every inch molding perfectly to mine. I brushed my lips against hers as my hand ran up her side, touching every part of her incredible body that had been taunting me from under her clothes for much, much too long.

I settled myself between her legs and gave a slight push, and she wrapped those luscious gams around me as I sat up on the couch, situating her on my lap. Our mouths were still joined as I slid a hand between us, swiping my thumb across her sensitive skin.

She let out with an exhale as she broke our kiss, tipping her head back toward the ceiling. "Oh God, Zac. You've always been way too good at this."

Her words made me chuckle, but not enough to stop what I was doing.

I grabbed the abandoned condom with my free hand and tore it open with my teeth. "You ready to try this again?" I asked.

Without another word between us, she raised her hips while I rolled it on, and the second I was done, Avery slid herself down on top of me.

I hissed an involuntary curse as she lowered her sweet, giving body down my length. I felt every inch sliding into her, her body stretching to take all of me. She closed her eyes and let out with a contented gasp as she sank down fully, my cock buried to the hilt.

And then, God help me, she started to move.

She rose and fell as I thrust upward and back, and before long, our movements synched. I had her ass in my palms as I devoured her perfect lips, the taste so unbearably sweet, the scent of cinnamon filling my senses. The beautiful vixen rocked herself against me, and I was more than content to let her take the reins, leaning back to enjoy the ride. And the view.

Her head was thrown back, her beautiful tits bouncing in my face... Even without the fact that I was buried to the balls inside her, I'd have been sent over the edge just from seeing that. But the fact was, I *was* inside her, and I was so close to losing it that I had to slow us down before I did.

I maneuvered us to lie down on the couch, my body covering hers. I wrapped my arms around her and slid myself inside again, hearing her moan, feeling myself coming apart. I went to lower my lips to hers again when the look on her face stopped me.

Her eyes were staring into mine, her hands were running in a slow caress against my back. Here was this beautiful girl giving herself to me completely, and for the first time in my life... I didn't want to simply *take* it.

It suddenly felt wrong somehow, just *fucking*. I'd been hoping for this for months, hell, for years. I *needed* to have sex with this woman. But until this moment, I never realized how empty that was. Because unexpectedly, with Avery, it didn't feel so empty anymore.

It was then that it happened. All at once, everything changed.

The feeling was almost beyond description. I was sheathed in the tight warmth of her amazing body, incredibly turned on, but even more than that, I was…

it felt like…

it was like I was…

coming home.

The thought came unbidden, but once it entered my brain, there was no turning it off.

It's a scary thing when you realize that the person you're with is the person you're *meant* to be with. There is no relief at having found them. There is only new torture. Because while you were so busy trying to make that person yours, you were distracted from the inevitable truth: Now that you have them, all that's left is the fear of losing them.

But not right now. At least for now, I had her.

I swallowed hard at the revelation, and there was a physical lump in my throat, obstructing the air from entering my lungs. I'd been with countless girls before. None of them ever felt like this. *Nothing* ever felt like this. Nothing ever felt this right, this perfect, this everything.

This was where I was supposed to be.

"*Avery*," I choked out, my voice unrecognizable. The single word an insufficient prayer whispered from my foolish lips.

Her eyes met mine, and I swear, I saw tears glistening within them. She knew what I was feeling, and more importantly, she felt it too. She swiped a hand across my jaw, and I turned my face to kiss her palm, never breaking contact with her gaze. She gave a bite to her lip and closed her eyelids, and that's when I saw the most amazing thing I've ever seen in all my life: I watched, stunned, as a lone tear escaped from under her lashes and ran down her cheek.

Holy shit. She *was* tearing up.

The sight of that innocent little rivulet completely broke me. A single tear that confirmed she was in this, too. One, tiny, inconsequential drop of liquid that rocked my entire world.

I love you.

The thought lingered on the edges of my brain, was so close to slipping from my lips. And it didn't scare me. It didn't freak me out.

It felt incredible.

I felt my heart splinter and soar, my past converging with my present, my future right there within my grasp. I welcomed the death of my past. I welcomed the sweet torture of the future that was sure to follow. She was it for me. Always had been. Always would be.

I was in love with this woman.

For the first time in my life, for the last, I was in love.

"*Zac*," she answered back, after an eternity. Her voice aching and seductive, so hot, yet so warm.

"Oh God," I said. My name on her lips at such a moment was the sweetest thing I ever heard. "Say that again."

"Zac," she whispered out.

My heart swelled, hearing her broken battle cry, her unconditional surrender.

Avery is mine.

* * *

245

The sun was just coming up, but we were only now settling in to get some sleep. Avery was curled up in my bed, contented, sated, and spooned in my arms.

Just when I was ready to pass out, she slipped out from my grasp and started to get dressed. I thought it was cute that she felt the need to put something on for the short trip to the bathroom.

I gave a stretch and said through a yawn, "Please stop putting your clothes on. You're only going to come back to bed anyway."

She chuckled, gave me a quick peck on the lips and said. "Can't. I've got to go."

I didn't like the finality of that statement. I sat up and asked, "Go? Where you going?"

"Home. Where do you think I'm going?"

Home? She's leaving? "I guess I thought you'd want to stay."

She laughed as she zipped up her skirt. "Zac. I'm a big girl. I know how this works. Tonight was fun, but I don't expect anything to come out of it."

She pulled on her sweater and grabbed the rest of her things, while I sat there, unable to speak. I watched, open-mouthed, as she slipped into her shoes and stuffed her tights into her bag.

"Oh, wait!" she added, as an afterthought. She opened her purse and pulled a few bills out of her wallet, depositing them on the dresser. "Here's that fifty I owed you from last week. Thanks."

She blew me a kiss and walked out to the living room. I heard the front door close as I sat in my bed, stunned.

What the hell just happened? *Have I just been used?* Is this what it felt like?

I just experienced the most earth-shattering night of my life, and Avery could just walk away as if it was no big deal?

I looked over at the bills on my dresser, feeling like a fucking gigolo. Fifty stinking bucks? If I were a girl, I'd be pulling a Coco and crying in the shower right now.

Instead, I dragged the sheets up to my chest and sank down into my bed, wondering where the hell everything went so wrong.

Chapter Twenty-Five

I'd just started playing with the Devils when I first met Avery.

This was back in the fall of '95, and I was unaware at that time that my run would be so short-lived. I was a cocky punk of a kid, having spent all those years in the high school and college leagues, just itching to get to the show.

I mean, I'd put in my time. I devoted the majority of my life to the ice, bypassing college at more prestigious universities in order to attend one where I could play, one where I had better odds of getting scouted by an east coast team. I thought my best shot was with the Flyers down in Philly, but soon enough, it was the Devils themselves that came calling.

Or, rather, *the* Devil himself.

Benny Brooks, General Manager. He was a local guy, too, and while he'd deny it, tended to keep a stronger eye on his fellow Jersey boys. Not to say I wasn't good enough on my own. I was. It's just that Benny's involvement made the difference between playing at the Meadowlands or being shipped down to Philly.

So, at first, of course I really liked Benny.

Until I didn't.

In between those two extremes, I met his daughter Avery.

I was busy banging anything with a heartbeat back then. And let me tell you, the girls were more than available during that time. They hung around our bar, lingered after practices, were waiting for us in the fucking parking lot after games.

So, you can't blame me for thinking Avery was a typical jersey-chaser that night we first met. Because why else would a girl show up to the bars we went to? The only reason for those girls to stick around was to get in on the after-party action. The game after the game.

I was captivated from that first moment; she was the kind of girl a guy would notice, whether or not she ever opened her mouth. Which she only started to do regularly after months of work on my part, breaking her out of her shell.

And as it turned out, I really, really liked her.

She would show up to Johnny's with a girlfriend or two, then spend the whole night doing her introverted thing. I used to catch her looking at me sometimes, but then again, she did it a lot. It was kind of nice, actually, to catch her staring at me like that. It was flattering.

One night—our last night—Avery showed up wearing some insane gold dress, and looking directly at it was like staring into the sun. But even still, I watched her every move from the second she walked through the door. I was practically drooling. We'd been hanging out pretty regularly by that time. Sometimes, we'd find ourselves alone, embroiled in some personal conversation or another. But mostly, our encounters were in a group setting, screwing around with the guys, goofing off. I was always impressed that she could hold her own.

But that night, we didn't spend too much time with the rest of the guys. I basically had her all to myself while we drank and shot some pool. I'd always kept her at arm's length, not only because her father was the GM, but because I thought I'd scare her off if I made any sudden movements. She'd pretty much made it clear that she was off-limits anyway. But on New Year's, for whatever reason, she was really laying it on. I always figured her friends had dared her or something, because Avery was acting really out of character.

Next thing I knew, we were hooking up in her car.

It was an explosive night in any case, for more reasons than just that.

Because I fell for her.

Hard.

I realized being with her was something I'd wanted for years, and was pissed that I'd denied it for so long. I thought the fact that she'd finally come to me meant there could be something more between us. Maybe I'd even date her exclusively, break ties with any of the other girls I was seeing and just be with one person for a while.

I thought it was the beginning for us.

The next day, I showed up for practice, and was welcomed with a red flag in my locker. It was a calling card from the manager's office, and a red flag never meant good news. It turned out to be the worst news I could get.

I'd been approached by the Stars a couple weeks before. The deal was, they were a great team and had an above-average chance of making it to the finals that year. They decided they wanted me as a backup for their front lines. Now, I wanted to win The Cup as bad as any other guy, but I didn't want to do it while sitting on the bench. The money they offered wasn't easy to ignore, so I figured I'd agree to their deal, sure that the Devils would up my salary in order to keep me. It may sound like a gamble, but that's just the way these things went down. Hell, it was their game, not mine. I was just following their rules.

But when I sat down in Benny's office, he broke the news: The negotiating term was up, and they weren't prepared to match the Stars' offer.

So, they let me go. Traded to Dallas, effective immediately.

The pronouncement was like a punch to the gut. I guess I never really considered the idea that I was expendable. I thought I was worth more, but it turned out I was wrong.

Wrong about my job, and wrong about the girl. At the time, I was convinced Avery had something to do with the decision.

Five years later, there she was, delivering another stick to my face.

I couldn't bring myself to call her yet. My emotions were too big and too mottled to talk to her in any normal way without coming off like a desperate loser. I almost told her I loved her last night, for chrissakes. I was sure it was just the heat of the moment.

A very heat-filled moment.

I mean, I really liked Avery. I always had. She was smart and fun and she didn't take any of my shit. She had this great dimple in her right cheek that would only show up when she was really laughing hard over something. I lived to make that thing appear. And I really liked the way her eyes would spark when she smiled, or soften when she was listening to me spill my guts, or crinkle at the corners whenever she was lost in thought. And yeah, sure, she'd swooped into my bar—into my *life*—and turned it right the fuck around. But come on. Did that mean I *loved* her, for godsakes?

Yes.

Shit.

I threw off my covers and got my ass out of bed, cursing the blinding white sun shining through my windows.

I fed Magnum.

I took a shower.

I did my paperwork.

I punched the wall.

Then I went downstairs.

We weren't scheduled to open until six on New Year's Day. I would have just closed for the holiday, but the bar was already going to be shut down for the wedding the following night as it was. My poor regulars would go into withdrawal.

Hank must have partied a little too hard last night, because he didn't show up this morning to do the sweeping. I grabbed the push broom from the storage closet and just did it my damn self. I needed something to take my anger out on anyway, and the repeated slamming of the bristles against the wood floor was just the thing to do the trick. There was more debris than usual: Scraps of confetti, the occasional paper hat, a few pairs of cheesy 2004 glasses. I shoved my broom at all of it, herding the mass into a pile in the middle of the room.

I was so caught up in my head about the Avery Situation, playing it over in my mind, trying to make some sense of what happened, that I didn't notice the banging in my brain was actually a knocking at the door.

When I finally looked up, there was *Julie*, cupping her eyes to the glass and giving me a wave.

Julie!

"Holy shit!"

She must've read my lips, because she was laughing as I unlocked the door. It had been forever since I'd seen her, and goddammit if she wasn't one hell of a sight for sore eyes.

"Holy shit, Jules! How are you?"

She came inside and gave me a quick hug, which I could only return with one arm because I still hadn't put down the damn broom. "Mmm. I'm good. It's good to see you!"

"You too."

My face mirrored hers, smiling ear to ear as she said, "I hope you don't mind the surprise visit. I've just seen so much press about the bar lately and figured I'd check it out for myself."

I directed her over to one of the hightops, answering, "I'm glad you did. It's been too long."

"Much too long." She scanned her eyes around the room, noting the new changes. "Wow. The old dive cleans up real nice, huh?"

"Yeah. I had some help. Landed myself an event planner who likes to decorate." At the mention of Avery, my stomach clenched.

"Well, whoever did all this must be some sort of genius."

"She is."

"Oh, it's a *she*, is it?" Julie shot a knowing smirk at me. It's not as though she wasn't aware of my depraved history with various members of the female persuasion. She was all *too* aware. "I should have guessed the reason you look like shit was because of some girl." She brushed a strand of golden hair out of her eyes and smiled as she asked, "So, who's the unlucky lady?"

I caught a glimpse of the small scar at her forehead. It was barely visible, but I couldn't look away.

Julie caught my stare. "Is it that noticeable?" she asked.

I reached a hand up to her face and ran my finger across it, feeling my heart break. "To the rest of the world? Not at all. To me? It's hard to see anything else."

"Great. I'm a walking scar."

"You're a walking *vision*." I didn't try to hide the warring thoughts playing across my face.

"Zac, you really need to stop beating yourself up over it."

As if I could. "I'll never stop beating myself up over it. I should have been able to stop it. What kind of man could do something like this to you? Why would you even let him within a twenty mile radius of you?"

"It's not your fault, Zac. I don't know why you insist on taking that on. You're not the one that hurt me."

"Wasn't I? Didn't I hurt you for months? Maybe I didn't take a whack at your skull, trying to intentionally scar you for life. But I hurt you all those months after I tore up my knee, when I was such a dick, Julie. And yet, you still stuck by my side. Why did you do that?"

"You needed me to."

"But... I didn't deserve it."

She sighed as she reached across the table to grab my hand. "You didn't deserve to bust up your knee. You didn't deserve to watch your father die. We don't get what we deserve. If that were so, I'd be a princess living in a castle."

"Yes, you would." I looked down at the table and directed my commentary toward our intertwined hands. "I want to thank you, Julie. For being a friend even when I didn't deserve it. I want to thank you for everything."

"You're welcome," she offered, without hesitation.

"And I want to apologize, too. I want to say I'm sorry."

"For what?"

I finally raised my head to meet her eyes. "For never saying it before."

Her face wore a mask of sympathy as she pursed her lips and gave a squeeze to my hand, banishing the last of my guilt. I felt it lifting off of me, my body finally shrugging off the burden I'd carried for too long.

Living with regrets is no way to live at all.

"So," she started in, breaking the sappy moment. "Tell me about this bar-fixing fairy that's got you all hot and bothered."

"Is it that obvious?"

She raised an eyebrow and said, "I don't think I've ever seen you like this."

"Yeah, well, I've never *been* like this." I ran a hand through my hair and admitted, "I don't think she's as into me as I'm into her."

Julie laughed and shook her head.

"What?" I asked, completely mystified.

Her eyes met mine as she smiled out, "Not into you? I don't think you realize what a ridiculous statement that is. It's easy to be crazy about you, Zac."

"Thanks."

"You'll figure it out. Besides, you've got your old Girl Expert back on the payroll. My advice never steered you wrong."

"The stakes were never this high, Jules."

She placed her palms on the table and ducked her head to meet my eyes. "Holy shit. You've really got it bad for this one, huh?"

"You have no idea."

"You'd be surprised." She clamped her lips together, hesitant to continue. "I didn't just come back here because of all the press about the bar. That was just an excuse to get you back into my life before this belly gets any bigger."

My brain couldn't compute her words, even though I knew what she was trying to say. "*What*?"

"I'm pregnant, Zac."

Holy shit. Holy fucking shit.

At first, my stomach dropped at the news. It was too much to register. But even then, I knew I was overjoyed about it. How could I *not* be?

My eyes were bugging out of my head and I couldn't find any words. Julie filled in the dead air. "And I'm getting married. To a great guy. Even if he *is* a Rangers fan."

I finally found my voice. "Holy shit, Jules! That's… fantastic!" My mind was spinning, but we were both wearing the same crazy grin. "Your parents must be flipping out."

"They are. I wanted to tell you myself before they had the chance to spill the news to your mom. They're really happy. Are you?"

I jumped up from the table and pulled her into a hug. "Are you kidding? I couldn't be happier." I wrapped my arms around her and gave her a big squeeze, joyful and astonished, relieved and overwhelmed. I was humbled to find that she missed me, still viewed me as someone important enough to want to share this with. I clutched her a little tighter and gave a kiss to the hair at her ear…

…just as Avery bounded in the door.

My face dropped along with hers when I realized what she had walked in on, how easily it could be taken the wrong way.

Before I could say the words, "Avery, wait!" she was in her car and zooming out of the parking lot.

Chapter Twenty-Six

There are moments in your life by which you can mark the passage of time. Those events that are so monumental, each milestone becomes a definitive line delineating Before from After. BC to AD. For me, that tick on the timeline was the year 1999. There was no denying that that entire year was fraught with some life-changing moments, and I've managed to jumble them all together as one.

When you're young, you get behind the wheel and hope you don't get in an accident, not because you're worried about getting hurt, but because you don't want anything to happen to your *car*. At some point in your life, you wake the fuck up and the opposite becomes true. You realize the stupidity of your past outlook, and recognize that a car can always be fixed.

People sometimes can't.

I don't know where that dividing line is, that point separating a cocky teenager from a realistic adult. In any case, back in '99, I was way too old to be straddling it. I still maintained that teenage conceit, that cocksure invincibility. I was a professional fucking hockey player, for godsakes. A physical specimen of the highest ranking—feared on the ice, desired by women.

Most of them, anyway.

Julie and I were childhood pals—more like cousins, really—considering that our parents were best friends and we'd known each other since birth. She had two older sisters, so by the time she and I came along, there were seven rugrats under the age of eight for our parents to contend with. We'd grown up in the same neighborhood together, but her family moved upstate about the time she and I started college. I went to BC; she went to some art school in Manhattan. We were separated for a couple of years, but once I got drafted to the Devils, her home base of New York wasn't so far away.

We were always pretty close, so it was good that we were able to maintain the friendship, even outside of the family connection. Our shared history solidified our bond and was one of the only things I knew I could always count on. She was a good friend.

There weren't too many girls I could say that about. I didn't particularly know a lot of women I liked enough to keep around for more than a few nights of debauchery, and it's not like any of them had been able to put up with me for any extended length of time either.

But Julie was different. She was fun, and unassuming, and cool. There was never any threat of a romantic relationship between us, so she never tried to stake a claim on me, and I was just as content to let her live her own life, too. She'd sometimes come and hang out at Johnny's with me and the guys whenever she didn't have something better to do. I relied on her for advice, and she relied on me as her go-to date for weddings or society parties whenever she needed a stand-in.

So, when I got shipped off to Texas, we both knew we were going to miss one another, but it's not like either one of us was crying into our pillows every night or anything.

We stayed in touch, though. One particularly lonesome night in April, I called her out of the blue. I found myself expressing my homesickness to her, which had the unintended effect of her showing up one day after practice. There she was, in all her Julie glory, right there in Dallas for a surprise visit. I couldn't have been happier to see her.

We bypassed the night out with the guys, and instead decided to take off for some alone time. It was raining that night, just barely a drizzle; that much I do remember. I was driving her stupid rental car. I must've taken a turn a bit too fast, and the weather conditions didn't help matters any. I swerved, the car fought me, we skidded off the road. Not a drop of booze in either of us; it was just one of those freak things.

The sickening rip of twisting metal and shattered glass roared through my ears like a freight train as we wrapped around a tree... and then everything went black.

I awoke to the sounds of sirens and bright, flashing lights... and a blinding white pain in my left leg. Julie was crying, her golden hair tangled with blood, her eyes focused on the red on her hands and shaking in disbelief.

And the thing that I remember most about that night? It wasn't the lights or the loud noises or even the pain. The thing I remember most was *not being able to get to Julie*. I couldn't move from my side of the crumpled car, pinned underneath the dashboard as I was. I had to sit there and watch her go into shock, just shaking like a leaf and staring at her bloody hands, her head matted in red. I tried to use my voice to soothe her, but there was no getting through.

The whole time the firemen were carving me out of my car, the whole time the cops were trying to keep us calm... I had to listen to Julie's scared little whimpers; feel her fear and her shock rippling through my broken bones. Every second knowing that *I* was the one that did that to her.

We were both brought right into the ER, and before I could even ask what was happening, everything went black again. I woke up dry-mouthed in a clean hospital bed, a shitload of tubes and wires sticking out from various parts of my body, a leg raised in a metal contraption, surrounded by a steel cage.

The first thing I did was ask about Julie, and thank God, it turned out her injuries were pretty minor. A few stitches in her forehead, some scrapes and bruises, but that was all. Not even a concussion. I was so relieved about that that I hardly registered the bad news the doc was giving me. My knee was shattered and there had been some irreversible nerve damage. Most likely a career-ender, the doc told me, but then, he didn't exactly know me very well, did he? He didn't know that hockey was my fucking life, and that of course I'd do everything in my power to come back stronger than ever.

Bash had been sent down to check on us, and he reported back to our parents and Julie's family with uncharacteristic regularity. At the time, I was confused as to why Bash had been sent down instead of Mom or Dad coming to see me themselves. I remember him looking away uncomfortably when I asked, but I was so drugged up that I didn't really think much of it until after I went home.

After a seemingly infinite stay at Parkland Hospital, arrangements were made for my conditional release, provided I continued my rehabilitation back at Kessler, which was a hell of a lot closer to home than anywhere down in Texas. I'll say one thing for the Stars franchise; they sure knew how to send a guy off in style. Bash and I found ourselves on the corporate jet which had been modified for my transit and outfitted with an on-board nurse. Not too shabby.

I was still in denial about my inevitable return to the ice, and it was hard to stay in a bad mood whenever Bash was around. Yet, I spent those hours on that private jet in miserable silence, playing the accident over and over in my mind.

As banged up as I was, I should have been reveling in that plane ride. Because while I was busy beating myself up with guilt and feeling sorry for myself, what I didn't know is that those were the last moments of peace I was going to have for a very long time.

Because once we made it home, I found out about my father: The chemo wasn't working. The cancer had spread. He had six months to live.

He only needed two.

Those days are such a blur to me, an endless stream of time divided between my own hospital stays and my dad's. I kept up the brave face for him, but whenever I was out of his earshot, I'd lash out at anything and everything within my sights. Most of the time, the closest target was Julie. I was such a dick over those months, just a snarly, bitter asshole flying off the handle, ranting about the unfairness of it all. She really tried her best to help me through the pain, but was eventually forced to put some space between us. I can't say as I blamed her. I was a black hole of bad luck and misery, a time bomb waiting to explode. Who the hell would risk sticking around for that?

That summer, when the Stars went on to make an appearance in the finals, I hardly even noticed. I was sitting in my father's hospice room, for godsakes, and couldn't really give two shits about the game playing out on his TV, much less the fact that we were winning.

That *they* were winning. I didn't contribute a goddamn thing to their victory. My father knew how frustrated I'd been during my run with the Stars.

So, you want to know the kicker of it all? Want to know the last fucking words my old man said to me before he never said another word ever again?

261

"We'll get 'em next time."

We'll get 'em next time. He had said those same five words after every game I'd ever lost in my life. It used to ease my mind some, take the sting off a devastating loss. Now he was trying to take the sting off a *win*, knowing I felt I had nothing to do with it, reminding me that I'd have another chance someday.

Problem was, there would never *be* a next time. There was no more "someday." Not for me… and not for him.

In the immediate aftermath, there was Dad's estate to settle, his final arrangements to be made. There was the inevitable squabbling with my brothers about every detail, the collective consoling of our mother to bring an end to it.

It was decided that I'd take over the bar (considering I had no other career options and I'd essentially purchased the place anyway), but those first months were really a team effort. Since Dad had kept all the pub's financial records in spiral-bound notebooks, we spent countless hours transferring all that data to the computer. My brothers and I had bought him the thing a year prior, but it was still sitting unopened in its box in the corner of his office. Apparently, he'd been using it as a table to display his scrapbooks, all the newspaper clippings and photos of his sons from over the years. When we flipped through them and saw the pride emanating from every page, the meticulous care with which he cataloged our accomplishments, it broke our fucking hearts.

That summer was absolutely the lowest point of my entire life. My career was over. My father was dead. But even then, I knew that if I let the events of my present consume me, I wouldn't have any sort of future at all. And I owed it to my old man to find *something* to salvage from the wreckage.

I'd been in limbo ever since.

Until Avery.

Because of her, I learned that you can't change the past. Shitty things are going to happen; you're going to make mistakes; life is going to knock you down at every turn. The important thing is that you *get back up*. The only thing that counts is what you do from here on out.

You can choose to let the past define you, keep going down a miserable road until you eventually shrivel up and die. Or you can blaze a new trail in life, set your sights on a brighter future, and just keep moving forward until you find out where your happy lies.

Maybe it's down a path you never thought to travel. Sometimes, it's right in front of you. Whether you choose to see it or not is up to you.

You always have a choice.

And I knew that I'd made mine.

Chapter Twenty-Seven

I came down to the floor way too early the next morning. There was a ton of stuff to get done before the wedding, but obviously, I only started my day at such an hour because I was hoping to run into Avery as soon as possible.

Only, she sent an assistant to precede her arrival.

I didn't know where she found the guy or how he knew where to put everything, but the dude was racing around the place as if his nuts were on fire.

Avery showed up a few hours later to put the finishing touches on the room. I was surprised that she'd waited so long to show up—let's face it, the girl was obsessed with details—but was happy she was even here at all. There was the smallest part of me that thought she'd back out and not show.

I gave her a wave from my post behind the bar, and she waved back before immediately shifting her focus to the task at hand. Seeing as she had a job to do, I left her alone so she could do it. I knew she was stressed out enough about pulling together a proper wedding, and I wasn't looking to add to her anxiety by cornering her just yet.

But I wasn't going to wait even one extra minute once she finally finished.

She'd transformed my modest sports pub into a winter wonderland. She left the white string lights and the paper snowflakes on the ceiling, which, I gotta admit, really worked. Especially since she'd had a dozen potted trees, hanging lanterns, and yards of *tulle* all lit up, too. There were white tablecloths over every table and white slipcovers over every stool. The hightops had been removed to allow access to the dance floor, which had a layer of fake snow scattered across the entire surface.

I thought all the white would just highlight the crappy brown wood in this place, but Avery managed to strike a great balance between rustic and... *pristine*.

Oh shit! Shabby chic! I totally got that now.

The band was warming up with a Fastball tune, and I hummed along as I double-checked my liquor stock. A bunch of my old teammates would be attending the reception today, and if the party back in June was any indication, I figured I'd rather be safe than sorry.

I took a look at Avery, busily fluffing flower arrangements, going over her lists, ordering her assistant around... and the sight made me smile. She was already dressed in a silver gown, and seeing her in that color surrounded by all this winter white, she looked like an ice princess—in the best possible way, of course.

A far cry different from the angry business-gal with the huge chip on her shoulder that walked into my bar seven months ago.

I guess we'd both changed over the past months. Funniest thing was, her transformation was in recalling the dreams of her past, and mine was in learning how to forget them. Somehow, we met in the middle. She helped me become a guy I never even knew I was supposed to be.

She taught me how to let go.

She taught me how to give.

And I got it now. I got why my father spent his life slaving away at this nothing pub. Because when you can bring people together—change their lives, even—you don't think about the money you could be making somewhere else. You can't save everyone, but sometimes, you can save *someone*. And when you have the support of the woman you love on top of that, the woman who challenges you to be the best version of yourself that even *you* didn't think you could be… you're a success.

Enough was enough. I pulled a white rose out of a nearby vase and walked right over to the woman in question. "Ave."

She turned, seemingly unaffected by my presence as she put her hands to her hips and answered, "Yeah, what's up?" Her brows were raised, trying to look casual, as if everything was fine.

"I didn't know if you were going to come," I said, holding out the flower. She took it, but she didn't seem won over by it.

Despite her attempt to seem impassive, there was no denying the bite in her voice as she said, "I was hired for a job. I know how to stay committed to something."

"Me too." I raised my eyebrows and dipped my head, attempting to meet her eyes.

No dice.

"I tried to call you," I continued. "Numerous times."

"I know."

"So, you're just avoiding me?"

"No," she lied, crossing her arms over her chest and gnawing on her bottom lip.

"I think I deserve a chance to explain."

She gave out a huff and started picking at the rose petals. "Explain what, exactly? That now that we've hooked up, it's time for you to check out again?"

"What you saw yesterday isn't what it looked like."

"Famous last words."

I knew she was pissed, but I found myself trying to fight a smile. She thought she wanted to stay mad, but we both knew there was no reason for it. We both knew the truth. "C'mon, Ave. The other night? You and me? You know that was real."

She wanted to believe it was true. She had to know that it was. But if she was afraid, if she needed me to convince her, I could do that. After all these years, I owed her at least that much.

"*I* know it was real," I offered, my heart beating out of my goddamn chest. "You know how I know?" I stepped closer and put a palm against her jaw. "I've never wanted to give anyone *forever* before." My thumb was moving on its own, tracing small circles against her cheek as I watched her raise her incredible topaz eyes to mine. "I could give my forever to you."

"Zac…"

"No. Stop fighting it, Ave. We're in love with each other. I know that now. I may have been an idiot about it for a long time, but I know I love you. You're it for me."

Her head dropped as the tears fell, her shoulders shaking. I pulled her against my chest, wrapped my arms around her, and just let her sob.

"I was trying to play it cool," she mumbled against my shirt. "I was trying to pretend that I could handle another one-night-stand with you. I was treating you as the guy you *used* to be, instead of the amazing man you've become." She raised her teary eyes to mine, adding, "And I'm sorry for that."

"You didn't want to leave?"

"It took everything I had to walk out that door."

"Sure didn't seem like it."

She offered a sheepish smile through her tears. "I can be a pretty good actress when it comes to protecting my heart."

"Ave," I scratched out, my voice unrecognizable to my own ears. "I promise you'll never have to protect your heart from me ever again." I bent down and stole a soft kiss from her perfect lips, amazed at the incredible woman in my arms. "I'll protect it for you."

267

My words brought a genuine smile to her beautiful face as she slid a hand up my chest and aimed those gorgeous eyes at mine. "Well, I should hope so. You know, considering it's yours and all."

She loves me. Was I the luckiest bastard in the world or what?

"Dammit, Ave. I can't even… I love you. God help me, but I do."

PART THREE

ZAC AND AVERY
2005

EPILOGUE

St. Patrick's Day was always a madhouse at The Westlake. I'd only experienced one of them prior to tonight, but this one was even crazier than last year.

Zac had added some new drinks to the menu board for the occasion, and was offering up an altered version of my Vodka Seven which he named "Thrown for a Loop," or "Loopies," for short. It had been on the board for over a year, but tonight, they were green, thanks to a few drops of Crème de Menthe. The girls seemed to like them.

I was sipping on mine while I looked over the buffet table. Felix had made about fifty pounds of corned beef which was sliced and heaped into Sterno pans along with a million pounds of red potatoes and bags upon bags of rye, compliments of Roy Bread himself.

He and the other regulars were already half in the bag, singing songs from the Emerald Isle and downing their beers. Zac's brothers were all here, too, which always made for a great night. It was awesome that they were all in the same room at the same time. That didn't normally happen unless a big game or major event was going down.

Mercifully, the river dancers showed up, temporarily calling a halt to the guys' crooning. Thank God. If I had to hear "Danny Boy" one more time, I might have gone insane.

The girls were adorable, with their green velvet dresses that swished as they danced and their ringlets piled on top of their bouncing heads. Seeing their talent—at such a young age—made me regret dropping out of ballet class at the age of nine.

273

Though, I suppose if I were going to be honest, I couldn't imagine I'd want to make a living as a ballerina when I was doing the one job that made me happiest. There was just something about the orderliness of my work that appealed to me.

Even if I took pride in the joy my parties brought others, I knew it wasn't the type of work that changed the world. That's what my sideline gigs at the bar were for.

The Westlake had become the hub of philanthropy in this town, and it seemed Zac couldn't go more than a month before people started sniffing around, wondering about our next event.

Which worked out great for everyone.

I always made some new contacts, Zac always gained some new customers, and the bar always made a ton of money for some really great charities. Highlighting some local businesses was simply a bonus.

When the dancers were through, I thanked them and handed their instructor a gift card, a donation from *The Celtic Shop* across town.

Once the guys caught the exchange, they immediately started in with their familiar chanting. "Give-a-way! Give-a-way!"

Zac hopped up onto the bar and rang the triangle which always got everyone's attention. "Okay! Alright!" he laughed, shooting a good-natured eyeroll at me.

He was so damned good-looking, that boy. Especially when he was wearing such a goofy grin.

Once everyone settled down, he started in with his schpiel. "I've got a very special giveaway planned for tonight. I wasn't planning on doing it until later, but I guess there's no better time than the present."

He pulled something from his shirt pocket and twisted it around in his fingers as all eyes turned toward me. My eyes went wide and my mouth dropped open as I saw the diamond ring he was holding in his hand. He smiled that perfect Zac smile in my direction, and I felt my knees go weak.

Maybe he found his little surprise funny, but I was ready to pass out.

"This little beauty is up for grabs to the first person who can tell me…" he scanned his eyes around the room, building up the anticipation. Every neck in the place strained to look from him to me then back again. Damn, the boy really knew how to deliver a line. "At the Meadowlands… in a single season… Who holds the record for most minutes spent in the penalty box?"

Oh my God. My hand clamped to my mouth as my eyes blurred. I couldn't even find the words.

"Maniac McAllister!" Jerry Liverwurst yelled out.

Everyone just cracked up with their jeers, throwing coasters and straws at Jerry.

Zac's shoulders dropped, and he was shaking his head laughing as he said, "No, Jerry. Good guess, though." His eyes met mine as he asked, "Ave, care to correct the man?"

My hand was over my chest, trying to keep my heart from escaping. I saw Zac's brothers at a nearby table, leaning back in their chairs and smiling proudly at me. *They knew* he was going to do this, the big lugs.

Major event going down indeed.

I looked toward Zac, the man I loved, standing there waiting patiently on my reply. My eyes were tearing up and my hands were shaking, but I managed to answer, "It's me."

He smiled and shot back, "Damn straight it's you."

He hopped off the bar and got down on his knee, right there in the middle of everyone. He held the ring up toward me as the hopeful look in his eyes shot straight into my heart. "I love you,

Ave. Whaddya say? You want to marry a broken-down, cranky old has-been?"

"No," I answered, smiling into his eyes. "I want to marry *you*."

A wide grin split his face as he stood up, grabbed my hand, and slipped the diamond ring onto my finger. "Here's your prize. Thanks for playing."

I threw my arms around his neck and kissed him as the entire bar cheered and started singing "When Irish Eyes are Smiling."

When I pulled back, I caught the elated expression on his face.

"You're happy," I said.

"I am. Because of you."

He gave a quick scan around the crowded bar, and decided to lead me into the pool room so we could have a bit more privacy.

Denny and Rachel were in the middle of a game, but Zac jerked his head toward the door, saying, "Shouldn't you two be working right now?" Neither gave any indication that they were planning on going anywhere, and they both looked at him blankly until he added, "I'd like a minute alone with my fiancée, alright?"

"Aww, hey, man. That's great! Congratulations," Denny said, coming over to clap Zac on the shoulder as Rachel piped in with, "Ooh. Lemme see the ring!"

Zac laughed, "Thanks, but guys! Get the fuck out of here already!"

"Yeesh," Rachel busted, as she grabbed Denny's sleeve and hauled him out of the room. "Check out Mr. Boss Man all of a sudden."

He shook his head in exasperation before leaning down to plant a sweet, soft kiss against my lips. "I talked to your parents, you know," he said, twirling a strand of my hair around his finger.

That was a surprising bit of knowledge. "You did?"

"Well, I needed to ask their permission to marry you."

"Oh my God! What did they say?"

Zac smirked and answered, "Well, your mother was crying too hard to say anything, so she just hugged the living hell out of me, which I'm going to assume was a good thing. But your father said we can thank him by naming our first kid after him."

My eyeballs almost popped out of my head. "He said that? About us having a *kid*?"

"Yes, and I think we should get started on that right away." He bent down to kiss me again as my mind raced, trying to register all the new information. Not only did we have my father's blessing, but our firstborn already had a name: Rudolph Benjamin McAllister.

Sorry, kid.

I tried to get lost in Zac's kiss until a thought occurred to me and I pulled back. "Wait a minute. Thank him for what?"

Zac gave a grunt, obviously not pleased about putting a halt to our liplock. "For two years ago. For suggesting the Stanley Cup party be held here."

My brows furrowed in confusion. There was no way my father planned that. He couldn't have... Did he?

Zac chuckled at the gears cranking in my brain. "He said he was good at putting together a winning team. Guess the guy knows his stuff."

Whether it was a calculated plan to throw the two of us back together or not, there was no way anyone could have predicted where we'd go from there.

But I couldn't have been happier about where we ended up.

"I love you, Zac."

His lips curled into a wicked smile as he slipped a palm behind my neck. "Well, that's good. Now I don't regret getting you that ring."

I held my hand out in front of me, watching as the light danced through the gorgeous, emerald-cut rock on my finger. "Wow. This is one hell of an ice cube you bought me. It must've cost a fortune. I have no problem with that, by the way."

He smirked at my appraisal, saying, "Some things are more important than money."

That beautiful man cupped my jaw and ran his thumb across my cheek, staring into my eyes with that knee-melting look he reserved only for me. "Besides, something tells me you'll be worth it."

THE END

ACKNOWLEDGEMENTS:

Of course I would like to start this gratitude train off with YOU, the readers! This entire book was only made possible due to your enthusiasm and participation. Your clever ideas and witty suggestions really helped to flesh this story out, and I am so grateful that you took such an active interest in our little project. So, thank you!

It was both easy and difficult to create a story that was locked into an established framework. Normally, I'll just tap away and see where the story takes me. TBH, sometimes I cursed the lack of freedom. But being forced to stay on point sometimes opened a new door that I never would have found had I ventured out on my own. It's been a really interesting experiment, and I feel a very successful one as well. Zac and Avery have evolved into two new favorite characters for me while writing, and I didn't think it was going to be possible to love anyone as much as Trip and Layla. To tell you the truth, I was more than a little paralyzed at the thought that *you* wouldn't, which is why it took me so long to get this story on the shelf. But I love the people we ended up with! I hope you do, too.

Special thanks goes out to Caro Clarke. Her website was invaluable to me years ago when I was first starting out. While dealing with the most debilitating writer's block of my life earlier this year, I sent her an email, and it was her advice that snapped me out of it. Thank you for your words of wisdom, Caro. I highly advise any author (or aspiring author) to go check out her site and soak up the pure awesomeness: www.caroclarke.com

To Kari Matthes: Could you BE any more of a cheerleader? Your constant words of encouragement seriously got me through some rough moments. I'm glad that I picked you as a friend, and I'm honored that you've chosen to be mine right back.

To LB Simmons. Gurrrl, sorry I didn't give you enough time for payback, as I know you would have enjoyed slashing this story to bits way too much during your read. But I can't thank you enough for what you *were* able to tackle. You offered some amazing suggestions, and I am grateful every day that we found each other. I love you to stinking pieces! Now get out of my head!

To Shay Ray Simmons: It's bizarre when you can find someone with whom you share a brain. I hereby relinquish all rights to said brain until further notice. It's all yours, so enjoy. It's a little fried around the edges right now, but don't worry, that thing will snap back into shape like Stretch Armstrong soon enough. Thank you for your advice and encouragement.

To Kay Miles: What to say here? Your brutal honesty during your initial read was exactly what I needed to hear. I am *so grateful* for your insight, because I *love* where this story ended up. Thanks for the nudge in the right direction.

To Stevie Kisner: As usual, you are the macaroni to my cheese, the chocolate coating to my chewy nougat. Thanks again for the offered shoulder, the tireless cheerleading, and all that lovely red slashiness. xoxo

To Casey Smith: Being a new mommy hasn't stopped you from acting as my ruthless book ninja once again. You are The Little Ninja That Could. If you were a founding father, you'd be Beninja Franklin. If you had red hair, you'd be a ginja. But as my editor, you're... awesome. Thank you for squeezing my life into yours. *mwah* (Now let's get cracking on DTS!)

To my bloggers: Kelly, Joanne... Kim... Jenny, Gitte, Sian, and the Rachels... Heather, Selene, and Brandi... Jennifer, you schmexy bitch... Every last one of you who has read my books and supported them—including the multitude that I *didn't* call out by name... Thank you. I sound like a broken record, but indie authors truly couldn't do this without you.

It's never redundant to thank my family and friends for their support and encouragement.
De Paul girls, thanks for your excitement. Special thanks go out to my high school friend Maria Chappa of Turnkey Productions www.turnkeyproductions.net for your event-planner insight.

Special thanks to Dad O., yet again, for the use of your house. Barb, I promise I'll write a clean book someday. ;)

Mom and Dad, thanks for dealing with my cranky self and for helping out with the boys so I could write. Diana, thanks for talking me through my nervous breakdown on Halloween. LOL

Michael, Tanner, and Mason: The three coolest guys I know. Thank you for letting me write this story even though we're Flyers fans. Also, thanks for not letting the house fall apart (too much) while I was working. You guys are incredible, and you own my heart. I'm so honored to give my forever to you. Xoxo

As always, I'll ask that if you enjoyed this book, to please leave a review, loan it out, and talk about it every chance you get. :)
Indie authors are only able to bring you new stories when there's an audience waiting for them, and we rely on word-of-mouth above all else to make a living.

If you haven't already, please come join the fun on my Facebook page!
https://www.facebook.com/pages/TTorrest-Author-Page

Here I am on TSU:
https://www.tsu.co/TTorrestAuthor

And here's my email:
ttorrest@optonline.net

You can also check out my webpage:
www.ttorrest.com

and join my mailing list for updates:
http://eepurl.com/318-n

NOW TURN THE PAGE FOR A PREVIEW OF MY NEXT BOOK!!!

DOWN THE SHORE
A rock-and-roll romantic comedy.

Livia Chadwick is a photographer by day and a self-proclaimed
rock slut by night.
Her dating life is a lackluster parade of evasive jerks and
her boss is an unrelenting nightmare of a human being.
What else can a girl do but rent a beach house with her girlfriends
And blow off a little steam every weekend?
But hey, she's from Jersey. Barhopping down the shore all season
is sort of mandatory.
All is going according to plan… until she meets Jack.

Jack Tanner is a contractor-turned-musician in a small-town
cover band
suddenly thrust into the limelight.
He's already had enough of the rock-and-roll lifestyle, and
groupies have never been his thing.
Then again… there's a gorgeous brunette in the audience tonight,
checking him out with the most incredible green eyes he's ever
seen.

She's looking for a fling.
He's looking for forever.

It's gonna be one helluva summer.

*Set in the summer of 1995, DOWN THE SHORE takes the reader
on a tour through some of the Jersey shore's hottest hot spots
over one, sleepless, flannel-clad summer.
It's a look back to a time when the music was groundbreaking,
the rock clubs were king,
and bar bands ruled the world.*

LIVIA
Friday, May 26, 1995

We had to cross over the crowded dance floor in order to shortcut to the other side of the large club. Jack was trying to carve out a path for us both when I saw him inexplicably reach his hand behind him and blindly grab for mine. I just as inexplicably put my hand in his, and had the oddest feeling as we wove our way through the crowd.

I became enigmatically aware of how… *electric* it was to hold his hand, even though I barely knew the owner of it. Our palms were flattened against one another's, our fingers intertwined... It was as though we'd performed this act naturally a million times over, not just for the first time one minute ago. The thought left me baffled, but fascinated nonetheless.

Before I knew it, he led me over to the payphones situated near the restrooms. He gave my hand a quick squeeze before releasing his hold and ducking into the men's room.

When Jack let go of my hand, I was surprised at the loss that washed over me. What the hell was that? I didn't even know the guy and he had me sweating from simply holding his hand? I couldn't even imagine what holding his dick would be like. I'd probably pass out.

I had to dig through a ton of junk in my purse to find the number for the beach house, but it finally appeared and I made the call. Even though I wasn't in the main part of the club, it was still loud, and I burrowed into the alcove as much as I could while covering my free ear with my hand in order to hear.

Samantha answered.

"Hey, Sammy! What are you doing there? I thought you were sick."

"I was. But I slammed down a few Sudafed and managed to catch the girls before they left. Where are you?"

"Tradewinds," I shot back. "Came to see a band."

"Any good?"

"Yeah, actually. They're fantastic."

I glanced up to find Jack leaning against the wall having a cigarette, waiting for me. Fuck. He heard that.

"So, I'm going to assume you'll be spending the night elsewhere?" Sam chuckled at her dig, but it wasn't like I could take offense. My girls knew me too well.

"Well, yeah, but not because... We ran into Monty. We're crashing there tonight."

I thought Jack would've headed back to our friends, but instead, he just stood there watching me as I talked to Sam. His eyes were squinted as he blew smoke through those delectable lips, and I felt my stomach drop. It was unsettling, to say the least, and I made myself turn away.

"Lucky bitch. Tell him we said hi."

"I will."

Before I could get another word out, I suddenly felt the length of Jack's body pressed against my back. *What the hell?* It caught me by surprise, to say the least.

I figured he was just screwing around, trying to be funny by distracting me from my phone call, but my heart leapt in my chest anyway. He chuckled against my hair, swiped some away, and lowered his lips to the back of my neck, my skin shivering at the touch. The whole time, I was trying to have a human conversation with Sam, no easy feat while this god was ravaging me from behind. I guessed he wasn't planning on wasting any time before getting this party started, and that was fine by me. I was more than game.

I snapped back to the real world when I heard Sammy taunt, "Well, have fuuun!"

As if that wasn't the understatement of the night. How could a hot rock star against my body be anything but fun? I offered a quick "I'm about to," before giving Sam a rather abrupt goodbye and hanging up, my body completely rebelling against all common sense. My knees went weak, and I braced my hand on the wall above the phone, pressing my backside against him.

At that, he gave out a snicker and whispered against my ear, *"Oh, so you wanna play, do you?"*

Oh, hell yeah I did.

There was an electric current running through my body as he turned me in his arms. He had his hands at my waist, running slowly up and down my sides, and a *just-kidding-around* smile playing at his lips.

He might've been kidding around, but I most certainly was not.

I took a quick look down the hall before backing him against the wall, sliding a hand up his chest and meeting his eyes. I could see the surprise in his, because he had no idea who he was dealing with yet.

"Do I want to play? I thought you'd never ask," I shot back, watching a sly smile eek across his lips. Lips that I was about to devour.

I brought my palms around behind his neck, grabbed a handful of that dark hair in my fist, and pulled. He was taken aback by the aggressiveness, but I didn't wait for him to figure anything out before rising on my tiptoes and meeting his mouth with mine.

His body stiffened at that, obviously caught off guard, but it didn't take him long to warm to my advance. Our lips were perfectly matched, our bodies fitting effortlessly against one another's. I felt his muscles relax as he returned my kiss, and soon enough, everything went insane.

His hands slid around my waist as he pulled me closer against his body, and well, *what do we have here?* It seemed Mr. Happy had decided to join us.

Jack turned us around to slam *my* back against the wall, and holy shit, I thought I was going to die. Our lips met again and there was a pounding in my ears beyond the blaring music, making me dizzy. His mouth opened, and I could taste his smoky, salty flavor, smell the shaving-cream scent of him, invading my senses, causing me to grip the shirt at his chest and hang on for the ride.

Or maybe I needed to take him on one.

I pushed off the wall and backed him through the nearest doorway… which turned out to be a storage closet. But there was a lock on the handle, so I took advantage of that before kissing him again. The smell of bleach and stale beer permeated my senses as we touched and tasted one another, the heat escalating off the charts.

Just as my hand slipped down to cop a feel, he asked, "Hey, whoa. Liv. What are you doing?"

The dark was pretty blinding, but I still managed to meet his face, a scowl on mine. "What do you *think* I'm doing?"

He grabbed my wrist and placed my hand at his waist. Trying to cover for my pounding heart, I slid my palms around to the small of his back, up his spine, across his shoulder blades, and went back in for another kiss. His hair was brushing against my cheek as his tongue invaded my mouth, and before I could stop myself, a slight moan escaped from my throat.

I'd been with lots of guys before, but something was different with him and I couldn't quite figure out what it was just yet. He was hot as hell, which was normally my only prerequisite for hooking up with somebody. But this guy had totally upped the ante. He wasn't just a rock star. He was a rock GOD. And from the first second I saw him on stage tonight, I knew I was going to wind up here at some point. Well, not here in a freaking closet for godsakes, but here in this guy's naked grasp doing the horizontal happy dance.

Or, I guess, vertical, in this case. TMI?

My hands went back to his jeans, ripping at Jack's fly, but before I could even get the first button undone, he braced his hands at my shoulders and nudged me away. "Whoa, whoa. Take it back some."

Still in a daze, I asked, "What?"

"This isn't happening. Not here."

Since when did a rock star give a shit where I did him? "I locked the damn door. No one's coming in here."

"You got that right. No one's coming *in here*. We can do better than this."

Was he serious? He started this whole thing, and now he was trying to put the brakes on? I was suddenly struck with the absurd thought that he really was only kidding around when he attacked me at the pay phones. No freaking way was that possible. Was it?

I crossed my arms as my sight adjusted to the dim light, eyeing him up and down. "Is this the part where you try to convince me you're a gentleman? Trying to pretend that you want this to be 'special for me'? Because trust me, Jack, I'm not looking for 'special.' I'm not asking you to work that hard. You can drop the wooing bit."

"*Every* girl is looking for special."

"Not this girl."

He crossed his arms, mocking my pose. "Then what are you looking for?"

"Fun," I shot back without hesitation. He eyed me in disbelief, so I added, "Do you have a problem with that?"

"Maybe I'm done with fun."

What is with this guy? "What's your game, player?"

"No game. Why?"

"You come on like gangbusters, but then the second you find out I'm into it, *bam!* Light switch off."

That made him chuckle. "Oh, you're a real maneater, aren't you? My mother warned me about girls like you."

"You've never met a girl like me, pal."

"Wanna bet?"

We were staring each other down, and I was trying not to let him see how humiliated I felt. There I was, practically throwing myself at his feet, and he was *turning me down*. Rejection can suck a bag of dicks.

He lowered an eyebrow and sighed, "Look, Liv. I've done this too many times to know that nothing good ever comes out of a situation like this."

"Out of what? A one-night stand? Who says I'm looking for anything more than that to come out of this?"

"Who says I'm *not?*" He let out an exasperated breath and ran a hand through his hair. "Look. I like you. Can't we just, you know, get to know each other? Do *you* have a problem with *that?*"

Yes. He was messing with my whole M.O. I didn't do the 'getting to know you' thing with rock stars. I had mind-blowing sex with them and went on my merry way. Why was he making this so difficult? "I don't date musicians."

"And I don't fuck groupies."

We stared each other down, caught in a heated standoff. Who the hell did he think he was?

"First of all, I'm not a *groupie*. I'm a music-loving girl with a healthy sexual appetite who knows how to say 'thank you' properly."

"Thank you for what?"

"For being talented as fuck, you fuck!"

That brought an unreadable smirk to his lips. I didn't have the patience right at the moment to try and explain anything more than that to him, so I continued with my rant. "Secondly, you're not fooling anyone with this chivalry bit. You're a red-blooded male with a working cock that rose to the occasion the second my lips hit yours."

Why the hell is he just standing there smiling at me?

I shook off his smarmy face and lined up the kill shot. "Thirdly... Since you don't fuck 'groupies,' feel free to go fuck *yourself.*"

At that, I stormed out, leaving him standing there gawking at my retreating form.

ALSO BY T. TORREST

The REMEMBER WHEN Trilogy

Come back to the '80s in this decades-long coming-of-age
romantic comedy between a smoking-hot, A-list Hollywood actor
and his high school sweetheart.
It's hysterically funny, super-steamy, rip-your-guts-out
heartwrenching, and incredibly romantic.

#1 Teen Romance
#1 Highest-Rated New Adult
#2 Romantic Comedy (Thanks a lot, Janet Evanovich.)

Find the ebooks and paperbacks at Amazon, BN, iBooks, Kobo,
and most other major bookseller sites worldwide.